WHEN WE LIED

CARLEY WOLFE

ISBN: 9798443937717

Cover Design: Olivia Pro Design
Editing: Sarah Hawkins

First Print Edition: 2022
First Electronic Edition: 2022

To all the adults who have told me my entire life I was capable of this.

PART ONE

1

November 4, 2019

It was the beginning of the end for Grace Simmons. Morning sunlight was peeking through the slit in the blackout curtains. She wasn't sure when or how she had fallen asleep. Just moments ago, she had dreamed she was back there, all those years ago. But instead, she was in her cramped apartment with her cat, Harold, crawling over her, begging for food. She blew out air in an attempt to get the orange fur away from her face, but she was mostly unsuccessful. As a tabby, his hair invaded every crevice of her apartment.

"Yes, I'm up. I'm going," Grace grumbled, pushing her coffee-colored hair out of her face. Despite falling asleep with her hair in what resembled the best bun she had ever made in her life, it was now in shambles, kind of like her life. Her body shivered against the morning anxiety as she thought about how her time was nearly up. She shook out her arms, trying to keep the jitters at bay, but it was useless. Instead, she bounced forward and backward on her feet before stretching down to touch her toes. Releasing a deep breath, she tried not to think about how much time she might have left at her current job.

Harold wove through her legs as she climbed out of bed, meowing frantically. Through her doorway, she could see the stove clock. 7:00 a.m. He was more reliable than even her own internal clock. Shuffling between her cheap Ikea dresser and bed, Grace moved to the kitchenette, but not without banging her shin into the coffee table. Cursing under her breath, she filled up Harold's bowl before glancing at the calendar on the wall.

"One month to go, Harold," she muttered, feeling her nerves bounce under the surface of her skin. Grace released a slow breath, practicing the calming techniques she had picked up from a few YouTube videos. "Well, I guess I better get moving."

When Grace was in high school, she was a dreamer. She wanted to be a preschool teacher or a baker. Both jobs seemed like femininity personified. She could practice being a homemaker before she became one full time. Her only real dream was to marry a handsome man who was indescribably wealthy but somehow humble, who would offer to let her quit her job, without demanding it. Of course, she would graciously accept and never look back. Now, that dream seemed more juvenile than when she thought she could find a prince. Back then, she never imagined she would see or do the things she had.

Instead, she now made her way to a small desk outside the office of Mr. Harris, a hedge fund manager.

If Grace was honest, she would say she didn't know anything about hedge funds, but when Mr. Harris asked, she did what she did best: pretend.

Mr. Harris was not in the office yet, which was typical on a Monday. Before Grace started, something had gone down between Mr. Harris and his previous secretary. When Mrs. Harris found out, she demanded they attend weekly counseling sessions together, probably as punishment for being such a cliché. All 37 employees in the office knew about it, but nobody said a word. The clock read 8:45, just as Grace planned for each day. Straightening her charcoal pencil skirt, she settled into her chair. Despite her slight frame, the chair groaned at the added weight, particularly as she unpacked her bag. She planned to check her phone one last time before hiding it, but a text caught her eye.

Mrs. Baker: *Hi, sweetheart. I hope you are doing well. I just wanted to tell you . . .*

The text cut off, and Grace hurriedly unlocked the phone to reveal the rest. Seeing the name "Baker" on her phone brought back the uncomfortable pounding in her chest. A small part of her hoped Mrs. Baker was wishing her an early birthday or that she saw a cat that looked like Harold and had to tell her about it. Deep down, she knew that wasn't the reason for the text.

Hi, sweetheart. I hope you are doing well. I just wanted to tell you that Jocelyn is back in treatment. She was checked in on Saturday night and should be able to accept visitors later this week. She is in Cold Waters Wellness Center.

Mrs. Baker didn't have to say much more. Grace knew why and that she was expected to visit. It was all implied. This was not Jocelyn's first rodeo at Cold Waters, and it probably would not be her last. In fact, Grace recalled visiting Jocelyn at Cold Waters at least two times before. It was the exclusive treatment center that the Baker's preferred when it had availability, as if it was a hair salon. Often all the spots were reserved or filled, and they had to take her to St. George instead. At least at Cold Waters, it felt like she was actually getting help.

As Grace moved to type her reply, her shaking hands fumbled. She set the phone down in front of her on the desk like she was handling a snake. Because of the tidy and minimalistic nature of her desk, the phone drew all of her attention. There were no family photos or colorful planners to distract her. Every time Jocelyn was checking in, it was for the same reason. A reason Grace might have played a part in.

Grace tried to take the calming deep breaths that all the self-help coaches wouldn't shut up about, but her loud breaths began to draw attention.

"Grace." Kate leaned across her desk to whisper-shout to her. "Are you good?" Kate was the office gossip, stationed mere feet away from Grace. She tossed warm-toned blonde hair over her shoulders as if it was impeding her ability to snoop. While it occasionally seemed as though Kate actually cared, Grace always assumed it was mostly a ploy to pry personal details from someone's life.

Grace tried to laugh it off and offer a quick smile.

"Oh yeah. I think I just had too much espresso this morning!"

Kate laughed and shook her head excitedly. "Have you tried those cold brews yet? They have a big kick." Kate turned her attention back to her own computer. Her concern was just as fake as Grace's would have been if Kate was hyperventilating at her desk. In fact, after a rather excruciating staff meeting last week,

Grace had seemed to have the exact same conversation with Kate, but vice versa.

Grace took a lap around the office, trying to keep her mind distracted as she made copies of Mr. Harris's quarterly report, poured herself a coffee in the kitchenette, and bit her nails down until they nearly bled. When she finally returned to her desk, it was past nine, and her hands had stopped shaking. She picked up the phone, prepared with her response.

Thank you for letting me know. I will visit on Friday. Please let me know if there is anything I can do for you.

There was so much more she could say, but this was the same dance they did every time. Grace would be the dutiful best friend who visited at least once, but not daily, and who would offer to help, but Mrs. Baker would politely refuse or ignore the request altogether. Grace didn't fault Mrs. Baker for refusing her help. She knew first hand that some things are easier to do yourself and others just slow you down. Mrs. Baker and Grace were the same in that respect. Each woman knew that they were the only person in the whole world they could trust to get a job done right.

Grace slid her phone back into her purse and pulled her hair into a low and tight ponytail. She could feel the ends sway against her shoulder blades when she turned her head as Mr. Harris arrived about a half hour later. There was a permanent grimace plastered on his face from his counseling session. She knew better than to ask how it went, but she jumped up to brew his morning coffee.

The day went off without a hitch, and after Mr. Harris had a particularly good business meeting that would result in padding his own wallet quite a bit, Grace popped her head into his office.

"Mr. Harris, may I speak to you for a moment?" she asked, working hard to keep her tone calm and neutral. He hated when people raised the pitch of their voice with questions. It was something his wife did that endlessly irritated him. In fact, he had refused to hire a woman for a position simply because she had that habit, despite being the most impressive candidate he interviewed. She was ultra-aware that all eyes, especially Kate's, would be on her through the large glass walls of his office. The silence in the room grew as he stared over the top of his glasses, reading something on his computer screen. When he peered through his glasses like that, Grace always thought he looked like Mr. Monopoly—if he ate too many Big Macs and hated his life. She knew better than to interrupt.

"Yes, Grace," he finally said, clearing his throat as he turned his attention away from the screen and locked his brown eyes onto her. "Take a seat."

"No, that's okay, sir. It will only be a moment."

He nodded and rested his hands on his oversized mahogany desk. "Well, get to it then."

"I was wondering if I could leave after the Steinberg meeting on Friday? I have a friend who—" Mr. Harris held his hand up to stop her. Grace bit her bottom lip, holding back her anger. Nothing pissed her off more than when a man interrupted her.

"Of course, you may. I have told you many times to use your PTO, but you haven't missed a single day since you started, have you?"

"No, I haven't." Grace had felt proud of this fact, but Mr. Harris was making it seem like it was bad.

"I respect your dedication to your career, but at a certain point . . ." He paused for a moment, drawing in a deep breath. She followed his eyes as he glanced down at the picture of his wife from their last vacation at a *Sandals* resort. "At a certain point, you will no longer have anything left to give of yourself if you don't care for yourself. Why don't you take the whole day on Friday? I don't need you for the Steinberg meeting."

Panic flashed through Grace's veins, but she concealed it, standing up tall and straightening her blouse. Grace held back the words she really wanted to say.

"Sir, Mr. Steinberg is a rather large client. I would feel more comfortable if I was there to assist you." He shook his head, crossing his arms with a sigh. She could see the irritation grow in his face, his cheeks starting to redden like they did whenever he was upset or drunk. She knew she had played her cards wrong.

"Grace, I do not need some assistant to take notes at the meeting. I am not incompetent, regardless of what my wife says." He offered a small chuckle in a failed attempt to lighten his tone. She knew he could sense her discomfort. Being a businessman, he learned to read people quite well. "If it would make you happy, I will record the meeting for you to review when you return Monday. Will that make you feel more comfortable?" His question took on a slightly mocking tone.

Fucking asshole, Grace thought. *No wonder your wife wants you to get counseling.* Grace plastered on what should be an award-winning smile.

"That would be great, Mr. Harris. Thank you for understanding."

He nodded, and she turned to leave. On the reflection of glass windows that made up his office, she could see him hang his head. Whether it was a gesture of exhaustion or frustration was unclear. Grace was not planning on ever asking for a day off again. She feared she might not even get the chance.

As she finished the workday, Jocelyn nagged at the back of her mind. Grace imagined her at Cold Waters, facing all kinds of stereotypes even though she knew those existed more in a place like St. George than at her fancy, resort-like center. She probably had a nicer room there than Grace's apartment. It was probably as nice as Jocelyn's bedroom at the Baker home, and Grace's entire apartment was smaller than Jocelyn's bedroom there, which was kept up even though Jocelyn no longer lived with her parents. Instead, she was somewhat of a nomad. She traveled from city to city, college to college, only staying long enough to have another relapse and end her world tour back at home for a mandatory extended stay somewhere. The longest Grace had ever seen Jocelyn stay in one place was the summer they first met. Although Grace loved her, thinking of Jocelyn's glamorous life, and particularly her childhood, sent jealousy pouring through Grace's veins. Jocelyn had everything. *She has always had everything, and she just throws it away.*

Grace shook her head and pushed the anger down. That wasn't true anymore, and she had no reason to feel that way. Jocelyn *used* to have everything. That was until Grace took it all away from her, and neither of them got to keep it. Grace's mind became carried away in thoughts of Jocelyn. She wasn't sure what to feel about her so-called best friend. Did she deserve so much space in her mind?

Before Grace could decide, she noticed that half the office was empty, and Mr. Harris was packing up in his office. Her eyes darted to the clock on her computer, but she had to jiggle the mouse to awaken it. It was already 6:40. She couldn't tell if she had just zoned out or if she had actually fallen asleep at her desk. Grace stood up and frantically gathered her things. *Did he notice I was just sitting there like an idiot? Did anyone else?* Grace winced at the thought, but nobody had noticed. Everyone else in the office was already home with their families. Her heart stung for a moment. *There was nobody who would come looking for me if I hadn't woken up on my own.* For just a brief moment, she was jealous of even Mr. Harris, who at least had his demanding and bitter wife at home. Mr. Harris hadn't finished getting his tan peacoat on by the time she scurried out of the office, hoping not to have another enraging conversation with the man who kept her afloat financially. She wasn't certain how much longer she could fake niceties.

The streets were already dark. Walking home from work would have been fine if Grace lived remotely close to the corporate office, but cities always seemed to make sure that business areas were well lit, while residential streets were nearly pitch-black the moment you turned a corner. Somehow, the darkness was comforting to Grace. *I can't see anybody, but they can't see me too. I'm invisible. And that's how you survive.*

2

July 15, 2011

Camp Willows was the perfect summer retreat—unless you valued things like air conditioning and warm showers, but this wasn't something that the wealthy clientele contemplated before shipping off their offspring to stay for two months of their summer vacation while they went off to vacation in the Bahamas or shop in Europe.

As the kid of working-class parents, Grace never had the luxury of attending Camp Willows as a camper. However, once she turned 17, she applied to become a counselor. It was on a whim that she applied, finding the camp after hours of searching online for a job where she could connect with wealthy families. For all her faults, Grace was dedicated to rising above her current life and finding her way into a new one. Even if her method wasn't so traditional.

Grace had a feeling she would get picked, as the camp was notorious for selecting a few counselors from lower-income households as a way of "closing the gap." Really, it was just so they could include that on their website. Charity was a more apt description.

Grace dreamt of eating grand meals in the dining hall and sunbathing by the lake wearing designer sunglasses. This fantasy was merely that, as the camp-counselor paycheck was not enough to push her into a whole new tax bracket. Regardless, Grace was excited. She stayed excited, even when her parents dropped her off at the dusty camp sign with her bags. The actual site was a mile down the turnoff, but her father claimed he was too frustrated by the two-hour drive to continue five minutes down the road to the main drag. This was typical for Harry Simmons.

"You want to get a job and be an adult, well then, we'll treat you like an adult," Harry spat as he pulled off to the side of the road. His fingers scratched at a dry patch of skin on the right side of his face. Grace could see the inflamed skin under the day-old scruff and the grime under his fingernails. He was deeply irritated by having to drive Grace anywhere. Grace hadn't told him before she applied to Camp Willows, and he didn't like the idea of her mingling with "rich snobs." Harry, who worked as a mechanic at a small garage, always thought people were cheating him. Cheating him out of money. Cheating him out of business. Cheating him out of a job. He was the ultimate victim of oppression. At least in his mind.

Grace's mother gave a sad wave as they drove off. Grace stood there, her hands filled with bags. She let out a deep breath and smiled. This was the beginning of a new life for Grace. At least she thought.

And just like that, Grace began the worst summer of her life.

* * *

"Hello there!" called a woman in her mid-thirties from the pathway by the front office. Grace assumed this woman must be Marge, the camp director. "Are you lost?" Marge began to walk toward Grace. Grace cursed herself for failing to make a good first impression. Bugs were already marking her body as their territory, and sweat was covering her reddened face. Marge, on the other hand, sported what seemed to be the iconic camp owner's attire, looking like she was ready for both a hike and fly fishing simultaneously. She appeared as though she was born to be a camp coordinator, and imagining her doing anything else was difficult.

"Hello! I'm Grace Simmons." Confusion spread across the woman's face. "I'm one of the camp counselors," she clarified. Marge nodded so emphatically it looked as though her head might detach completely from her neck.

"Oh, well that makes more sense! I thought you were a runaway or something." Marge let out a belly laugh, and Grace's mouth twitched upward in a smile. "I suppose I should introduce myself. I'm so flustered I've forgotten my usual spiel. Gosh darn it." Marge closed her eyes and took a deep breath.

"Well, anyway, welcome! I'm Marge, the coordinator here."

Grace set her bags down on the pavement and reached out to shake her hand. Despite her face looking young and full, her hands revealed she could probably be Grace's grandmother. Grace attributed it to her fuller frame and the likelihood that she applied sunscreen religiously. "It's nice to finally put a face to the name!"

"Hello! It's lovely to meet you." Grace plastered on a big smile, but felt a moment of hesitation. *Am I acting too friendly? Should I be more serious?* Grace had never had a serious job like this, one where she signed a contract and was expected to be present at all times.

Nestled behind Marge, surrounded by large elm trees, sat the small camp office. On the outside, it was covered in wood that made it appear as though it was decades old, but the interior had been entirely updated. On the front porch of the office, a teen girl sat, engrossed in her cell phone. She looked up at Grace for just a moment. Grace was struck by her piercing-green eyes as Marge led her up the front steps.

"Let's bring you in and get you all set up," she said.

The girl immediately returned her full attention to her phone. As Grace passed by, she saw the girl was intensely playing a puzzle game on her phone. She had seen some kids at school play the same one, but she'd never gotten close enough to learn its name or rules. The way she was staring at the phone made it look like she was in the middle of a life crisis.

Inside the camp office was a kitchenette, along with a few desks. Dark hardwood flooring spread throughout the building, and Grace admired the large windows at the back of the building. While Grace couldn't quite put her finger on it, something about the space screamed money. It was likely just in her head.

Marge took a seat at one of the desks covered with mountains of paper. She stared at her desk for a moment, her brow furrowing, and then, she took another deep breath. The woman emanated chaotic energy.

"I thought I left all the room assignments right here," she mused, fumbling through the stacks haphazardly. Grace couldn't imagine functioning with a desk like that, but somehow, it seemed some people did.

After knocking over at least three stacks of papers, Marge pulled out one singular sheet. "Here it is!" As she pulled, the paper tore in half under the weight of the stack. "Oh, shoot!" She forced the two pieces together and squinted.

"Let's see here, you're in the Elm bunks with a group of 14-year-olds. I hope that's okay. I try to leave at least three years between the counselors and the age of the campers. But you will be paired with—" She paused for a moment, shaking her head. She adjusted her large rotund glasses. Her voice lowered as she went on. "You will be working directly with Jocelyn. Now, you should know—" The door swung open, and the girl with the piercing-green eyes entered. Grace glanced over before looking back at Marge.

"Margie, are you talking about me again?" the girl asked, offering a small smirk.

"Why, actually this time, I was, Jocelyn. Grace, here is your co-counselor!" Jocelyn strode toward Grace and looked her up and down like a model at fashion week. After what felt like a full minute, she nodded and smiled back over at Marge.

"Well, I think you actually did okay, Margie," Jocelyn said. "She seems like a decent human being. Not like that horrible Abigail you tried to stick me with last year." Grace was about to smile, but frowned as Jocelyn continued. At school, Grace had her fair share of experiences with mean girls. While Jocelyn's personality seemed repulsive due to her arrogance, something about her made Grace want to be her best friend. Grace bit her bottom lip as she felt her stomach twist nervously. She said a small prayer that her anxiety wouldn't make her stomach act up. More than anything, Grace wanted to impress Jocelyn, but at the same time, she knew if she tried too hard, Jocelyn would hate her.

"I'm Grace." Grace reached out a hand, but Jocelyn just smirked again and rolled her eyes.

"I deduced that myself, Einstein. Maybe we found your nickname." Marge glanced at Grace, fearing for the wellbeing of her newest employee. Grace knew she had two approaches: allow Jocelyn to get under her skin or pretend she was the same as her.

"Einstein. I like it. Except I think your hair might suit it a bit better." The words tumbled out before Grace had decided if she made the right choice. There was a second where Jocelyn didn't know how to react, as if she was determining if this insult was innocent or malicious. Jocelyn's eyebrows raised, and she let a smile spread across her face.

"Fair enough, Grace. Here, I can show you to our cabin. But don't ask me to help you with your bags. I'm not the damn bellhop."

Marge frowned.

"Jocelyn, you remember you will have to help the children with their bags when they arrive tomorrow, right?" There was an edge of hysteria to her voice as if she was only one false step away from a breakdown.

"Calm down. I know. Anything for the kids—" Jocelyn paused for a moment before adding, "Margie." The way she spat the nickname was thick with venom.

Grace tried to stop herself from cringing before Marge nodded and looked away. Jocelyn seemed to be in charge of the situation. Grace got the feeling it was like that everywhere she went.

"Please show her the campgrounds. Keep in mind she was never a camper with us, so she is not familiar with the area. Dinner is around six, girls."

Without a look back, Jocelyn traveled out the door and back into the humid summer air.

"Thank you, Marge." Grace emphasized her name, quietly hoping to instill a little confidence back into her fragile employer without allowing Jocelyn to hear. She nodded before collapsing back into her desk chair.

"Good luck, Grace. Let me know if you have any issues with Jocelyn." She whispered the final part, afraid Jocelyn may hear and react. Grace tried to give her a sympathetic smile, hoping Marge would not think she was the same as Jocelyn just because of the comment she made. More than anything, it was an act of self-preservation.

Jocelyn stuck her head in the door and rolled her eyes.

"Come on, Einstein. Now or never." She began to walk off again without looking back. Grace hurried after her, knowing her words rang true. If her hope was to experience a wealthy lifestyle for once in her life, Grace needed to move and keep moving. Grace's main plan was to pretend she fit in until it was actually true. *Fake it till you make it,* she chanted in her head.

She trailed after Jocelyn, trying to take in the scenery around her. Cabins spread out in uniform rows, a main asphalt path that branched off to each one. Her observations were disrupted by Jocelyn's fast pace, especially with her two heavy bags slowing her down.

Before she had left for camp, her mother had taken her shopping to buy all the supplies. Her mother had taken the time to find an online list of suggested camping supplies. Grace had looked over the list and frowned.

"Mom, this is way too much stuff. I probably won't—"

"Sweetie, it is fine. I have a little bit of money saved up that your father doesn't know about, and we will use that." At that moment, Grace wanted nothing more than to cry. What that money was for, Grace could only guess. None of those guesses were good. So Grace didn't ask any more questions and let her mother take her on her first ever shopping spree. Almost nothing was off-limits, but Grace kept herself reigned in. Now, she was saddled with a couple bags and pounds of guilt.

Grace was half running in order to keep up. She was not going to be left in the dust, like her father had been, and resent it for the rest of her life. Jocelyn looked like the beginning of a way out: Grace was going to take it.

3

November 8, 2019

Even though Mr. Harris assured Grace multiple times this week that she could take the whole day on Friday, she couldn't allow herself to sleep in. Grace lay in bed, the yellow sheets roped around her legs. Her eyes focused on the clock on her wall and watched the second hand rotate. She began to wonder what was happening in the office without her there. At 8:55, Mr. Harris would be walking toward his office. Would he remember she had taken the day off? Or would he be irritated and think she was late? He was a busy man, and Grace doubted he would have remembered any conversation, let alone one that involved her. Grace could feel her heart beginning to race. *What if he didn't remember? What if he plans to fire me because of it? What if he only let me take today off because he wanted to fire me to begin with?*

No secretary lasted with Mr. Harris for more than six months at a time. Either they fizzled out, had an affair with him, were falsely accused of having an affair with him by Mrs. Harris, or were fired for some unknown reason. Last week marked Grace's five months as his secretary. Grace closed her eyes and tried to take deep breaths to calm herself, but it only seemed to make her breathe faster.

Somewhere in the building a toilet flushed, summoning Grace back to reality. Today was the day she had to pull herself together, not fall apart. Jocelyn needed her. It wasn't the first time. Grace swung her legs out of the bed and sat up. If she could focus on Jocelyn, she could get through the day without a full-blown panic attack. *You sure about that?* a voice chirped inside Grace's mind. She pursed her lips. *No, I'm not.*

Grace played outdated pop music to distract herself as she applied makeup heavier than usual. Although the residents of Cold Waters would not be dressed to attend a gala as they may normally be, she needed to look the part. Like she belonged there as a visitor. The music reminded her of that summer, and despite the bad memories, it forced her into the right mindset to deal with Jocelyn.

On one occasion, Grace had run into Mrs. Baker when she was entering the lobby to visit Jocelyn at treatment. A large fountain and meditative music could be heard in the background, but Mrs. Baker had a tendency to draw all attention to herself with a full face of makeup, contoured like a Kardashian, along with Louboutin heels and a Michael Kors bag. Of course, she had matching sunglasses too. For a moment, she didn't recognize Grace since she was barefaced and dressed in leggings and a sweater. Recognition flooded over her, and she lifted her glasses and reached toward her for a hug.

"Oh, Grace, dear," she murmured into her hair. Grace cringed at the pity in her voice. Her body smelled of the kinds of perfume Grace had only experienced from magazine samples at the hair salon. The scent of roses overwhelmed her. To Grace, Mrs. Baker simply smelled like money.

"Mrs. Baker." Grace hugged her back. She was simultaneously relieved to see her and horrified. She had become like a mother to Grace, replacing her own when she passed from cancer a few years back. Although she was not necessarily the nurturing type, she probably did more for Grace than her own mother had ever done. Her mother had loved her and tried her best, but she didn't understand that Grace couldn't follow in her footsteps. She refused to live in a double-wide and live life paycheck to paycheck.

"Shush, no, sweetheart. Please call me Claire." She pulled away briefly, holding firmly onto Grace's shoulders, before embracing her again. "Jocelyn is so lucky to have a friend like you to depend upon in times like these. All her others are too busy chasing waterfalls in the Amazon or something."

"Real waterfalls are overrated," Grace replied, gesturing to the fountain a few feet away. She hoped to ingratiate herself by making Mrs. Baker laugh. Instead, she nodded and smiled graciously.

"Today is a good day. She seems better. She will be so excited to see you." Mrs. Baker glanced down at the ground for a moment and hesitated before continuing. "Please don't stay with her for too long today. I don't want her to get worn out. Her energy is already low."

"I will leave as soon as I notice she needs rest."

"Grace dear, she won't show you that. You know how she likes to keep up appearances."

Grace nodded. *No, that's me, not Jocelyn. She couldn't give a flying fuck what people thought.*

"Of course. I'll only stay a moment then."

Mrs. Baker grinned and squeezed her arm.

"That's my girl. Thank you again for tending to her. I will see you again soon, I'm sure." She leaned in and kissed both of Grace's cheeks before replacing her sunglasses over her eyes and disappearing into the busy street. Heat spread across Grace's face. *Thank you again for tending to her?* Grace was left feeling like she was the paid help. She knew she couldn't let Mrs. Baker see her like that again.

Since then, Grace tried to pick times to visit Jocelyn when Mrs. Baker was unlikely to be there. Grace felt like she needed to maintain appearances with her. It was pointless since Mrs. Baker already knew she wasn't cut from the same cloth as the prestigious Baker clan. Grace couldn't afford to keep up appearances all the time without Jocelyn offering up makeup and her closet. Instead, she avoided Mrs. Baker whenever Jocelyn was having a "rough time," as her mother liked to call it.

Just in case, she dressed as closely to how Mrs. Baker had that day, even with her limited budget. She saved her more valuable items all for Cold Waters, just for a half-hour visit with Jocelyn. Grace couldn't risk running into her again looking so unpolished, and she never knew who else would be at Cold Waters. Perhaps her ticket out of Mr. Harris's office would be checking out after their latest relapse. Grace opened the door to her tiny closet and pushed aside her normal business wear to pull out the plastic-wrapped Michael Kors dress she found at Goodwill. Careful to not mark it, she slipped on the navy-blue satin over her shoulders and tied the belt.

Once Grace was satisfied that she looked like a mini-me of Mrs. Baker, she headed out the door, holding her purse close to her as she headed toward the subway. She braced herself for the scent of urine and humiliation as she boarded the car.

Most of the passengers she typically shared the car with were already at work for the day, increasing Grace's anxiety that Mr. Harris would think poorly of her. Her brain was trying its best to convince her that she was going to get fired. Grace reached into her purse and pulled out a small water bottle, taking a gulp and hoping it would settle her nerves. As she struggled to screw the cap back on, water splashed onto her dress.

"Shit!" The few passengers nearby glanced over. Grace offered a tiny smile and mouthed "sorry."

Within a few minutes, she was at the station closest to Cold Waters. She disembarked and checked her makeup in her phone's camera one last time before stepping into the daylight. The demographic of the city already seemed different, even what seemed a few short minutes from her apartment. Women dressed like Mrs. Baker were everywhere, pushing strollers and carrying dogs in their handbags. They were heading to brunch or getting a quick workout in before a shopping spree. Grace found herself caught up in daydreaming about their lives. Maybe one day she wouldn't have to worry about money or bills or a job she hated.

Cold Waters was a block from the station. She pulled open the glass door and entered with confidence. This was not her first rodeo. She moved to the visitor desk and smiled at the nurse working.

"Hello, Grace Simmons to visit Jocelyn Baker, please." The nurse was unfazed by Grace's directness. Little did she know, Grace had practiced that exact phrase at least twenty times before leaving her apartment.

"Sign here please. Can I have your ID?"

Grace picked up the pen to sign, but paused.

"My ID?" They had never asked for that before.

"It's a new procedure. Now that we accept minors in our program, we are required by the state to obtain ID from all visitors."

Grace pulled out her wallet and handed her ID to the nurse. Her scrubs were pulled tight across her large frame, and for a brief second, Grace imagined the stitching screaming for relief.

"Thank you." She entered the ID into a small scanner and printed a temporary badge for Grace with her picture plastered black and white on it. She handed back the ID with the badge.

"Miss Baker is on the third floor in room 320, but she will likely be in the dayroom at this time, so check there first. Your badge is only good for 30 minutes, as she has a limitation on the length of visits currently."

Grace took pause once again. She could never remember Jocelyn having this type of restriction before, at least formally.

"Is that a new policy, as well?"

"No, it does not apply to all our patients. Her doctors have decided that visits any longer could be detrimental to her recovery." The nurse rolled her eyes but attempted to hide it by turning away from the desk to a filing cabinet.

Mrs. Baker would be devastated by these restrictions. The only time she really spent with Jocelyn anymore was during her stays at Cold Waters and St. George. She would come after lunch and stay until Jocelyn's afternoon therapy session around four, depending on the facility. It didn't make sense why the doctor would put such a strict restriction on Jocelyn. She had never needed that before.

Before entering the elevator, she passed through a set of metal detectors. Pausing after she went through, she looked to the security guard to make sure she could proceed. Instead of speaking, he grunted and swiped his badge on the terminal outside the elevator. The door glided open for Grace.

The elevator brought Grace to the third floor. The doors opened to reveal a very different picture than the stereotypical mental hospital. Although it smelled faintly of antiseptic, there was a distinct effort to conceal it with lavender and eucalyptus. The furniture was new and mostly white or shades of beige. The walls were painted bright yellows and blues. Grace stepped directly into the dayroom, which was accompanied by a nurse's station (or the prison guard station as Jocelyn always called it). Grace trudged forward, her legs feeling heavy. Despite being a regular visitor, being here always brought alive a deep fear inside her.

The dayroom was nearly empty, with a few people scattered about. One pair was playing Scrabble in the corner, while another sat cross-legged, paging through a book. The room could easily be mistaken for a recently renovated college library. Grace scanned the seats in the dayroom and saw no trace of Jocelyn.

Grace turned and scanned the sign directing visitors to different patient room numbers. There was no room 320 listed. Grace trotted back to the nurse's station, where a much friendlier face awaited. She was a young blonde nurse who looked like she hadn't had her spirit crushed yet by the pains of working at Cold Waters. Not only did they face needy patients daily, but they had to cope with their even needier families, who demanded only the best and were ready to sue at the drop of a hat. Families like the Baker's.

"Can I help you find someone?" Her head tilted to the side and she looked genuinely concerned.

"Hi, I'm looking for Jocelyn."

The nurse's demeanor shifted. She glanced down the hallway to the right.

"Jocelyn is not having a great day today. Perhaps you could come back another day?" she asked. Grace matched her frown and shook her head after a moment.

"There must be more than one patient with that name. I'm looking for Jocelyn Baker. The woman downstairs said she would be in the dayroom now." The blonde nurse bit her bottom lip for a moment and glanced at Grace's badge.

"We are talking about the same Jocelyn. The receptionist doesn't have access to all of her files, so she didn't know. Honestly, Jocelyn shouldn't be approved to see any visitors at all."

"What? Can you pull up her file and check? I've never had an issue like this before." Mentally, Grace praised herself for taking on such a superior tone despite the overwhelming feeling of nervousness. Her parents had raised her to be kind, but she wasn't sure how successful that had been for any of them. The nurse, out of obligation, searched Jocelyn's name on the computer and met Grace's stare again after a moment.

"As I said, she is not having a great day today. The

doctor has written in her file that no visitors other than family should be permitted today specifically. Maybe tomorrow you could call and see if she is getting along better?" the nurse offered, trying to smile through the tension Grace was omitting.

"I took today off from work specifically to see her." She bit her bottom lip for a moment before remembering she was supposed to be acting entitled and confident. Instead, she placed her hands defiantly on her hips. Grace scolded herself for asking Mr. Harris for time to visit Jocelyn. For years, Grace had put Jocelyn ahead of herself. She knew that needed to change. The nurse tried to give Grace a hopeful smile as she read the name off her badge.

"Miss Simmons, why don't you have a seat, and I will go check to see how Jocelyn is doing? If she seems better, maybe she could handle a very brief visit. Only about five minutes though." The nurse glanced at the elevator nervously, looking like she was afraid her boss would walk in as she was breaking the rules. Grace knew that fear all too well. For her sake, she nodded and moved toward the nearby seats.

"Thank you." She moved away from the desk and turned down the right hallway.

Grace peeked around the corner to watch her. There was a door separating that section of the floor from the rest, something she had never noticed before. The nurse scanned her badge to enter. The lights were dimmed in the hallway, contrasting greatly with the airiness of the dayroom. At the end of the hallway, just before the door began to swing shut, Grace thought she saw a man. It was a flash of broad shoulders and black clothes. And even though she could barely see him, she felt like she knew exactly who it was. Before she could get a better look, the door clicked shut, and he was gone.

Grace picked at her cuticles and stared at the white tile floor. Her heart was smashing itself against her ribcage. It wasn't really possible that man was here, just like it wasn't really possible that Jocelyn wasn't allowed visitors. None of it made sense, and for a moment, Grace considered the possibility that she was dreaming. With a pinch, she pulled a hangnail loose, and the nail bed flooded with blood. No, it was not a dream. It just felt like a completely different reality.

4

July 15, 2011

The cabin was deceiving. It shared the same classic exterior as the camp office. Grace was hopeful for a moment when they approached, believing that maybe the interior was updated as well. She had seen the pictures online, so she held out hope they had remodeled. They had not.

There were ten bunks in the cabin, including two beds near the front of the cabin for the counselors. Grace set her bags down and ran her fingers over carvings in the wood of the bunks. Hearts with initials carved inside were a common theme, though there were quite a few that had been scratched out in a poor attempt to erase some unrequited love. Jocelyn had already claimed hers, closest to one of the few windows in the cabin. Her clothes were strewn about as if she had already been here for a week. The base of Jocelyn's bunk had *"Marge sux"* carved into the wood. Grace wondered if maybe Jocelyn had done that herself.

"You've gotten comfortable." Grace gestured to Jocelyn's things.

Jocelyn plopped down on her bed, not bothering to move the clothes and magazines on it. Buried under it all, a gray quilt was bunched up near the foot of her bed, along with white sheets that looked silky and expensive. The idea of white sheets always made Grace nervous.

"After a few days here, you will too."

"A few days?" Grace thought she meant that she was already comfortable because she had been a resident at Camp Willows before, but something in Jocelyn's tone didn't sound so light.

"Yeah, my parents dropped me off on the 11th because they had to attend some gala in Europe or some shit."

"Your parents dropped you off early?" Grace found herself asking if that was really an option and why hadn't she thought of that herself earlier.

"They basically pay Marge's salary so she said yes. Plus, I think she felt bad." Jocelyn had dropped the nickname now, demonstrating that she only used it to irritate their boss. Grace paused at the four-drawer dresser at the foot of her bunk and turned to face Jocelyn fully.

"What have you been doing the past four days then?"

"A whole lot of this." Jocelyn gestured to her current position lying on the bed. It seemed like for just a second, her tough exterior cracked. Grace could see that Jocelyn was suffering just like she was. That they were both unhappy.

"Right." Grace nodded, unsure of what else there really was to say.

"I've had my phone, which is basically what I would be doing if I was at home anyway, so no biggie." She tried to brush off the sadness she had let leak into her voice before. Grace felt sympathetic to Jocelyn's tough girl facade: sadness meant weakness, and Jocelyn did not want to ever be weak.

As Grace pulled out her underwear, Jocelyn began to comment, "You should really get something sexy. Nobody wants to get into ugly granny panties." Jocelyn barely glanced up from her cell phone. Grace hadn't even realized she was watching closely enough to see them.

"That's not really why I came here this summer, but I suppose you're right. Too late now." Grace shrugged.

"Everyone comes to summer camp to get laid. You mean, you didn't?"

"I don't think that's true."

Jocelyn raised an eyebrow and sat up.

"Let me get this straight: you've never been to camp before and you suddenly think you're an expert?"

"I guess," Grace replied, sitting down on her mattress.

"Maybe you're right. I guess there is one other reason people come to camp. To run away from something," she suggested, nodding along in agreement with herself.

"And I'm guessing some people are doing both." Grace smirked and glanced Jocelyn's way, wanting to see if she agreed. She grinned but didn't look up from her phone to meet Grace's eyes.

5

November 8, 2019

"Miss Simmons. Miss Simmons." Grace jumped as a hand touched her shoulder. The blonde nurse looked at her with concern. "Are you alright?" Grace had disappeared in time once again. Just like she had at her desk earlier in the week. This time she felt confident she hadn't fallen asleep, but she didn't have a clue what had happened in the last few minutes. The couple in the corner was gone, along with the reader sitting alone. She hadn't noticed them leave.

"I'm fine. I must have been daydreaming." A drop of blood sat on the floor before her. Grace covered it with her foot and hid her finger that was now stained with dried blood. Last she could remember, she had pulled a hangnail. Now the blood was dry. *How long was I out?*

"Jocelyn seems to be up for a very short visit if you are ready."

31

Grace looked up at her, confusion spreading across her face.

"Who?" she asked before shaking her head and offering a small laugh out of embarrassment. "Of course. I'm sorry. Like I said, you caught me in the middle of a daydream. Should I wait out here for her?"

The nurse grimaced.

"Miss Simmons, are you close with Jocelyn?"

"Yes, she's my best friend. Why?" Grace bristled at the nurse's new set of questions. She tried to hide her resentment since this nurse seemed to be going out of her way to help. Grace just didn't like being questioned.

"I think you should know before you see her that she may be worse off than you are expecting. She has lost her dayroom privileges and isn't allowed around other patients at the moment. She has been suffering from outbursts. The doctor thinks it may be delusions but . . ." She trailed off and sighed. "I really shouldn't be sharing this with you, but I want to prepare you. She is likely nothing like the Jocelyn you are used to seeing." Grace shook her head and glanced down the hallway where Jocelyn was being kept.

"I've visited Jocelyn many times here. I don't understand. She has never had issues like this before. Is her medication causing this? It's not like her."

"I've already said more than I should, Miss Simmons. But I will tell you, her mother said yesterday when she was here that she didn't understand it. She had never seen her daughter this far"—she paused, searching for the right word— "so far gone." Chills wrapped around Grace's spine.

"Oh" was all that she could manage to say. The nurse placed a hand on her shoulder again and offered a tiny smile.

"It can be difficult to see someone you care about like this. Are you sure *you* are ready?" she asked. Grace gave a small nod and got to her feet, careful not to smear the drop of blood she had left.

"I'm ready." Without another word, the nurse led her through the security door and down the dim hallway. It was eerily quiet. After the nurse's description, Grace expected screams. Patients rattling the door handles. Desperation hanging in the air. There was none of that.

Finally, they stopped at room 320. The nurse knocked before unlocking the door, as if Jocelyn had some semblance of privacy in this place. The door looked like it wasn't made of much more than the ones Grace would find in her apartment, though it did have a small window to look through. The glass was webbed with some kind of metal to reinforce it, and Grace wondered if the door was actually stronger than it looked. *Could it hold back someone who was having a breakdown?*

"Miss Simmons is here," she said, opening the door gradually as if it was a warning. Grace stepped inside, trying to stop herself from shaking. This was not the visit she had planned.

Jocelyn was sitting cross-legged on the bed, staring at the beige wall. The bed looked less like one from a hospital and more like a prison. The only exception was the metal frame had padding covering it. Her black hair looked like it hadn't been washed or brushed in days. Upon closer inspection, patches of hair were missing entirely.

Grace glanced back at the nurse. She moved close and whispered into Grace's ear, "She keeps pulling on it and making it like that." Her warm breath against

Grace's face sent shivers rolling down her back. Grace took one step farther into the room, toward Jocelyn's bed. She didn't look up for so long. It was almost as if she was asleep with her eyes open. Grace imagined herself looking the same when the nurse had discovered her in the dayroom and unsuccessfully attempted to push the thought away.

"Jocelyn." Grace's voice cracked on the second syllable. Jocelyn's head turned gradually toward Grace like she didn't care who she was or that she was there at all. No recognition crossed her face. "It's me, Grace." Grace was nearly whispering. Jocelyn uncrossed her legs.

"I know," she murmured. The nurse offered a hesitant but encouraging smile to Grace, who wanted to bolt back out the door. This was not Jocelyn. But it was.

"I am just going to step out into the hallway. I will leave the door cracked. Just call if you need me." Grace wanted to shout no and grab the nurse's hand, but she stopped herself. She wasn't sure how well Jocelyn would react to sudden movements. The nurse left the door open halfway as she disappeared into the hall.

"Can I sit?" Grace asked, pointing to the bed. Jocelyn nodded, and Grace slowly settled in next to her friend.

As the awkwardness of the moment grew, Grace ran her finger along the quilt covering the bed. It was the same one Grace had seen each time she came to visit Jocelyn. She could imagine it bunched up in the back of Mrs. Baker's car, ready to be whipped out whenever Jocelyn's mental health took a nosedive.

"Why are you here?" she asked after they were both silent for over a minute.

"What do you mean? I always visit you."

She shook her head.

"Not always. Not when I needed you."

Grace reached over and touched her shoulder. Even through the fabric hospital gown, she felt clammy. Normally, Jocelyn sported her own athleisure clothing at Cold Waters. She would rather be caught dead than wearing a hospital gown. And yet, here she was.

"What are you talking about?"

Jocelyn didn't meet Grace's eyes. Instead, her eyes were fixated on the wall straight ahead.

"At camp. You weren't there."

A burst of anxiety bubbled from Grace's stomach and into her throat, burning like acid.

"At camp? That was forever ago." It had been eight years but Grace knew exactly what she meant. The blood drained out of her face, and her hands began to tremble.

"That night." Jocelyn whipped her head to face her, and Grace withdrew her hand from her shoulder. "You weren't there that night. The only night I needed you."

Grace drew back, rising to her feet and shrinking toward the wall. For just a second, she wanted to shout back. She wanted to ask if Jocelyn wanted her dead, because that's probably what would have happened if she had been there. Guilt nagged on the edges of her mind and stopped her from questioning her.

"Jocelyn, I'm sorry I wasn't there. I didn't know. I couldn't have known." Grace's voice shook.

The tension in Jocelyn's face eased, and she nodded continuously, unable to stop.

In seconds, her face contorted from anger to devastation as she began to cry. "I know. But I still needed you." Her voice cracked now. Her head collapsed into her hands, the sobbing becoming uncontrollable in mere seconds. Grace wanted to console her, but fear overcame her instinct as Jocelyn began to moan and gasp for air between her breaths. She began beating her arms against the bed. It wasn't until that moment that Grace noticed the large purple bruises covering Jocelyn's forearms. The door began to open and the nurse re-entered. When she saw Jocelyn, her eyes darted back to Grace.

"What the hell did you say to her? She was doing better!" Grace frowned and moved toward the open door as the nurse approached Jocelyn cautiously. "Jocelyn, it is Li—" Before she could even get her name out, Jocelyn ripped the white pillow off her bed and began swinging at the nurse, screaming.

"Get away from me! Grace, get him away from me! Please!"

Immediately the nurse backed away, holding her arms up to protect her face as Jocelyn dropped the pillow and resorted to scratching at the woman's face. Grace stood, paralyzed, watching the scene unfold. This was not the Jocelyn she knew. It never had been the Jocelyn she knew. Grace pressed herself against the wall, hoping she could just disappear. Hoping she could make it all disappear.

The nurse barked orders at Grace as she attempted to grab Jocelyn's wrists and restrain her.

"Get the hell out! Now!"

Trembling, Grace edged along the wall and out the door, feeling her breathing becoming strained. She glanced to the right, disoriented about how to get back to the dayroom. Grace's eyes fell upon the man from before. Dressed in all black, hands in his pockets, watching. Fear seized her as she spun on her heels and ran to the left, grabbing desperately at the handle of the security door. It was locked.

6

July 15, 2011

Jocelyn led Grace down to the lake by their cabin after dinner. As they trotted down the gravel path, Jocelyn reached into the pocket of her hoodie and withdrew a silver flask. In the setting sun, Grace could see the glimmer of an engraved family crest.

"Want some?" Jocelyn asked as she unscrewed the lid.

"I don't drink."

Jocelyn put her hand out across Grace's chest and stopped her midstep.

"What you mean is you haven't drank in the past. If you're going to be my co-counselor, you're going to have to drink." *This bitch is pretty pushy.*

"So that's how this works?" Grace chuckled. She nodded and tried to pass the flask to her. Grace pushed it away.

"I'm serious. Take a sip or I'll tell Margie I found it in your suitcase and that you were getting wasted the night before the kids arrived."

Grace turned her body to face Jocelyn fully. Grace was waiting for her to laugh, but she didn't. There was a glint in Jocelyn's eye, daring anyone to challenge her.

"You're bluffing."

"I'm not." Jocelyn shook her head before she took a swig from the flask and wiped her mouth with the back of her hand. "Who do you think Margie would believe? The rich girl who she has known since she was ten, or the poor girl who is only at camp to run away from something—my money is on me. Also, I would like to place a bet now that you're running away from some serious daddy issues."

Jocelyn pushed the flask into Grace's hand and continued down the path toward the water without looking back. Grace wasn't positive Marge would believe her. There was no choice: Grace had to drink. What felt like lighter fluid swirled down her throat, but after, she could taste cinnamon. She wanted to hate it, but she wasn't sure she did. She decided to take a second sip for good measure.

For a moment, Grace was unsure how to feel. It seemed like Jocelyn could be the big sister she had always wanted. Now that Grace had someone like that, she understood why people hated their siblings.

Perched on the dock, they dipped their toes into the cool lake water to relieve themselves from the humid summer air. Grace had never drunk alcohol before. It seemed silly to feel buzzed, but Grace felt a giddiness she had never experienced before. Jocelyn encouraged her to take another sip. Grace did. For the first time in her life, she actually relaxed. The girls giggled together as they chatted. It was as if they both had transformed into completely different people.

"Leonardo DiCaprio is definitely hot," Jocelyn argued.

"But he's super old now," Grace shook her head a little too far in each direction, a smile spreading across her face.

"Just because he's old doesn't mean he isn't hot. And now, he's super rich. I'd take old Leo over young Leo any day." Jocelyn nodded triumphantly as she saw Grace smile.

"I can't argue with that logic." Grace wondered if they were more alike than she initially thought. Jocelyn took another long sip from the flask.

"You know what?"

"What do I know?" Grace asked.

Jocelyn broke into a laughing fit that caused tears to fill her eyes.

"You're so formal." There was a pause as she tried to contain her laughter. "I am glad you're here. You are so different from the normal trash that floods this place. It's nice to have some fresh meat."

Grace began to laugh too. For once, she felt like she fit in. In a place where she had only hoped to belong.

"Jocelyn, are you calling yourself trash?"

Jocelyn shrieked and dissolved back into giggles, her face turning red. Her feet flailed over the edge of the dock, kicking water up onto both of their thighs.

"I guess so." She held up the flask once she contained herself. "To being trash!" She held the flask up as though she was making a toast and drank the rest. She attempted to push the empty flask back into the back pocket of her jean short, but she kept missing the hole. Ultimately, Jocelyn had lay down on her side to accomplish the task, but not without struggle. Grace found herself almost falling into the lake as her body shook with laughter.

After a moment, they pulled themselves back together while they stared at the sun setting over the lake. The blue of the lake mingled with shades of orange, yellow, and purple. Grace would have wanted a picture, but she knew moments like these never photographed well.

"It's so beautiful—" Jocelyn began.

"You are definitely different from what I'm used to, too. I don't like my kind of trash either." There was a sudden heaviness in the air that hadn't been there a moment before. Grace wasn't sure why she had said it, but the words had tumbled out. The alcohol had loosened her tongue and mind.

"Guess we'll have to deal with all the rest of it tomorrow." Jocelyn shrugged, not bothering to take Grace too seriously.

"What do you mean?"

"All the rest of the trash. Once the kids come, this place is completely different. We will be catering to spoiled, rich brats. And the ones who aren't brats, they're the ones getting picked on by the brats. And a lot of the time, there's nothing we can do because the brats have parents who aren't afraid to pull the extra funding from the camp. Margie is basically a politician running this place: taking bribes and keeping her wealthy constituents happy."

I guess it isn't so different from the real world then, Grace thought.

"Is it really that bad?"

Jocelyn stood up and offered her hand to help Grace to her feet.

41

"Guess you'll find out tomorrow, huh?"

A beat passed between them.

"Which one were you?" Grace asked. Jocelyn tilted her head at Grace, confused. "Which one were you: the brat or the bullied kid." She moved her eyes back out onto the lake, not returning Grace's gaze.

"Which do you think?" Her tone was solemn. Grace began to consider the question. Jocelyn was so strong and quick-witted. She couldn't imagine her being a victim, but at the same time, she seemed like damaged goods, just like herself. Grace opened her mouth to speak, but Jocelyn was already turned to walk away. Her silence was enough to answer the question.

* * *

The end of the next day smelled like sweat and bug spray. Their 14-year-old campers were settled into their bunks, exhausted and homesick but quiet. Jocelyn and Grace sat on the steps of the front porch of the cabin, enjoying the quiet after a day of chaos.

"14-year-old girls suck," Jocelyn remarked, glancing back at the cabin behind them.

"They aren't too bad. They're just . . ." Grace burst out laughing. "I can't think of a single word to encapsulate a 14-year-old girl. Just something, I guess."

Jocelyn let out a genuine laugh, the only one from her all day, with the exception of when she saw a young boy from another cabin fall headfirst into a mud puddle while he was carrying all of his camp bags.

"Something for sure." Jocelyn stared down the path at a group of male counselors sitting on their own cabin steps. "I think I need to do something to unwind . . ." She brought herself to her feet and tied a knot in her teal camp shirt so it looked more like a crop top than the giant rectangle it truly was. Her jean shorts sat low on her hips, revealing her olive skin. Grace contemplated how she had achieved such an even skin tone, especially in the summer. Jocelyn turned and began prancing down the trail, shaking the tiny curves she had. "You coming?" she called back. Grace glanced back at the cabin, nervous.

"What about the girls?"

She shrugged and carried on. Grace felt like she shouldn't leave them on their own with no counselor, but she was just going down a few cabins. She couldn't see any harm in it. She jogged to catch up with Jocelyn, tucking the front of her counselor shirt into her jean shorts. Jocelyn was right. The boys were cute. Even from a distance, it was like she could sense it.

"Hey, boys!" Jocelyn said, a smirk already painted upon her face. She stood with her hands on her hips, staring down at the boys on the cabin steps. Grace stayed a little off to the side, since Jocelyn looked like she was trying to frighten them into submission.

"Hi, Jocelyn," the boy with brown hair replied. "This is Matt. He's new this year."

Jocelyn nodded her head in his direction and offered a friendly smile. Matt sported longer dark hair that was somewhere between brown and black. He looked up at Jocelyn and nodded, but his expression remained unchanged. He did not offer a smile or a hello. He simply looked at the girls.

"This is Grace. She's obviously new too. This is Alex. We go way back." Jocelyn winked at Alex. Although he smiled, his eyes looked fearful.

"Hi, Grace. Are you a girl of few words too?" he asked, gesturing with his thumb at Matt. Matt remained unfazed by this comment and continued to watch the conversation unfold.

"I don't think so? Maybe sometimes." She glanced at Matt and tried to offer a friendly smile, but still, he had no reaction.

"I'm going inside," Matt remarked, getting to his feet and turning to go inside the cabin.

"Good night, then," Alex said, holding out his hand to Matt for a handshake. He ignored the hand and went inside without another word. Jocelyn settled next to Alex on the porch and frowned.

"He's a weirdo," Jocelyn whispered.

"He acts normal around the kids, but as soon as it's just him and me, he gets that way. Doesn't say a word. When I asked him about it, he just said he's not talkative and that he just likes to soak everything in. His dad is like a congressman or something. I guess he used to go to a different camp, but he didn't want to be a counselor there because it would be weird being in charge of friends. At least, that's what Marge told me this morning when I asked her about him," Alex said, keeping his voice low.

Grace leaned against the column of the porch so she could hear their conversation better. Jocelyn tried to move closer to Alex, but he jumped up instead.

"I need to go to the bathroom," he said. "I need a shower after being around these kids all day."

"Wait, you had the one that fell in the mud, didn't you!" Jocelyn exclaimed, checking his clothing for signs of mud that may have hit him as well.

"Yeah, don't remind me. That kid was a sobbing mess for hours. Apparently, the bags he had were brand new and his mother had told him specifically not to get them dirty. Total meltdown. Anyways, I'll see you around." He popped up from the steps and turned into the cabin, the door swinging shut behind him.

"Did you see that?" she asked brusquely as she stood and headed back toward their cabin.

"See what?"

Jocelyn's demeanor had flipped on its head. She went from flirty to enraged in seconds. Jocelyn's personality was a light switch. Sometimes she was on, and when she was off, she was someone else entirely. There seemed to be nothing in between.

"The way he moved away when I sat near him. And once Matt left, he bailed as fast as he could. He spent all last summer begging to get me in bed, and now that he did, he's no longer interested."

Grace reached out and grabbed her arm.

"Wait, you had sex with him last summer?" Grace whispered, shocked. She shrugged off Grace's arm and kept walking, passing their cabin without stopping.

"That's what I'm *saying*. Are you not listening? Jesus Christ, try to keep up, Grace." Her pace was quickening and the distance between them spread. "He wants to just pretend it never happened, and that he wasn't chasing me like a lost puppy all last year. Instead, he thinks he has the right to act like I'm just his friend. Nothing more." Her voice was raised, and she was nearly sharing her sex life with the entire camp.

"Wait, Jocelyn!" Grace ran to close the distance between them. "Are you actually interested in him?" She put her hand on Jocelyn's shoulder and tried to turn her around. For a brief second, her face met Grace's. She was crying. Grace let go of her shoulder, surprised to see she was genuinely hurting. Jocelyn turned her body away and moved off the path and into the woods, disappearing while Grace said nothing.

7

November 8, 2019

Grace was curled up in the corner by the security door when the nurse found her. Jocelyn's door was shut, and the man was gone, but her face was red with tears. When the nurse first tried to help Grace get up, Grace crumpled back to the floor and dissolved into the terror once more. Her chest felt so heavy she couldn't pull in air. She made a wheezing noise each time she tried to breathe. It was like she was drowning in panic.

Grace wasn't just afraid of the man who had been haunting the end of the hallway; she was terrified of the way Jocelyn had acted. The fear in her eyes and voice had never been there before. Jocelyn was convinced the nurse was that man, just like Grace was convinced she had seen him in the hallway. She had thought she had seen him out of the corner of her eyes a few times over the years, but never twice in one day.

Finally, the nurse got Grace to her feet. Grace wiped her tears and snot on the sleeve of her sweater and gripped onto the nurse with the other arm.

"I'm so sorry. I don't know what I said," Grace whimpered, taking shallow breaths in between words. If the nurse wanted to yell and scream at her for triggering Jocelyn, she did not let it show. She scanned her badge and let Grace back into the dayroom, which must have been cleared by the security team, as all the patient doors were shut. They were all locked up. Not to protect other patients from each other but to protect the other patients from Jocelyn. The nurse led Grace to a high back chair by the window. Grace gripped the white armrests so tightly her knuckles nearly matched it.

"I'll be right back," she instructed before walking back to the nurse's station. She kept looking over her shoulder to ensure that Grace hadn't moved. She returned with a small bottle of water and a box of tissues.

"Here. Take some deep breaths. You're safe now. Jocelyn is safe. Everyone is safe." Her voice took on a soothing tone. She waited patiently as Grace regulated her breathing. Grace blew her nose, too overwhelmed about the event to even remember she was supposed to be acting like a wealthy family friend.

"I've just never seen her like that. Even at her worst." The tears started again, and the nurse rubbed her back in a small, circular motion.

"She didn't know where she was or who I was. It can be scary for anyone to see that." She paused and glanced toward the nurse's station. "Yesterday, she did not recognize her mother."

Grace covered her mouth with her hand.

"She thought her mother was that man?"

The nurse shook her head.

"No, it wasn't quite the same, but she didn't know it was her mother. She thought she was someone else. Mrs. Baker wasn't even sure who." The nurse released a sad sigh. Grace took a small, polite sip from the water bottle, trying to regain her posture.

"I should have listened to you originally. I'm sorry to have caused that." Grace took a moment before continuing. "Would it be possible for you to call me with an update of how she is doing tomorrow?"

"Do you know how much—" The nurse was winding up to go on a tirade about how she had violated policy for Grace already, but paused and shook her head. Grace could tell she pitied her, and she hated it. Even if it helped her get what she wanted.

"Yes." She pulled out a pen and a piece of paper from her black scrubs. "Write down your number," she told her before standing up. "I have to go check on Jocelyn and make sure she has settled. If I'm not back, just leave your number at the nurse's station." She turned back towards Jocelyn's room.

"Thank you!" Grace called after her. She didn't turn back this time. Grace feared she had stretched this woman's patience too far, but she was worried. If even Grace was seeing this man, Jocelyn must have been obsessing over him.

Once Grace made it onto the street again, it felt like hours had passed. The sky was so dark it seemed like night had fallen over the city, despite it only being lunchtime. There was a storm approaching, and the women that had been joyously moving through the streets were now tucked away in their little townhouses and brownstones, putting their babies down for naps.

Even though it was the middle of the day, Grace felt exhausted. She took the miserable trip on the subway back to her apartment and collapsed on her bed as soon as she walked in the door. Although she worried her mind would be racing too much to fall asleep, it seemed like she instantaneously fell unconscious, regardless of Jocelyn's outburst and her delusions or even the man in black appearing once more. Sleep wrapped her in a cocoon that blacked out all the world.

Grace awoke hours later with drool crusted to her chin and Harold demanding dinner. He kneaded into her thigh, letting out soft meows. She rubbed the sleep out of her eyes and sat up, her own stomach rumbling with hunger. She hadn't eaten anything all day, and her back ached from how she had passed out on the bed. Her mouth was dry, and her muscles felt tight.

While her body protested, she climbed out of bed and moved into the kitchenette to fill up Harold's dish. As she bent to drop his kibble into the bowl, her eyes fell upon her apartment door. Over the top of the kitchenette counter, she could see the pure white lighting of the hallway. Her apartment door was cracked open. Tingles raced up her arms as she rushed toward the door. But once she was there, she wasn't sure if she should close it or leave it untouched. *Should I call the cops? Could they dust for fingerprints? Was it even worth calling?*

Realizing how paranoid she sounded, she pushed the door shut and engaged the lock and chain, tugging on it a few times just to reassure herself. Grace tried to think back to when she arrived home. *Had I closed it when I got back? Did I remember to lock it?* She had been so tired she couldn't be certain she had done anything. But locking the door, that was something you did on autopilot. She shook her head and tried to convince herself that it was her mistake, but she wasn't sure. It seemed unlikely she would compromise the only thing keeping out the world and keeping in Harold. But at the same time, the other possibility was too daunting to consider.

Harold meowed at her feet, begging for the food that still hadn't come. If the door had been open the whole time, why hadn't Harold raced out? He always was trying to make a mad dash out the door whenever she opened it to leave. The reality of that thought was something she couldn't focus on. She tried to shake off the paranoia and fill his dish.

As she watched him scarf down food, she was reminded of her own hunger. She debated her options: order in and stay safe in the apartment, all the while inviting a stranger into her space, or go out, pick something up and bring it back, exposing herself to a whole world of potential dangers. Ultimately, it made more sense to go pick something up, as she believed safety would rest in numbers. She picked up her purse and keys and headed out, wrapping up in a scarf as if that would protect her from an attacker.

There was a small sub shop a few blocks down from her apartment that was well lit and close by. She decided that would be her best option, as her hands had still been shaking when she locked her apartment door. Once she made it out to the street, she walked fast and held onto her purse tightly. The street lights reflected off the wet cement sidewalks. She had slipped her house keys into her jacket pocket instead, in case someone tried to mug her. She was willing to give up her things, but not her safe space with Harold. Her legs moved almost as fast as her heartbeat.

Despite the nerves and anticipation, nothing happened on her way to the sub shop. Since it was a Friday night, it was busier than usual. The line wrapped around the shop, encroaching on a few patrons trying to eat at their tables. As she waited in line, she felt her phone buzz with a call. It was Mrs. Baker.

"Hello?" she called into the phone, plugging her other ear with a finger. Mrs. Baker's voice cut through the noises of people waiting in line and music playing overhead.

"Grace?" she asked. "Where are you? A club?"

Grace laughed. *Did that sound insensitive?* She thought she probably shouldn't laugh at a woman when she had just caused her daughter to have a mental breakdown.

"No, I'm just out getting dinner." She didn't want to disclose she was alone, getting a hunk of bread filled with deli meat. Somehow "dinner" sounded far more glamorous.

"I'm sorry to interrupt, but I had to ask you what happened today with Jocelyn." The tone of her voice became confrontational midway through the sentence. Taken aback, Grace stepped out of the line and weaved through the filled café tables to the corner of the store where the restrooms were to hear her better.

"Why? Is something the matter?" She could hear Mrs. Baker scoff on the other line. Mrs. Baker had never acted this way around her, but she could certainly tell where Jocelyn had gotten her personality from.

"Is something the matter?" Mrs. Baker repeated in awe. "They are kicking her out of Cold Waters and sending her to St. George. They said she attacked a nurse while she had a visitor today."

Grace frowned. The word "attack" brought back to Jocelyn's room, watching her scream at the blonde nurse, believing she was someone else entirely. Someone terrifying.

"Why on earth would they do that? She needs their help!" Grace protested, and she could feel Mrs. Baker rolling her eyes through the phone.

"She *attacked* an employee. That's where they draw the line, apparently. They said that St. George would be better suited to care for someone with such *severe* needs. Jocelyn's never been described as having severe needs before. That doctor there is a crackpot. And when I told them I would be contacting my lawyer because I believed there was malpractice going on, they told me their legal team had already"—she released an exasperated breath—"their legal team was already ready to fight such a claim because of her violent outbursts." If Mrs. Baker hadn't been so angry, Grace was certain she would be dissolving into sobs. She understood that it would be far easier to be angry than sad, so it made sense for her to take this out on someone else.

"I'm so sorry," Grace whispered into the phone, uncertain of what she could say to make her feel any better.

"Sorry doesn't mean anything, Grace. What the hell happened today!" she demanded. She was on the edge of breaking down, and Grace paused and tried to think of the best way to retell the horrific scene that had unfolded.

"I was speaking to her and she was thinking back to what had happened at camp," Grace started. Mrs. Baker knew this already. What had happened at camp was the source of all of Jocelyn's problems. Grace bounced her weight from one foot to another. She could no longer feel the hunger eating through her stomach. After moving aside so an elderly man could reach the bathroom, she decided to forge forward. It was likely Cold Waters had already told her the story. "She became really upset, and then, the nurse came in to tell me our time was up. Well, Jocelyn—" She struggled to find the right words to describe what Jocelyn had done.

"Jocelyn what!" Mrs. Baker barked. There were tears in her voice now.

"Jocelyn thought the nurse was the man from camp." Mrs. Baker was silent on the other line. Grace rubbed two fingers against her eyebrow, trying to ward off the first signs of a migraine. "Then the nurse told me to get out, and Jocelyn started attacking the nurse. She didn't know what she was doing. She thought she was in danger."

The silence on the line grew an uncomfortable length before Mrs. Baker replied.

"She didn't know where she was."

"Yes." Grace felt a bit guilty she was delivering this news over the phone.

"The doctors told me she was suffering from delusions or hallucinations or something but I didn't believe them."

"She seems to be in a really bad place," Grace finally admitted, just as much to herself as to Mrs. Baker. The sobs grew on the other line. She frowned and stared at her dingy sneakers. Her eyes traced the white-and-black tile of the floor as she waited for a reply. She couldn't imagine being Jocelyn's mother at this moment. Eventually, Mrs. Baker pulled herself together and returned to her usual formal tone.

"Thank you for visiting her. I'm sure she appreciated seeing a friend there," Mrs. Baker stated.

"Can you let me know when she arrives at St. George so I can see her again?"

Again, silence returned to the line. In the shop, the owner dressed in a white apron smudged with a variety of sauces yelled out a name three times before a person stepped forward.

"I don't think it is a good idea for you to visit her anymore, Grace."

The words smacked her in the face. Her mouth opened to ask why, but she already knew. She understood. Mrs. Baker didn't want someone like her to trigger her daughter again, and if St. George refused to help her, their options were limited. She would have to be sent somewhere outside the city.

"I understand." Grace hesitated for a moment before adding, "Please let me know if there is anything I can do." It was an offer she always made to Mrs. Baker, but this time, she knew more than ever that she would not be accepting it.

8

July 18, 2011

"Wakey wakey."

Grace's eyes jumped open. Jocelyn was leaning over her, nearly whispering in her ear.

"What the hell?" Her voice was a raspy whisper. She could barely make out Jocelyn's face in the dark. "It's the middle of the night!" The girls around them were all asleep.

"Don't be dramatic. It's like 4:00 a.m. I have something I want to show you."

Grace rolled her eyes and pulled her thin cotton blankets up against her face.

"So show me!"

"No, it's a place. Get up."

This piqued her interest. Jocelyn, smirking down at her, leaned away so Grace could get up. She rubbed at the sleep in the corners of her eyes.

"Put on some sneakers and follow me." Jocelyn went out the door without hesitation.

* * *

Grace trudged through the underbrush as Jocelyn led her through the woods.

"Come on. Where are we going?" Grace moaned. Water splatted against their legs from the morning dew.

"Trust me, it's worth it."

"I bet you're leading me straight into the arms of a serial killer. I bet that's what this is. He said he would let you go free as long as once a year—" Grace chuckled.

Jocelyn looked back at her and grinned.

"Go on. Once a year what?"

"You have to bring a young virgin to sacrifice. Obviously, I'm the young virgin in this scenario."

"Obviously." Grace reached out to hit Jocelyn's arm but stopped midway.

"We're here."

They had entered a clearing. Around them sat cabins in various states of disrepair. Some had windows broken, others were missing entire windows or doors. One's roof had caved in. Sections of the gray wood were covered with vibrant green moss.

"Is this the original campground?"

"You bet your ass."

Grace approached the closest cabin, amazed. It still had a large sign that read OFFICE. The sign now hung vertically as one of the nails had come loose. When a strong wind came by, it swung side to side. She had no idea these had still existed. Marge had talked about the original camp during their orientation, but she hadn't shared that it was still standing. Mostly.

"Disappointed that there's no serial killer?"

"Only a little bit," Grace murmured as she entered the cabin. Jocelyn followed behind. A wooden desk sat next to a beige filing cabinet with peeling paint, exposing the dark brown metal beneath. Both were covered with layers of dust. There were a few handprints here and there. A wooden chair sat broken in the corner.

"Wait, check this out." Jocelyn led Grace outside of the cabin and around to the side.

"A payphone?" Grace ran her fingers along the cool metal.

"Pretty cool, right? These things are like relics."

"Does it work?"

Jocelyn shrugged. "I haven't tried. Believe it or not, I don't carry around quarters with me."

They moved back around to sit at the front of the cabin and started talking.

Shortly, Grace and Jocelyn fell into comfortable conversation. "That one girl, with the red hair—"

"Catherine," Grace provided.

"Yes! Her! She's the most annoying one of them all." Grace rolled her eyes and shook her head.

"You only think that because she is exactly like you."

Jocelyn gave Grace a death stare before dissolving into laughter.

"Okay, you might be a little bit right, but you don't have to be a bitch about it."

"Jocelyn, I think I am the only person in this world who isn't a bitch to you." They both paused at this statement. Grace had meant it in a lighthearted sense, but there was a heaviness to it that they weren't prepared for.

"What I mean is—" Grace began before Jocelyn set a hand on her knee.

"No, you are right. And you are the only person who is honest with me."

Grace couldn't meet Jocelyn's eyes, so she looked at a tree just past her.

"That's a good thing, right?"

"Definitely." They could hear the cicadas around them chirp as they sat still, waiting for the other to speak.

"I kind of thought you had it easy, you know? Because of the money." Grace felt heat spread across her cheeks as she plunged deeper into honesty.

"I mean, I do. It's just hard in different ways." Grace thought about how the Bakers dropped Jocelyn off four days early just so she wouldn't be an inconvenience to them. She thought about her own mom spending her only savings so she could pursue this stupid camp dream.

"I came here to network. I don't know who the hell I thought I would be networking with." Grace let out a bitter laugh.

"With me, silly!" Jocelyn stood up and twirled in a circle before holding out her hand to shake Grace's. "Jocelyn Baker, heiress to the Baker estate, at your service." Grace smiled and shook her hand.

"Grace Simmons, heiress to my father's Budweiser collection." She expected Jocelyn to laugh, but instead she held onto her hand with both of hers.

"Budweiser? I cannot say I am familiar. Is that a brand of cars?" Jocelyn kept a straight face and Grace chuckled.

"You are quite the actress!" Jocelyn shrugged and settled back onto the cabin porch steps.

"It's a good skill to have. It's gotten me out of a lot of tight spots."

"Guess you could teach me a thing or two."

"You have come to the master of deception, after praising yourself for your honesty. Grace Simmons, you are quite an interesting character."

"You might be good at acting, but I'm good at secrets."

Jocelyn smiled and leaned in. "Oh yeah? Any good ones yet?"

Grace laughed and leaned back, with her arms supporting her weight.

"Not yet, but I'll let you know once I do."

9

November 8, 2019

"Grace! Grace!" The fog in her head was beginning to clear. "Order for Grace!" The man behind the counter called as she stumbled over her feet. The moments had slipped away from her again. She hadn't even remembered ordering food, but she must have. The man stared at her, suggesting there wasn't some other Grace that had ordered. She stepped forward and grabbed the bag he held out, her hand shaking a bit. Concerned, the man suggested, "Is this not what you ordered? A turkey and cheddar? Your usual?"

Grace nodded and turned to walk out of the shop, stuck in a daze.

Grace paused at the door and tucked the sub into her oversized purse, clutching it to her side. As the memories came flooding back, she felt an overwhelming sense of fear. She couldn't quite remember why, but she knew she had to be careful.

Setting off into the cold November night, she wrapped the scarf around her neck a few more times. With each inch she got closer to her apartment, the past few hours came rolling back in waves: Jocelyn attacking the nurse, the apartment door being open, and Mrs. Baker's upsetting phone call. Even larger than those memories was the anxiety building in her stomach. It was a bubble waiting to burst, leaving her in fragments. She thought back to the sandwich in her purse and felt sick at the thought of eating it.

Grace glanced down the alley a block before her building and stopped. Her purse fell to the ground. At the end of the alley, he was there. A light above him flickered, casting shadows across his face. His legs were shoulder-width apart, his hands crossed in front of his body. He wasn't moving, just watching. He knew where she lived.

Grace stared back at him, entranced. The overwhelming smell of the alley made her eyes water, blurring his shape. Her mind screamed at her legs to run, but she was glued to the pavement, a signpost declaring she was an easy target.

"Here you go, miss."

Grace pried her head away from the alleyway to see an old man with fuzzy eyebrows and large, round glasses holding out her purse to her.

"Are you okay, dear? Do you need directions?" he asked after she didn't respond. Finally, she reached out and took the purse from him.

"Thank you," she mumbled before glancing back at the alley. He was gone. It was as if he hadn't been there at all.

Grace pushed past the old man and raced down the

street toward her apartment, her legs finally receiving the message from her brain. She heard the old man yell something, but she couldn't process it over her labored breath and the static in her ears. All she could hear was the terror rising up her throat, like acid creeping to the surface. She made it to a trash can outside her building just as the bile poured out of her mouth. There was no food in her stomach, just acid and fear.

Wiping her mouth with the back of her hand, Grace glanced back and searched the crowd for the man in black. She took a quick moment to catch her breath, gripping onto the cool black metal of the trash can.

"Calm down, Grace," she whispered to herself, focusing on breathing in and out. The world around her was spinning and the only thing keeping her upright was this trash can.

Once she gathered herself and confirmed that there was no man nearby, she raced through the lobby, nearly knocking over a fake plant coated in a thin layer of dust by the stairs. As she rushed up the two flights to her apartment, she scrambled to get her keys out of her coat pocket. Finally, she yanked them out, ripping her coat as the keys finally appeared.

She jammed the key toward the lock, her hands trembling like a washing machine. After two failed attempts, she finally got the key in. Desperate, she pushed herself inside just as Harold slipped past her into the hallway.

"Harold, no!" she yelled, but her body didn't stop. She slammed the door shut anyway, just as the cat raced down the hallway and turned the corner.

She collapsed, laying her back against the door, sobs racking her body. Black dots clouded her vision, and her skin felt like it was on fire. She tried to breathe, but it felt like she couldn't get any air. Her belongings fell in a puddle onto the floor around her.

Grace reached up behind herself and slide the chain lock into place, knowing she couldn't go back out there, even to save Harold. She couldn't go back outside, knowing what could be out there. He wouldn't listen to her calling anyway and would easily escape out into the street.

Grace wanted to say that the man hadn't been there. That she had imagined him. Over the years, he had appeared infrequently, at moments of high anxiety, but never three times in one day. He was not in her imagination. He was out there, he was following her, and she was pretty sure he knew where she lived.

* * *

After taking twice the recommended amount of NyQuil, Grace forced herself onto her bed with the turkey sandwich in hand. The apartment door was locked. She had triple-checked, along with her bedroom door. She contemplated pushing the nightstand against it too but decided it would only confuse her more when she woke up in the middle of the night and ran into it.

She focused on force-feeding herself the turkey sandwich. In a way, it was comforting to eat something that was so normal when it felt like her entire world was falling apart. The soft, fragrant bread brought a bit of warmth to her, as she had been fighting a chill that wouldn't go away since she had recovered from her latest panic attack. She wanted to cry about Jocelyn and Mrs. Baker. She wanted to fall apart after seeing that man and allowing Harold to roam the streets free, but there were simply no tears left. She felt like a broken woman, so she forced herself to sit in bed and come up with a plan. Grace retrieved her journal from her nightstand. She only used it on rare occasions when she felt too overwhelmed. Mostly, she wrote about things from her past that still troubled her. She opened to a fresh page and began writing.

1. Find out when Jocelyn is being transferred to St. George.

Grace could visit her there and try to get to the bottom of why she was suddenly so ill. For a moment, the chills worsened as the thought crossed her mind that the man was really there, haunting Jocelyn just like he was with Grace. Perhaps her delusions weren't fake. Grace shook her head, trying to shake away the thought, but it stuck to the outer corners, taunting her and making way more sense than it should.

2. Find Harold.

That sounded like a job for tomorrow in the light of day, when the man in black couldn't rely on the shadows to hide. She would print out missing cat posters and hang them around.

3. Tell Jocelyn everything.

She had to tell her the truth about that night in words. Jocelyn said that Grace wasn't there when she needed her. She was right, but she didn't know the whole story. If Grace was going to fix this mess Jocelyn was going through, Grace needed to reveal what she had done, and it was a lot worse than her hiding a flask in their cabin.

10

July 21, 2011

Grace sat in Marge's office, awaiting punishment for a crime she didn't commit. For the most part. In front of her, on Marge's desk, sat Jocelyn's silver flask amongst precariously stacked paperwork. Marge stood behind the desk, staring down at Grace with an anger she had never seen on her boss's face before. Her tan complexion had shifted to a beet red. Grace could feel her own face redden as tears slipped out of her eyes.

"I always try to give new counselors the benefit of the doubt. From everything I have seen, I thought, wow, this Grace girl will be a great addition to our camp. She will be a great influence on the kids, and even a good influence on Jocelyn: something that girl desperately needs. I thought you were kind and responsible, but you have endangered the safety of our campers. That is something I cannot ignore." For a moment, Marge seemed like she might begin to cry, but she gathered herself before continuing.

"When I decided to do random room checks, I thought I would find some prohibited items from the campers, but never my own staff!" Grace had been told that Marge had decided to do room checks after she caught a few kids drinking in the woods. They were 16, so it didn't seem too bad, but it was enough to put her on the warpath. When she and the other adult staff began searching the cabins, they found Jocelyn's metal flask stuffed into Grace's dresser.

"I'm so sorry," Grace murmured through tears. Her body had caved in on itself. Her back was folded inward, and she avoided Marge's eyes. There was no point in denying whether the flask was hers. Marge had already interviewed Jocelyn, and she had told her Grace had been drinking from the flask since the day she had arrived.

"Sorry is not enough!" Marge jumped up from her chair as she spoke before beginning to pace back and forth behind her desk. Apparently, she didn't want to look Grace in the eyes either. "You are very lucky we are in the middle of camp season. It would look so much worse for camp if you were fired and a cabin was left without a second counselor. I admire that you have admitted to your mistake, but I do not trust you. For the time being, you are still an employee of Camp Willows. But if you make one more misstep, you will be gone." Grace nodded. "Now get out of here." Her tone started strong like an order, but by the time she finished her words, she just sounded tired. Grace stood up and left without saying another word.

Outside the camp office, Grace knew she could not go back to her cabin and face Jocelyn right now. Rage bubbled under the surface. She hadn't felt this angry since her father gave away her pet cat after she gave him too much attitude. She was nine. She also knew she couldn't go anywhere the campers were because she didn't want them to see her like this. Instinctively, she strode straight for the woods, following a gravel trail, knowing there would be comfort in being alone.

Once Grace was shrouded in the safety of the pine trees, she made her way to the lakefront that was secluded by the woods around it. There was an old picnic table there with one leg unsteady, and the noises of children and people disappeared into the distance. When Grace took the campers on a hiking adventure, which ended mostly in sprained ankles, bug bites, and tears, she had discovered the entrance to the trail and became curious.

She sat down on the top of the picnic table, staring out at the water. Tears dripped down her face and anger pulsed through her veins. Jocelyn had thrown her under the bus. Grace knew that Jocelyn shouldn't be trusted, but she had started to anyway. She didn't understand why she would do this. Grace was desperate to make a better life for herself. Jocelyn was here, being the stereotypical rich bitch, ruining everything. Just like Grace's father had anticipated.

A twig snapped behind Grace, and she spun around to find Matt approaching. He had wired earbuds in and was staring down at an iPod. Grace didn't know much about iPods, but she knew it had to be expensive with the large display screen it had. When he looked up and their eyes met, she could tell he was surprised to see her there.

"I'm sorry. I didn't realize you were here." He paused by the edge of the clearing, seemingly contemplating whether he should turn around and leave her to be alone.

"It's okay." Grace rubbed the tears away from her eyes, trying to conceal that she had been crying. Matt took that as a sign it was okay to approach. He walked over to the table and the table swayed to one side as his weight settled onto it. Grace was grateful for the comfortable distance he had left between them.

"Are you okay?" he asked, trying to make eye contact.

"Oh, yeah, I'll be fine," Grace replied, looking down at her hands. When the silence between them grew, she continued, "Just a little girl drama." He nodded but didn't look away.

"With Jocelyn?" he asked. Grace nodded. He laughed. Grace had never heard him talk this much, or laugh, apart from when he was around the campers.

"Why? What's funny?" she snapped. He finally turned and looked out at the water.

"Nothing. Just some of the stuff that Alex has told me about her." She frowned and folded her hands in her lap.

"What did he say?" Matt paused for a moment, debating if he should share. He shrugged and ran his hands through his hair.

"Just some things that happened last summer."

"That they slept together?" she asked, an eyebrow raised.

"Not just that. That she basically slept with everyone here." Matt took a deep breath and pushed forward. "Alex said he got crabs from her."

"What?" Grace tried to understand how this was possible, but she couldn't wrap her head around it. Sure, she could imagine Jocelyn sleeping around, but she couldn't imagine her having wild, unprotected sex all across Camp Willows to the point where she contracted a disease.

"Yeah. Lucky for him, it was curable."

Grace nodded as if she knew anything about STDs.

"That must be why she thought he was acting weird on the first day of camp. . ." Grace remembered how cold he had acted and how angry Jocelyn had gotten.

"And that's why I disappeared as soon as she showed up. I could tell right away she was on the prowl. If she thinks I'm a freak or whatever, she'll stay away." He chuckled, and Grace smiled.

"I think you did a good job doing that." *So we are both pretending,* Grace thought. *Me, to get a better life, and him, to keep Jocelyn away.*

"It's a pretty fool-proof defense mechanism I've developed over the years."

Grace found herself laughing again. Her anger had faded into the background, barely a dull roar in her mind. Matt was surprisingly charismatic. Splashing could be heard in the distance with faint screams from children. Closer, cicadas called out to them.

"Is that part of being a politician's son?" Grace asked. She worried he might be offended by her prying into his personal life. He let out a long and slow sigh.

"So my secret's out, huh?" he asked. Grace frowned and moved to touch his shoulder before she realized that they barely knew each other.

"Oh, I'm sorry! I didn't know you were trying to hide it," she urged, feeling like an idiot for even bringing it up. Grace wasn't really used to making friends. She had always been a loner, which is part of what attracted her to Jocelyn. It seemed Jocelyn was a loner by choice though, rather than necessity.

"I'm just kidding," Matt teased, unleashing a large grin. He looked like a politician's son: a big grin and attractive features. The only thing that set him apart was his wild hair.

"Oh my god. That is not fair!" Grace whined, pushing him. He barely moved. For a brief moment, she felt a tingle of something she had not experienced before. He was strong and attractive and different. She blushed, feeling her attraction but hoping to hide it, looking back out at the waterfront. It didn't hurt that he probably came from a different world than she did.

"Hey, I was just trying to get you to laugh! You can't blame me for cheering you up," he reminded her. He was right. The idea of Jocelyn and the flask had faded into the background.

"I guess you're right. I definitely can't blame you for that." They stared at each other for a moment. She felt the heat on her face as she tucked a loose strand of hair behind her ear and saw a glimmer in his eye. "That probably comes from being a politician's son too." He chuckled and nodded.

"Now you're catching on." He paused. "So, what about you? Where do you come from? Probably the daughter of some hedge fund manager or something."

Grace shook her head and stared back to the horizon, the water glistening from the sun above, hoping to hide her shame.

"Not quite, but something like that," she lied. Harry Simmons wasn't exactly a father to brag about. She didn't meet Matt's gaze, fearing he would sense her discomfort.

"You're really good with the kids," Grace pivoted, changing the subject.

"Yeah, I want to be a teacher when I get older, but

my family is pretty against it, considering how they are always cutting back my future salary." He let out a bitter laugh and stared at his own hands now. "It's hard when you feel like you were born into the wrong family, like you belong to a whole different type of people. I just wish I could let them see how important this is to me without money clouding their judgement."

"I get it," she replied, reaching out and touching his hand for a moment. Her heart pounded as she saw her hand on his. She hadn't consciously thought about this action, but it appeared her subconscious was braver and smarter than she was. "More than you can ever know." Their eyes met once more. Grace could hear her blood pulsating in her ears. For a moment, she thought they were going to kiss, but the moment ended. Grace withdrew her hand and stood up, still wondering how they had gotten here.

"Thank you for the company, Matt."

He nodded and offered another large grin.

"No problem. I come here a lot. You can join me any time," he offered before replacing his earbuds and pulling his iPod out of his pocket. Grace had planned on coming to Camp Willows to network with the rich, but she couldn't figure out how Matt fit into that plan.

11

November 9, 2019

Grace was running. There were screams, and they felt close, so she kept running. The underbrush of the forest scraped her ankles, leaving rivulets of blood across her calves. She couldn't remember the last time she ran in her life. Her body raced through the woods, her breath becoming labored and elusive. She wanted to stop; her legs and lungs begged her to stop. All of a sudden, the forest was the hallway of Cold Waters where Jocelyn was being kept. And she wasn't running away from the screams; she was running toward them.

Grace jolted upright in bed, sending a half-eaten turkey sandwich across the room. Her body was shivering. She felt like she had been sleeping outside, but she was covered in sweat. Morning light was streaming into her apartment. Immediately, she checked the door to her bedroom, discovering it was still locked from the night before. Grace let out a sigh of relief and rubbed her arms, feeling little goosebumps as she did, hoping to erase the chill within her body. But the chill was on the outside. The air inside her apartment was freezing. She realized the cars and noises from the street were magnified this morning. Her eyes flashed back to the window. It was wide open to the outside world, the black curtains waving in the breeze. It wasn't from a NyQuil hangover; it was because her window had been opened.

Grace rose to her feet and inched toward the window. Fear tumbled through her stomach as she thought of the possibility that someone could be inside her apartment after all. She glanced out to the fire escape, searching for any potential evidence of what had happened. Grace wasn't sure what she expected to find. Something like what they discover on those crime shows: a lost glove, a cigarette bud, maybe even a forgotten convenience store reward card. There was nothing. She pulled shut the window and locked it. She stepped away, wondering for a moment if she should check under her bed. Someone could easily have stowed themselves away there overnight. She forced herself to bend over, terrified of what she might find. Once again, there was nothing.

A cool breeze struck her back, and she yelped. It was as if a ghost had embraced her. She turned on her heels and stared at the window. It was open again. She pulled it shut again, harder this time, believing that it would resist. It fell right back into place. She attempted to latch it again, only to realize the latch was broken. She wasn't sure whether to find comfort or fear in this. In a way, it meant that someone had not necessarily broken into her apartment while she was sleeping, but it also meant the window was a ticking bomb, waiting for the right person to take a chance. She contemplated placing a call to her landlord, but remembered the way he had licked his lips when he handed her the keys to the apartment. The last thing she wanted was to invite him in. Her thoughts spiraled as she realized he definitely had a key regardless. Manically, she imagined him standing over her while she slept.

"This is fine," she lied to herself. "You are overreacting."

In her closet, she began throwing boxes full of school memorabilia to the side, searching for the beginner's crocheting kit Mrs. Baker had bought her last Christmas. She had handed it to Grace and declared, "Because you are always wearing little homemade things!" She didn't tell her that she often bought homemade things at Goodwill because that's all she could afford in the cold winters or that she had no idea how to crochet. As she finally pulled out the kit, she felt the breeze hit her lower back as her shirt rose up. With some beige yarn in hand, she returned to the window, wrapping it around the latch until it seemed to hold it shut. If someone wanted to get in, they probably still could, but at least they would wake her this time. Staring at the window, she could feel panic swelling. One or two things, those were a coincidence. Four or more, those were connected. Letting out a deep breath, Grace planted herself on her bed and decided to call the only person she had left.

"Hello," the voice grumbled from her cell. Grace wasn't sure if he even had her number saved.

"Hi, dad." Grace failed at trying to hold her voice steady. He didn't respond. She balanced her phone against her shoulder as she picked at her cuticles. "It's me, Grace." She felt stupid saying that. She was his only child, and it wasn't like he needed to be reminded of that. What his silence was really saying was "What do you want?"

"It your mother's birthday already?" His voice was soft for a moment. While the man didn't care about much, and he didn't seem to like her mother when she was alive, he was torn apart by her death.

"No, that's not for a couple more weeks." Silence hung in the air. She could hear the TV in the background. She could almost see him in the armchair, surrounded by that dirty shag carpet, in the same spot he had been last night when he fell asleep.

"Oh" was all he managed to reply.

"I was just calling because I've had some weird stuff happen." An armchair creaked on the other line as though her father was leaning forward to focus better.

"Weird how?"

"Well, I think someone has been following me."

"Jesus Christ, Grace. This shit again?" Her father groaned and she nearly dropped the phone, feeling as though he had slapped her.

"There's been other things—"

"Grace, listen here. I know damn well you've been watching way too many of those cop shows where women get sexually assaulted. You live in a white neighborhood. Ain't nothing bad gonna happen to you. 'Cept they might try to steal your paycheck." He chuckled to himself.

"It's the same person as before. I think he's been after Jocelyn too." Grace could hear him crush a beer can.

"Oh, is it now? And why the hell would they come back all the sudden? Unfinished business? Bullshit.

People don't wait eight years to finish something like that." Grace bit her thumbnail, waiting for him to finish speaking. "You are overreacting. Again. And that Jocelyn girl? That money has gone right to her head. She's lying about seeing shit just so her mommy will bail her out."

He wasn't wrong. Jocelyn did have a tendency to have breakdowns at the most convenient times. Convenient for her, at least. Usually when she ran out of money or she had just started a new job she hated. How could Grace explain that this was different? This wasn't a routine stay at Cold Waters. But he would never understand that.

"You're probably right, Dad. Thanks." Her voice fell just short of sincerity, but based on the TV volume in the background, he wouldn't notice.

"You are welcome. Now, I have to go. The game is on in a bit and I have to head over to Tony's."

A single tear fell as she thought about all the times Tony's was more important than herself or her mother or anything else.

"Bye," she managed just before the line cut out. She let the phone fall down and looked back at the window, the string of yarn dangling below the sill. If her own father didn't believe her, who else would? Mrs. Baker wouldn't. Jocelyn couldn't help. That was it. That was the whole list of people she had.

She forced herself to take a deep breath and focus on the plan. There was no time to waste worrying about whether someone was breaking into her apartment. She had to figure out if someone was breaking into Jocelyn's room at Cold Waters.

Even though she knew she would have seen it already, she checked for a missed call from the nurse at

Cold Waters. There was nothing. Mrs. Baker had probably given her strict orders not to contact Grace or involve her with Jocelyn. Instead, she looked up the number for St. George. She leaned back against her bed, the springs creaking below her, and waited, staring at the cobwebs in the popcorn ceiling.

"You've reached St. George Hospital. This is Lenore. How may I help you today?"

The woman seemed to maintain the same amount of friendliness as the receptionist in the lobby of Cold Waters. Grace took a deep breath and prepared for her best performance.

"Hello. My name is Fiona Baker." The name sprung into her head, remembered from a conversation where Jocelyn told her it was the name her father had originally wanted. Claire thought that Fiona was pretentious. Grace laughed so hard that she snorted when Jocelyn had told the story. "I am Jocelyn Baker's sister. I was just calling to see if she had been admitted yet and whether she was accepting visitors at this time." Grace almost shocked herself with this performance. This woman would have no idea that Jocelyn was an only child. That wasn't the type of information they kept track of at St. George.

"One moment, Miss Baker. Let me check that for you," she replied on autopilot. Her typing could be heard in the background. Grace tried to keep her breath even so she wouldn't tip the receptionist off that she was nervous. "It seems that your sister was admitted late last night. She is meeting with the doctor in an hour, but then she should be available for visitation." She paused. "It does say on her file that she is not permitted visitors, but it will depend on what the doctor decides after evaluating her."

Grace sighed. It seemed like the entire universe was working against her. Just like her father used to say, "No good deed goes unpunished."

"Thank you. Would it be possible for you to call me after her meeting with the doctor and tell me if I can come?"

"Sweetie, I get off in twenty minutes. We don't do that kind of thing here. Maybe she should have stayed at Cold Waters." She laughed. "Bye-bye now." The receiver clicked, and she flinched. Seeing Jocelyn the old-fashioned way might not work, but if the man in black could get in to see her, so could she.

12

July 25, 2011

The cabin porch creaked, and Grace opened her eyes. She hadn't been asleep. There was no sleeping when she knew Jocelyn was out.

Every time Jocelyn walked out the door by herself, Grace could feel all the nerve endings in her body electrify. She was wild and unpredictable. There was no way of knowing what kind of mood she would be in when she returned. She was either drunk and happy or angry beyond words. Sometimes it all depended on whether she had sex that night. Jocelyn would try to share the details, but Grace always tried to tune her out. She didn't want to know what positions she had tried or which counselor was her flavor of the week. When Grace confronted her about it, along with the flask incident, Jocelyn tried to flip the entire situation around.

"You are just a bitter virgin, aren't you?" she'd accused.

The memory unsettled Grace. Confronting Jocelyn felt like a mistake.

"Just because I'm not going around giving everyone at camp an STD doesn't mean I'm a virgin," Grace had snapped. Panic crossed Jocelyn's face. At the time, the campers were off at movie night, and they were duking it out in their cabin.

"Who told you that?" she hissed, moving so close Grace could feel the heat from her breath. Grace tried to move back but her calves were against the frame of her bed. She hesitated. She couldn't throw Matt under the bus. He seemed like a good soul.

"Alex," Grace lied.

Jocelyn put her hands on her hips.

"So you're sleeping with him, then!" she yelled.

Grace put her hands up and shook her head.

"I'm not sleeping with anyone!" Grace almost laughed at how ridiculous she seemed.

"So you are then! A bitter little virgin, who is pissed off she can't find a guy crazy enough to get anywhere near her vagina. You couldn't find anyone back home, so you ran away here, hoping you could prey upon some desperate little kid."

Shock radiated through Grace's body.

"Are you accusing me of having sex with the campers?"

"Well you are always disappearing out in the woods. You think I don't notice! You always come back with a silly grin on your face. You're meeting up with some pimply preteen!"

Grace's hand acted independently of her mind. It flew across Jocelyn's face, a red mark growing in its path. Jocelyn's own hand flew to her face. Grace stood stock still, uncertain that she had really hit her.

"You're psycho!" Jocelyn whispered before turning and rushing out of the cabin.

They hadn't spoken since. Now, the door creaked open, and Grace stared from her bed, watching as Jocelyn crept back into the cabin. She closed the door cautiously, trying not to wake the campers who would ask her a million questions about where she was and who she was with. Jocelyn had fallen victim to gossiping campers the year before, which is how Alex found out about her galivanting with other boys.

Jocelyn's eyes looked directly at Grace's. For a moment, she thought about shutting them and pretending she was asleep, but she forced them to stay open. *She will not intimidate me,* Grace thought. Jocelyn stood in the moonlight, staring back at her, and Grace felt the rage between them growing. She had felt bad for hitting her, but she was certain Jocelyn deserved it. Jocelyn finally looked away and climbed into her bed, facing the wall. Grace had won this time.

Grace forced her eyes shut and told herself she needed to sleep. According to the wall clock, there was only two more hours before the day would start again. Grace was going to have to spend another day pretending everything was fine. Pretending to like Jocelyn, but fighting with her silently when nobody else was around. Her heart broke a little, as she remembered thinking only a few days ago that maybe Jocelyn would be her first best friend.

13

November 9, 2019

Snow was floating down onto the streets. Grace pulled on mittens as she walked through the building lobby. She was heading off to the library to print some flyers for Harold, then she was going to try to see Jocelyn at St. George, even if it seemed hopeless. As she headed through the lobby toward the street, she saw something on the front stoop outside. Grace approached it, stopping just before opening the door. She stared down through the glass.

Under the snow that was building up, there was something orange. She opened the door and reached down, clearing away some of the snow. It almost looked like a package. That didn't make much sense, though, as that wasn't how deliveries were handled at her building.

As the snow cleared, Grace gasped and drew back. Amongst the fallen snow was a collection of fur and blood. It looked like roadkill. Whatever it was, it was even missing its head. Grace felt nausea wash over her, but she couldn't look away. The animal was nearly unrecognizable, but Grace knew. *Harold.* She shrank back. She moved too quickly, and the ice on the step sent her falling backwards into the building door. A hollow crack sounded as her head made contact with the glass. Grace's last thought was, *He killed my cat.* And then, there was nothing.

* * *

Grace heard a humming noise, followed by a high-pitched tone. She grimaced and tried to open her eyes, but then, the pain sunk in. Her head was aching too much for her to open her eyes. She shut them tighter. Her hand reached up to her forehead and she groaned. She shaded her eyes further with the hand. It was way too bright. She felt something in her other hand and tried to open her eyes to see what it was. At first, it was like she was getting smacked in the face with whiteness. Eventually, the room materialized before her.

A hospital room. Grace blinked multiple times, thinking the image before her might change. It remained the same. A long curtain was drawn next to her, presumably hiding another patient. A TV was perched in the corner by the door, turned off or broken, she couldn't tell. An IV trailed out of her left hand, attached to the machinery next to the bed she was in. She tried to sit up, but pain crashed over her body like a wave, stopping her.

"Hello," she moaned. There was nobody in the room. She couldn't quite see out into the hallway. It was like her vision was fragmented. She attempted to sit up again, but the pain flashed back into her head, reminding her she had just tried. Grace took a few deep breaths, trying to focus.

"A hospital?" she whispered, her fingers touching her lips as they moved. If she hadn't felt her own lips move, she wouldn't have thought she was the one speaking. She tried to do a mental inventory of her body. Was everything still attached? She wasn't even sure at this point, and opening her eyes to the bright lights hurt so much.

She attempted to move through her body mentally, trying to focus on what was damaged. Her brain was fuzzy, but she felt something hard digging into her hip. Her mouth dropped open.

"Was I stabbed?" She moved her right hand away from her face to her hip, where she felt plastic. Through squinted eyes, she investigated. It was a remote. For the bed. For calling a nurse.

Grace pulled the remote up to her face, trying to keep her eyes as closed as possible. Finally, she stumbled upon the red call button and pressed it repeatedly. Nothing happened.

She began to panic, shouting "Hello?" over and over. Gradually, she got louder. The noise echoed in her brain and rattled around until it sounded like a chorus of her voice begging for help. Grace shut her eyes so tight it hurt and tears escaped through her eyelashes. *What happened to me?*

"Miss Simmons?" A man's voice. It sounded distant and for a moment, Grace thought she had imagined it. But footsteps came next. She pulled a slow breath through her lips before opening her eyes. A middle-aged man in a doctor's coat had entered the room and stood at her bedside. He met her gaze, looking over her tears, and then frowned.

"It's all okay. I am sure you are feeling very overwhelmed right now."

"Where am I?"

"Miss Simmons, you don't know where you are?" Grace began to nod but grimaced, the pain in her neck stopping her.

"No. I mean, I guess I'm in—" She paused, closing her eyes from the pain. "The hospital."

The doctor nodded and moved closer, pulling out a penlight.

"I'm just going to check a few things before we can chat," he explained, turning the light on. He shone the light into her eyes, and her eyelids flew shut.

"Please, no."

"I have to examine you. Try to bear with me." She pried her eyes open against all instinct. He moved from her left to right eye, and back again. She groaned as he clicked off the light.

"Good job. Now can you sit up?"

"Maybe with help." He reached around and helped her sit up and forward as she pushed against the bed with her arms. He held her forward and pulled out his stethoscope. He reached up and moved her hair to the side. Pinpricks of pain dotted the inside of her eyelids.

"Just a moment," he murmured, obviously too busy with his examination to notice the enormity of her pain. "You can lay back." Grace slid back down slowly, trying to cushion her head as it touched the pillow. It felt as if someone had yanked out a clump of her hair, and the skin was left raw. Tears trailed out of her eyes again, and the doctor sighed. A nurse wheeled in the computer and passed it off to the doctor. Grace heard clicking and typing. She wondered what there was to say about her.

"Can you tell me what's going on?" Constant white noise filled Grace's head and she couldn't focus. She tried to open her eyes to help focus, but the pain was equally distracting.

"Miss Simmons, you have suffered a brain injury." He paused to check if she was listening. "Did you know this?"

She held back a laugh.

"How was I supposed to know? I mean I—" Grace pulled in a sharp breath before continuing. "My head feels like shit."

"So you do not remember speaking to me earlier?" He enunciated each word.

"What?"

"You do not remember discussing the severity of your brain injury with me a few hours ago?"

"No . . . We have never even met." Grace would have laughed if she could. The doctor couldn't even keep his patients straight. How many young female patients did he have with head injuries?

"Well, Miss Simmons, I can tell you that is certainly not true." He moved to the edge of the bed and showed her a page from a file folder. "Is that your signature there?"

Grace forced her eyes open and reached out to the page. As her eyes skimmed the page, she saw words like mental state and psychiatric unit. She couldn't put together what the words above her name meant. "Yes. But I didn't write that . . ."

"Miss Simmons, do you remember my name?"

Grace responded with silence.

"I'm Dr. Carter. I watched you sign this paper an hour ago. Your injury must be more severe than we originally thought." He paused and glanced back at the file. "When you first arrived, you told the staff here something about St. George." He hesitated again before clearing his throat. "Have you ever been a patient at St. George?" Grace shook her head immediately, letting out a little squeal as her neck resisted the movement. "Miss Simmons, I'm going to ask you to remain calm."

"What?"

"Miss Simmons, you are displaying symptoms of more than a brain injury. In fact, I'm not sure your brain injury is causing your symptoms at all. I am wondering, perhaps, if you were on your way to St. George this morning before your incident."

"Incident?"

The doctor carried on as if she hadn't spoken at all. "You helped a nurse unlock your phone so she could find an emergency contact, and your most recent outgoing call was to St. George's facility."

"I did call them. I think ..." Grace tried to concentrate and retrace her steps, but nothing came. Finally, a small crumb. "I think someone I know is there."

"Maybe your doctor?" He stared down at Grace expectantly.

Jocelyn, her brain screamed suddenly. The thought was so loud she flinched. The doctor reached out and touched her arm.

"Miss Simmons?"

Snapshots crept into her mind. A hallway with a locked door. Someone chasing her. Someone in black.

"No," she whimpered. The doctor interpreted that as an answer to his question.

"A friend, perhaps?" He prompted, beginning to type on the computer once again. Her brain was whispering in her ear: *He's going to hurt Jocelyn. He's going to hurt you.* She gasped and forced her eyes open all the way. They darted across the room, checking for the man. She could hear beeping from the machines, both close by and from behind the curtain next to her. Each beep sent a shock through her brain, like a strobe light being flashed in her face. The white sheets that covered her legs suddenly felt like sandpaper, and sweat dripped down her back.

"Grace, I am going to recommend you meet with one of our psychiatrists so we can get to the bottom of these issues you are having. Depending on what they say, we will make a treatment plan from there."

"I don't need a psychiatrist! I need to see my friend."

The doctor nodded and offered a gentle pat on her shoulder.

"I understand," he insisted. He turned away and disappeared into the hallway. Grace was left to stare at the empty space to the right of her bed, where the doctor had once stood.

"What does that mean?" None of this made sense. The last thing she could remember was making the call to St. George. Everything after that was just gone.

* * *

Grace had fallen asleep before the psychiatrist had entered the room. The woman rapped her knuckles against the wall as she walked in. Grace stirred in bed, forcing her eyes open. The pain seemed to have faded a bit. That was mostly thanks to whatever was in her IV. The woman approached the bed slowly, as if she would a frightened animal. She was a short, older woman with thick glasses and "dress" pants that were held up by an elastic waistband.

"Grace," she cooed, touching her hand. "I'm Dr. Campbell. I heard you'd had quite the accident."

"I don't even know what happened."

The woman nodded sympathetically and sat in the navy chair next to the bed. There was a softness in her brown eyes that most people didn't have.

"That's what they tell me. But we don't have to talk about that if you don't want to. I'm sure you're tired of being asked questions about that."

"I really am." Tears collected in her eyes. Confusion still lingered at the surface of her mind. Flashes of Jocelyn's fear and anger as she thought the nurse was the man in black played on repeat. Grace tried to grab onto Jocelyn's face to keep focused. Instead, it felt like she was being jostled about.

"So why don't you tell me what's going on? You seem very upset." Tears ran down her face, and she finally noticed she was in a thin pink hospital gown, the ties bunched uncomfortable against the back of her legs. *Had they changed me? Had I done it?* The lost minutes and hours were starting to add up more and more.

"I'm just very confused. I was on my way to visit my friend, Jocelyn, and—" Grace took a moment, trying to choose her words carefully.

"Yes?"

The truth came spilling out. "She's not well. She's at St. George. I saw her yesterday and she was having delusions. But I don't think they are delusions." Grace began rocking forward and back ever so slightly, trying to soothe herself. "They're real. She's in danger. I'm scared. For her and myself. There's a man. He's been following me. And I saw him there when I was visiting her. I think he's trying to hurt us, but he keeps disappearing. He wears all black." The psychiatrist's softness gradually disappeared as she forged on. Her eyes searched around the room, checking to make sure he wasn't there, listening. Her eyes landed on the window, and she stared at it for a long moment before continuing, trying to remember its significance.

"Oh! And I think he broke into my apartment. My door was open and the latch on my window doesn't work anymore."

Dr. Campbell pulled out a pen and retrieved a small notepad from her coat pocket.

"I see." She nodded to herself and poised her pen on the paper. "And when did this all begin?"

"Yesterday! I went to visit Jocelyn yesterday, and I saw him three times. He knows where I live. He must have followed me home from Cold Waters!" It was all beginning to click in her head. He had just been stalking Jocelyn. But she visited Jocelyn. *I put a target on myself*, she thought.

"Cold Waters?" She paused, looking back at what she had written. "You just said St. George a moment ago." She looked down at the floor and tried to focus on one green tile. There was a smudge of something brown stuck to it. *Had I said that? Which one was it?*

"I think I was at Cold Waters yesterday, but I don't remember. I just know I called St. George this morning . . ."

"Okay, so back to this man in black. He broke into your apartment?" she questioned. Grace tried to nod but only let out a small yelp. She was so caught up in the conversation she had forgotten about her injury. Dr. Campbell reached out and touched her arm. At her touch, Grace froze, unable to move away. She gazed at the age spots speckling her skin. "Please don't hurt yourself. Be cautious."

"I'm sorry. It's all just beginning to make sense. I was wondering why I had seen him so many times, but it was because he followed me. I led him right to me."

The psychiatrist returned her notepad to her white coat and put her pen away with a satisfying click.

"Grace, did you call the police when this happened?"

"No." *Why didn't I? I must have had a good reason.* Grace remembered the uncertainty she felt about the whole situation. She felt fuzzy on the details, but she remembered doubting herself. "I guess I wasn't sure if I had just left the door open. But then something happened to the window."

"After the window, did you call the police?"

"I thought maybe it was a coincidence." Grace's eyes had now fallen upon the string dangling from the window blinds, and Grace thought back to the phone call with her father. He had convinced her there was nothing to worry about. He was why she didn't call the police. Her gaze didn't move from the blinds.

"Okay, let's move on from that then. Your friend, Jocelyn. You said the doctors believe she is suffering from delusions. What was your visit with her like yesterday?" she asked.

"Horrible." Flashes of Jocelyn attacking the nurse played before her eyes. The palms of her hands were pushing down into the mattress, so hard she was almost lifting herself off the bed. She closed her eyes to try to make the images stop, but they only grew more distinct. Her breaths grew shallow as she remembered how Jocelyn accused her of not being there when she needed her.

"What happened?"

Grace's mouth felt dry as she began to speak. She tried to wet her lips with her tongue, but everything felt like cotton. "Could I have some water?"

Dr. Campbell nodded quickly and walked over to the countertop near the entrance. Grace could only see her shadow in the distance. The dark image made her head shake slightly, and she pried her eyes away, trying to tell herself it was just the doctor. She returned with the drink and passed it to Grace, who lifted it to her lips, her hand shaking faintly, and she took a large gulp.

"Better?" Dr. Campbell asked with a small smile.

Grace nodded her head before draining the rest of the cup.

"Good. Now you were just about to tell me about yesterday. Can we continue?" Dr. Campbell tilted her head to the side in what Grace thought was an attempt to seem warm and welcoming. Really, it just made Grace feel like she was being observed like a tiny insect.

"Yes." Grace cleared her throat. "I've never seen her look so bad. At first, they weren't even going to let me visit. But finally, the nurse agreed. I was only there for a few minutes before Jocelyn attacked the nurse because she believed she was the man who is stalking us." The words came quickly. Dr. Campbell grabbed a tissue from somewhere and handed it to Grace. She wiped at her cheeks. She hadn't even realized she was crying again. Immediately, the tissue was wadded up and moist all the way through. She clutched it in her hand and tried to meet the doctor's eyes but her glasses reflected the bright fluorescent lights from above instead.

"And when did the man first start appearing?"

This question caused Grace to pause. He had been

appearing for eight years, off and on, ever since that night at Camp Willows, but his appearances had not increased until yesterday. She couldn't explain everything that they had gone through to the psychiatrist. Everything Jocelyn had gone through. She had tried therapy after Camp Willows, but since she couldn't be completely honest, it never helped. She quit after the second session.

"Yesterday," Grace lied.

"I think that's all I need to know. Is there anything else you would like to share, Grace?" she asked, her smile slowly reappearing on her face as if she wanted to part on good terms. Grace noticed a small fleck of lipstick on one of Dr. Campbell's front teeth.

"I just need to get to Jocelyn. I need to help her."

The psychiatrist gave one quick nod.

"I understand. Thank you for sharing this with me, Grace." She gave her arm a final squeeze before turning and disappearing again from view. Relief swelled through Grace's veins. *I can finally help Jocelyn,* she thought. Grace believed she was no longer alone in her rescue mission, which was more important than ever since she could barely think straight. Pulling the hospital blanket up to her chest, Grace shut her eyes and tried to focus through the static in her brain. The pain radiated like a migraine.

A conversation began in the hallway. Grace tried to listen, tuning out the beeps of the monitors.

"I think you are right," Dr. Campbell declared. "Based on what she just told me, I believe she had a mental break . . ." Their conversation went in and out of range and Grace strained to listen. "They are both suffering from similar delusions, from what she described. I definitely believe she needs further treatment before we can . . ." Confusion and betrayal punched Grace in the gut.

"Hello? Doctor?" Grace could feel the words rip out of her throat like a scream. *I am not crazy*, Grace repeated over and over in her head. Footsteps echoed in the hallway outside of her room. She stared at the doorway, waiting for the doctor to appear. Instead, it was him.

14

July 26, 2011

The cabin was silent, but the tension was palpable. Grace's back was to Jocelyn as she made her bed. She kept arguing back and forth with herself if she should say something to Jocelyn. There were three more weeks of Camp Willows, which meant three more weeks of bunking with Jocelyn. Finally, Grace's desire for peace overtook her grudge.

"I'm sorry I hit you," Grace mumbled, not turning to look at her. Jocelyn didn't respond. At first, Grace assumed she was giving her the silent treatment still or maybe she hadn't heard her. She glanced over her shoulder and saw tears falling down Jocelyn's face.

"Jocelyn!" Grace rushed to her side. "I said I'm sorry. What's wrong?"

She sniffed and swiped at her splotchy cheeks, doing a halfhearted job of clearing away the tears.

"It's not you." She took a moment to regulate her breathing. Jocelyn's eyes stared at the foot of her bed, rather than Grace. "I forgive you. I just feel awful for saying those things to you. Sometimes I get so wrapped up in what I'm feeling, I lose control. I don't know what I'm saying. I just say them."

Grace nodded and sat next to Jocelyn on her bed, rubbing her back.

"It's okay. I shouldn't have hit you either. We were both irrational. I was just so angry about the flask."

Jocelyn sniffled and let her hair fall over her face.

"I understand. I just can't take the fall for it. The flask, I mean. If I had one more letter in my file here, I wouldn't be allowed back. Marge only keeps me on the staff because she knows my mother would pitch a fit if she didn't."

"I didn't know."

Jocelyn had only thrown her under the bus because she knew she would be screwed otherwise. Grace was pretty sure she would have done the same thing.

"I know you didn't. But you had a clean record. I knew Marge wouldn't get rid of you for the first offense. Besides, the flask was empty. She can't bust you for an empty flask."

Grace nodded, finally understanding. A piece of her ached despite that understanding. Jocelyn had betrayed her regardless. Anger bubbled deep in her stomach, but she tried to push it away. *Just forget about it,* she begged herself. But the betrayal still tugged on the edges of her mind.

"I understand. Hopefully we can move on from here," she suggested, offering a small smile through her tears.

"We can certainly try."

Later that morning at the canteen, as Grace reached for the scoop for scrambled eggs, her hand collided with Matt's. She jumped back and looked up at him.

"Sorry," he said, pulling his hand away and gesturing for her to go ahead.

"It's okay." She reached cautiously to grab the eggs, wanting to make sure they didn't touch again. It was as if electricity had jumped from his hand to hers, leaving her feeling tense.

"How are things going? Better than the other day?" he asked, watching her face closely. His eyebrows were scrunched together and a strand of dark hair fell across his face. Grace gave a small nod as she finished scooping eggs onto her tray and handed the spoon to him.

"Yes and no." Things couldn't be good while she was still trying to cope with Jocelyn's wild moods. And the anger she couldn't let go of.

"Do you wanna go outside and talk about it? There's a picnic table we can eat at."

Grace glanced over at her cabin's table. Jocelyn was with them, and Marge was doing crowd control.

"Sure."

They turned and headed for the door together. In an instant, Marge was at Grace's side, grabbing her upper arm firmly.

"Hello, Grace!" Her voice dripped with fake friendliness. "Where are we off to?"

Grace cringed and turned to face her head-on.

"Hi, Marge. Matt and I were just going to eat outside."

Marge shook her head.

"I'm sorry, Grace, but I can't allow that. I need to keep a close eye on you after what happened the other day."

Grace suppressed a laugh. *What were we going to do?*

Have mimosas with our breakfast? Matt frowned and glanced from Marge to Grace, uncertain of what was happening. She was clearly targeting her, but not him.

"Okay, I get it," she grunted, turning back to the cabin's table. "I'm sorry," she called over her shoulder. It wasn't clear if she was apologizing to Marge or Matt. Jocelyn had screwed her over more than she realized. Grace always flew under the radar. It was a matter of survival. If nobody notices you, they won't hurt you. Now she was losing freedom, privileges, and trust because of Jocelyn. This job was supposed to be a stepping stone into something bigger and better. Then, in a turn of events, she thought maybe she had made a friend instead. Now, everything was in pieces.

Grace sat at the end of the table and glanced over at Jocelyn as she laughed with a few girls from their cabin. She was the wild one, not Grace. Even after their fight was resolved, Grace was left picking up her mistakes and taking the blame. She tried to eat her scrambled eggs, but she couldn't even taste them. Grabbing her water, she drank to force the eggs down. She felt empty. Grace wasn't going to allow some bully to control her life. She was going to come out on top.

15

November 10, 2019

"Grace."

To Grace, it sounded like the voice was coming from underwater. Her head was pounding, and she felt like she couldn't move her limbs. She opened her eyes slowly, although her lids felt heavy. The room swirled and shifted as she struggled to focus. Eventually, her eyes locked onto Dr. Campbell. She forced her eyes to stay open, looking at her skin, but it seemed as though she was wavering, swaying back and forth like a ship.

"Wh—"

The psychiatrist shushed her instantly.

"It's okay, dear. You're safe here. Please just listen." Her tone was like the one a mother used on a child who had just awoken from a nightmare. "You need your rest. I was just checking to see if you were feeling better."

Grace glanced around. Although her vision was blurred, she could tell she was no longer in the hospital. Now, she could see the entirety of the room, as there was no floral curtain dividing it. There were also no windows. The room felt small and barren. Confusion smacked her in the face. The room looked vaguely familiar. Her eyes caught on a fleck of white paint that had chipped off to the expose yellow paint underneath.

"St. George."

The psychiatrist nodded. "Yes, Grace. We transferred you here for an involuntary 72-hour hold."

Grace moaned, closing her eyes.

"What?" The word came out garbled. With each moment, it felt harder to stay awake. She drifted off but came back at the sound of her name.

"Grace. We are going to help manage and treat your condition. We have you on a pretty strong sedative for the moment so you don't injure yourself further."

Her eyes shot back open. "Injure myself . . ."

"Grace, after we spoke earlier, you suffered from another delusion. You attacked a nurse who came into your room to check your vitals. You gave him a concussion."

She shook her head just slightly. *That doesn't make sense.* Grace had never physically harmed someone in her life. Though she had imagined it quite a few times.

"No, how? I can't . . ." Grace wanted to argue. She couldn't move. How could she attack someone? Through her hazy memory, she remembered bits and pieces. She had seen the man in black, but he had no face. He could have been anyone. Her memory disappeared from that moment on. There were more lost minutes and hours. Maybe even days. After a few moments of silence, the psychiatrist spoke again.

"Hopefully, in a few hours, you will be feeling more like yourself, so we can began trying some therapy." She smiled, but Grace could still feel resistance inside herself. A smudge of lipstick still sat on Dr. Campbell's teeth, but Grace couldn't remember if it was the same color, and she couldn't shake the feeling that there was something she needed to be doing. *Jocelyn!* She could almost hear Jocelyn's voice yelling at her within her head. This doctor was stopping her from helping Jocelyn. Rage ignited in her.

"I need to see Jocelyn! I need to get out of here!" Grace screamed the words, but they came out slurred together. She attempted to stand up, but her legs didn't move. "Do you have me tied up!" she accused, reaching for the blanket wrapped around her. Grace's arm swooped through the air, missing the blanket entirely before flopping back against the mattress.

"You are not restrained, Grace." Dr. Campbell lifted the yellow blanket to reveal her feet. While they were sporting a pair of socks, there were no restraints. Dr. Campbell was telling the truth. Grace tried to wiggle her toes, but nothing happened.

"Then why can't I move!" Grace struggled against the bed, trying and failing to lift her head.

"It's the sedative." She paused for a moment. "I doubt it is from your head injury, though it is possible, so you should probably remain calm." There was a sense of condescension in her voice that only made Grace's blood boil more. Grace grunted as she continued to struggle, focusing on individual pieces of her body, trying to get them to follow her brain. Dr. Campbell walked out of the room as Grace stared at her body in terror. Now, a dark-blue hospital gown was wrapped around her, this one without any ties on it. At least, Grace couldn't feel any ties underneath her. It felt like her entire body was stuck in mud. Dr. Campbell returned moments later with a nurse. The nurse reached into her scrubs, which were covered in a pattern of characters from Winnie the Pooh, and she retrieved a vial and a needle. The nurse extracted some of the liquid from the vial and approached Grace.

"What the hell is that! I refuse! I do not consent!" Grace was trying to argue with the nurse, but the words were only clear to herself. Her hair stuck to the sweat on her face as she turned her head side to side.

"Miss Simmons, please remain calm. You are going to injure yourself further," the nurse stated matter-of-factly. Her slender hand held the needle poised in the air, and Grace imagined her jamming the needle into her chest. The psychiatrist leaned closer to her, whispering something.

"What are you telling her? You can't do this to me! I know my rights!"

The nurse moved toward Grace with the needle, frowning at her struggle. Grace felt like the characters on her scrubs were dancing in front of her. "We don't know what you are saying. Please stay still."

Grace continued to wiggle her neck and shoulders. Adrenaline had made the pain from before disappear almost entirely. The nurse stuck the needle into her IV and pushed down the plunger. She stared in shock at the needle, then at the nurse's face.

It didn't happen instantaneously like in the movies. It was slow as her mind gradually began to grow quiet. The last thing she could feel before the darkness swallowed her, mind and body, was the dull pain radiating from her neck and head. *What had happened, again?*

16

July 26, 2011

The campers pranced off to another movie night, a time when Marge gave certain counselors time off to make up for their 24/7 service. Grace felt lucky that tonight was hers to have off. When Marge pulled her aside earlier that day, after breakfast, Grace thought Marge would tell her that she had to attend anyway.

Now Marge stood in the Elm bunk, glancing around, her eyes pausing a beat too long on Jocelyn's unmade bed, before meeting Grace's eyes.

"Grace," she stated cautiously, as though she was trying to stop a cat from pushing an object off an end table.

"Yes?" Grace forced herself to keep a straight face. She avoided her eyes and leaned over, smoothing out the edges of her own bedding before sitting down on the edge. She had an overwhelming feeling Marge was going to punish her once again for the flask. It felt never-ending. Instead, she surprised her.

"How are you doing?"

Grace blinked, unsure of what Marge wanted her to say. *Does she think I'm a legitimate alcoholic? Does she think I'm going through withdrawals or some dumb shit?* Grace was dumbfounded.

"I mean, how are you adjusting to camp life?" Marge clarified when she saw Grace's confusion.

"I'm doing okay, I think." She scanned Marge's face for any signs of fear. Her face gave nearly nothing away, but her eyes looked slightly wet. *Had she been crying?* Grace wondered. *Maybe she thinks I'm a danger to myself?*

Marge gestured to the bed. "Do you mind if I sit?" Grace shook her head immediately, afraid to refuse. Marge settled her wide hips down onto the bed and sighed. More than anything, she looked tired.

"I know camp can be tough. I always try to choose counselors with some kind of fierceness to them. Not like in a mean way. Just that they are survivors. They adapt and move on. Oddly enough, being a camp counselor can either foster that, or destroy that."

"Makes sense to me." Grace shrugged, but she suddenly understood why Marge kept Jocelyn around. She was a fighter, a survivor. She had a wildness that it seemed no one could tame. Her eyes stared at the empty space where Jocelyn normally sprawled on her bed, scrolling through her phone.

"So you're okay?" she confirmed one more time, staring into Grace's eyes, waiting for them to say something different. Grace swallowed hard and pulled her pillow onto her lap, hugging it to her chest. In that moment, she felt like a small child, hiding from the truth.

"I'm good."

Marge watched her for a moment longer before she grinned.

"Enjoy your night off tonight then." She hesitated a moment as if questioning whether she should add more. She decided against it and spun on her heels, trotting back toward the camp office.

As the noise of the campers walking down the trail and away from her cabin faded, Grace got up and moved outside. She couldn't stand to stay alone in silence while everyone else was off having fun. Grace made a beeline for the only place she found peace: the picnic table in the woods.

The night was just beginning to spread its darkness through the woods, and the last rays of the sun were disappearing on the lake's edge. As she approached the clearing, she saw a figure sitting on the picnic table. Grace paused at the edge of the trees, staring. It was difficult to see, but she knew it must be Matt. His long hair was barely discernible, along with his headphone wire dangling from his ears. Through the noises of the woods, the sound of bass from his music could be heard. Slowly, Grace approached him.

"Hey, stranger," she greeted, although she wondered whether this was ironic or true. Even after a couple weeks had passed at camp, she still knew remarkably little about anyone here. She didn't even know Matt's last name, but she still remembered what he had said the last time they had spoken about feeling like you didn't belong.

Matt pulled out his earbuds and smiled.

"I was hoping you would show up here."

Grace settled next to him on the picnic table, anticipating the sway of its weight before it happened. She could smell the bug spray he must have applied before heading out to the woods tonight, along with the faint scent of men's shampoo.

"Well, here I am."

"I see that. After this morning, I definitely need to know what was going on the other day. I try not to be too nosy, but you must have done something to seriously piss off Marge for her to talk like that."

"I didn't do anything." As the words fell out of her mouth, she could taste their bitter flavor. Matt didn't seem phased by her reply. After spending so much time with Jocelyn, her temperament seemed to be rubbing off on Grace.

"You know you would make a great politician someday. I don't know a single politician who would own up to their mistakes." He used a teasing tone, but she still felt the anger surge through her at the suggestion that she was lying.

"It was Jocelyn."

"Now there's something I can believe." He chuckled, but after he glanced at Grace's face, he could tell he wasn't meant to be laughing. "What happened?"

"On our first night here, she brought out this flask. I was trying to impress her, but I'd never drank before. I told her I didn't want to drink. She threatened me that if I didn't, she would tell Marge that it was my flask." Grace picked at a hangnail on the edge of her thumb. After she finished talking, she repeatedly clenched her fists and then slid her hands down her legs, making a conscious effort to try to keep her hands open.

"That's awful." Matt groaned. Grace didn't meet his eyes but instead stared down at the backs of her hands against her thighs.

"That's not even the worst part. I did drink that night. I didn't even want to, but I felt like I needed to:

to protect myself and to impress her. Nothing happened that night, but the other day—" Grace pulled in a slow, deep breath. She could feel tears gathering in the corners of her eyes. She gripped her thighs and squeezed, trying to distract her brain. *You will not cry*, she told herself. *You are not weak.* "Marge did searches of the cabins. You remember that?" He nodded but didn't speak. "She found the flask hidden in my things."

"Why did you have it?"

Grace sat up and stared directly at him. "See that's the thing. I didn't. Jocelyn put it there."

"What?" he questioned, not following. "That doesn't make any sense."

"She said she hid it there because she knew I wouldn't get fired but she might."

Matt shook his head and put his hand on her shoulder.

"No. If she knew there was going to be searches, why did she hide it? Why didn't she just throw it in the trash or into the lake?" Grace met his eyes. "Wait a minute, did she know there was going to be a search?" Her heart skipped a beat before it began pounding.

"What?" The thought hadn't crossed her mind. *Why had she hidden it in my stuff to begin with?*

"Would she have hidden it if she didn't even know there was going to be a search? I'm not sure that she is that good at covering—"

"Okay, hold on a minute," I sputtered. "Do you think . . ."

"That she knew there was going to be a search? Definitely."

"So she did it on purpose, knowing I would get busted." He nodded, squeezing her shoulder. Her breath caught in her throat for a moment as he touched her, but the moment was gone as soon as he continued. "But why? That doesn't make any sense."

"It seems like a lot of things about Jocelyn don't make any sense." Grace bit her bottom lip to hold back tears. "Maybe she was jealous about something dumb."

Their fight after Marge found the flask came flying back to her mind. Jocelyn had accused her of having sex with Alex, and then campers. *She was jealous because she thought I was sleeping with Alex, and just like a little kid, she doesn't want something until somebody else has it.*

"That bitch." The tears were nonexistent; only anger pulsed through her body. She rocked back and forth on the picnic table, unable to stay still. "What the hell?"

"You know her better than I do, but do you think she was the reason Marge did a search to begin with?"

Grace's brain short-circuited.

Matt pulled in a deep breath before continuing. "Do you think she *told* Marge to search the cabins?"

They sat in silence for a few minutes as Matt let her process this idea. She opened her mouth to speak but found she had nothing. She stared at Matt now, but her eyes were unfocused and far off, contemplating. It was entirely possible. Jocelyn could have felt jealous and come up with a plan to get her in trouble. She could have been the one who reported the campers drinking in the woods *after* she hid the flask in Grace's things.

"So there's only one question left: what the hell are you going to do about it?" Matt paused for a minute. "And how can I help?"

17

November 11, 2019

The sedative had worn off around midnight. Or at least, that was what time Grace thought it was until she realized the clock in her room was wrong. Without a window, it made it impossible to keep track of the hours. Even before the door opened, Grace could smell the scent of fried food nearby. The nurse brought in breakfast a few hours later, and she undid the straps that had been fastened around Grace's wrists since her last *outburst,* as the doctor called them.

"Okay, Grace, in order for you to eat, I'm going to undo the straps around your ankles too. The last thing we want is for you to choke on your food." The nurse glanced cautiously at her face, gauging if her anger from earlier had dissipated.

"I won't do anything." Grace felt like a child. Or a hostage. She felt hopeless. Her body was already aching from the fight she put up earlier, and she didn't want to make it worse. The nurse released the straps and backed away as though Grace would spring into action immediately. Grace stretched her muscles out, feeling the tension that had built up in them. She hadn't realized she had thrashed around so much. It wasn't clear if the soreness had come from earlier, or even before that, when she saw the man in her hospital room. After giving Grace a moment to stretch, she brought over the tray of food.

"Can I get you anything?" she asked.

"Can you help me sit up?"

She bit her bottom lip, still clearly afraid. Grace wasn't sure whether this was a good or bad sign for a nurse in a psychiatric hospital. *Is it better to always be on high alert or remain calm?* She moved to her side and reached under her arms.

"Here, let's rest your back against the wall." Together, they maneuver until Grace was sitting up, back resting on the cool wall.

"Thanks." Grace didn't really feel thankful, but she felt obligated to say it.

"Just be careful of your head, okay? The doctor doesn't think you need to be in a brace or anything, as long as you don't move too rapidly." She frowned, clearly thinking back to the day before. The scrubs she sported now were covered in hearts in varying shades of red, purple, and pink. Grace glanced at her ID badge: Samantha. She seemed young and timid. *Is this the only job she could find fresh out of college?* Grace questioned.

"I will. When can I leave the room?" Her thoughts were beginning to come into focus. Finding Jocelyn was back to the top of her priority list.

"That's up to the doctor. It depends how quickly you improve." She hesitated.

"What?" she demanded just a touch too fiercely. Samantha recoiled.

"The doctor said they would like to see you go at least twenty-four hours without any delusions before granting you additional privileges." Grace wanted to laugh. Suddenly, this felt far more like a prison than a hospital.

"Okay, thank you." She gave a small nod that almost appeared like a bow due to her petite frame before disappearing out the door.

Grace turned her attention to the breakfast tray. Scrambled eggs, a mushy hash brown, and an orange Jell-O: the breakfast of champions. The wheels in Grace's brain began to turn as memories oozed out of the dark matter and into her consciousness. Orange Jell-O was Mr. Harris's favorite snack ever since he had his second heart attack and Mrs. Harris made him go low-calorie everything. Grace had a running theory that this was to emasculate him and deter other women.

Grace had been so distracted that she had completely forgotten about her job. She counted the days in her head. It was Friday when she first saw Jocelyn. She had been at the hospital Saturday. Then, she stopped. *Was it Sunday or Monday?* Either way, she was screwed. Grace Simmons was officially just another statistic as one of Mr. Harris's secretaries. A no-show on a Monday would infuriate him. Even if he encouraged her to take Friday off, he would be irate if he had not heard from her at all. Grace's imagination ran loose, anxiety fueling her thoughts. She was done at that company. It was a miracle to get hired there to begin with. Now her chances were slim-to-none at finding something else. *He's probably blacklisting me with all his associates already.*

"Fuck," she groaned. She wanted to erupt and scream, but she knew her doctors would just put her under again. Grace began to cry as she silently shoveled the eggs and hash browns into her mouth, avoiding the orange Jell-O at all costs. She had to make them think she was trying to get better. The image of Mr. Harris storming through the office played on repeat in her mind. *Was I willing to sacrifice all this for Jocelyn?* Grace didn't have to answer. She already had.

18

July 26, 2011

Grace was back at the cabin after talking to Matt for what felt like hours. Moonlight slid in through the windows in the front of the cabin, and she gazed up at the wooden rafters above. The girls were still out with Marge and were probably in the middle of roasting marshmallows and telling not-so-scary ghost stories. Grace looked over at Jocelyn's empty bed and smirked because now, she had a plan.

Grace reminisced on her night with Matt. After he had calmed her down, they chatted about anything and everything. Matt talked about what it was like being the son of a politician. At first, Grace hesitated, but then, she shared too. How she wanted to do better than her dad. To be better than her dad. Matt didn't say much, but he sat and listened. Exactly what Grace needed. Eventually, Matt leaned in and his lips reached hers.

Grace touched her lips at the memory. It was her first kiss since that awkward one at an eighth-grade dance at the YMCA. It felt perfect. Moonlight was shining on their faces, and for once in her life, she had someone else looking out for her.

In the distance, giggling approached the cabins. Movie night was over. The clock hanging above the door read 11:00. The girls would probably fall right asleep after they crashed from their sugar highs. *What would my life be like if I had never come here?* she wondered. There was genuine companionship and love between the kids. *What is it like to be fourteen and feel like you are a part of something? Like you aren't an outcast?* Grace still wasn't sure what that felt like even now. *But Matt . . .*

The door swung open, and Jocelyn led the gaggle of girls into the cabin. She was laughing along. Her straight black hair swayed as she shook her head with giggles, and for a moment, Grace finally saw how beautiful she was. No wonder she could sleep with every guy here. The pit of jealousy in her stomach grew. If the circumstances were different, if Matt had been here last summer, would he have slept with her? Whatever the answer was, she didn't want to know.

"Time for bed!" Jocelyn called. Jocelyn had never been so joyous before. She always looked determined or angry or drunk: there was nothing in between. She thought back to the few times they had laughed together. Grace had forgotten that Jocelyn looked happy then too.

The girls took a few moments to get settled, but eventually, they made their way into bed, putting their hair into buns or braids before resting their heads on the pillows. Grace stood up and turned off the overhead lights one by one. After a moment of watching the girls settle into their dreams, she opened the door and stepped out into the night, hoping Jocelyn would follow. The air outside the cabin was cooler from the slight breeze. Shaking out her t-shirt to dry some of her sweat, she settled down on the cabin steps and stared out into the night, waiting and hoping. *Come on, Jocelyn. Come talk to me.* She tapped her fingers impatiently against the wooden porch.

Finally, the cabin door opened.

"Stop making all that noise," Jocelyn hissed as she stepped out. Grace hadn't realized how much noise she had been making. She pulled her hands into her lap.

"Sorry."

She dropped down next to Grace on the cabin steps and shrugged.

"It's fine. I don't think it woke up the girls anyway."

Why had she seemed so mad then? She didn't ever make any sense.

"How was movie night?" According to everything Jocelyn knew, they were on good terms again. Grace tried to put on her best fake smile. She was used to pretending anyway. But anxiety flowed through her limbs now that it was the time to set her plan in motion.

"Boring. We watched *The Lion King* for the third year in a row. The really little kids cried." Jocelyn yawned. Grace offered a small chuckle but it came out sounding more like a cough.

"So tomorrow is your night off, right?"

Jocelyn nodded.

"You're stuck on talent show duty," she replied, laughing at the concept. "Meanwhile, I'll be checking out some of the new talent here." She smirked and glanced down at the other cabins.

"Do you already have plans with someone?" Grace

shouldn't be surprised. Even after Alex had warned some of the other counselors, it wasn't like he wanted to go around advertising that she had given him an STD. Jocelyn having plans wasn't something they had accounted for. Jocelyn was usually a spur-of-the-moment girl.

"Oh, no. Not specifically. Just a general idea of what I might be doing." She made a lewd gesture with her hands. Grace nodded and bit her lip. *Come on, Grace. Do it. Do it now!* her brain hissed at her.

"I was talking to Alex," she lied. She hadn't talked to Alex really apart from that very first day at camp. This piqued Jocelyn's attention immediately.

"Is he trying to have sex with you?" Jocelyn spat instantaneously. She was like a snake poised to strike, venom ready to kill.

Grace shook her head rapidly.

"No." She paused, trying to calculate how to play this out. "At least, I don't think so. I'm not interested in him at all. But I mean, he did invite me to a party." Grace glanced away, afraid to see her reaction.

"Oh?" she asked, her voice curious but restrained. Grace knew the tone: she knew she wouldn't get the information she wanted if she freaked out, and she still didn't trust that Grace wasn't interested in Alex.

"Yeah." Grace rubbed her hands together, hoping to exert some nervous energy.

"When?" She acted like she wasn't interested. Grace knew she was.

"Tomorrow night. But obviously, I can't go because I'm scheduled to be with our cabin."

Jocelyn rolled her eyes. "So you're going to ask me to cover your ass. I don't think Marge will fall for that."

Grace took a deep breath. None of this was how

she had imagined it, even though she had played through the conversation a million different ways.

"I figured she wouldn't, but I didn't think that would stop you from going."

Jocelyn looked at Grace, concealing whatever emotion she was feeling. When Grace had envisioned this part, Jocelyn had looked shocked, and like Cinderella attending the ball, she was honored. Instead, she just looked bored.

"Hmmm, maybe I'll check it out. Though if Alex is there, I don't know."

Internally, Grace groaned. They definitely hadn't thought it through.

"Maybe you could make him jealous though?" Grace surprised herself at how easily the lie came off her tongue.

"Grace Simmons! You know, that might actually be one of the best ideas I've ever heard come out of your mouth." Her anxiety had crescendoed and was now receding. "So where is this party?"

"The old campsite." Since they had traveled there a few days ago, Grace had now learned it was a popular hook-up site amongst the counselors. It wasn't usually used for parties, because normally those didn't happen, but it was believable enough.

"Okay. Yeah, that makes sense."

"It's there. Around nine." Grace's pulse slowed as Jocelyn nodded.

"I will be there. Sorry you can't make it. Maybe you can sneak away after the girls go to bed. The talent show will probably be over by like 9:30 at the latest. You could meet me," she offered.

"Yeah, totally." Grace flashed a fake smile back.

Matt had told her everything would work out

perfectly, but she hadn't been sure. However, after hearing how easily Jocelyn had accepted the fake party invitation, she believed him. She believed every word.

19

November 11, 2019

The door of the room slowly opened, and the petite nurse entered again.

"Grace?" she asked cautiously. Grace had hoped that the nurse would start to trust her, but remembering back to what she had done before they had pumped her veins full of sedatives, she really couldn't blame her.

"Yes," Grace answered, trying to sit back up in the bed. Her body was feeling incrementally better. *Had they given me a painkiller?* She couldn't really remember. Maybe they hid it in the food.

"How are you feeling?"

"A bit better."

"The doctor wanted me to ask how your memory is?" Her voice rose at the end of the sentence just like Mr. Harris hated. Grace closed her eyes and tried not to break down at the reminder of her long-lost job. Even though her head was no longer pounding, there was still a dull ache and absolutely nothing left in those lost hours.

"Nothing."

"I see." She looked just as disappointed as Grace felt. "How about the pain?"

"It seems better, but I"—she hesitated to ask if she had been given secret painkillers in her sleep. The nurse seemed so kind, so she decided she could trust her—"I don't understand why it feels so much better." She tried to play it off a bit like it was just general confusion. The nurse nodded.

"Well, it's probably from the morphine we gave you earlier."

"What do you mean? When did you give me morphine?"

"The doctor came in after your breakfast to do an evaluation on you. You were complaining about the pain, and she gave you some morphine."

Her mind was blank. There was no evaluation, no morphine, not even a doctor. Hesitantly, she attempted to wiggle her toes. She could see the scratchy blanket undulate with her movement. She let out a breath she didn't know she had been holding.

"You must have me confused with another patient."

"Grace, we only have four patients in this wing. I don't think I would have you confused with anyone else," she insisted with confidence, placing a hand on her hip. "You don't remember that at all?" Grace shook her head slowly, noticing how little the movement hurt. She was certainly right. She must have had some painkillers. *I must be on a hidden camera show.*

At any moment, someone is going to pop out and yell, "Gotcha!"

"Is it a possible side effect of painkillers or the sedative? Memory loss?"

"No. The doctor wouldn't prescribe anything for you that had a memory-related side effect, considering the condition you were in when you arrived, but I will let her know." She turned to leave, but she stopped short of the door.

"Oh my goodness, I completely forgot why I even came in. You must not be the only one with memory issues. Maybe there's something in the air," she chuckled, but stopped, realizing it was a little insensitive. "The doctor said if you were feeling better, you could have a visitor."

"That's great news, but I don't have anyone interested in visiting me."

Her mom was gone. Her father probably wouldn't show up, especially based on their last conversation. Jocelyn was locked up somewhere in this building, and she was pretty certain Mr. Harris wouldn't come looking for her.

"Well, you're certainly in for a surprise then. You have a visitor."

"Who?" None of this was making sense. The nurse stuck her head out the door and called out to someone. Moments later, she was in the door, eyes piercing-green and staring at her.

"Hello, Grace, dear," Mrs. Baker greeted tensely, still upset. Her hands were clasped tightly together in front of her, turning whiter by the moment. Grace's mind pressed play on the memory of their conversation in the deli, where Mrs. Baker had told her that Jocelyn was being moved because of her. She felt the pang of disappointment she had caused deep in her heart. If only she could express how much she was disappointed in herself as well. Grace pulled in a breath, trying to avoid breaking out in a sob, but instead, it turned into a violent coughing fit. Mrs. Baker rolled her eyes as she waited for Grace to regain control.

"Mrs. Baker." Suddenly, her throat and tongue felt dry, as if she had swallowed flour. Her lips stuck together, and it felt like there was a gummy substance stuck inside her throat. "What are you doing here?"

The nurse turned and disappeared outside. Grace remembered the fear she had felt when she was left alone with Jocelyn. *Was Mrs. Baker afraid to be left alone with me too?* Instead of cowering in the corner, she glided, head held high and straight ahead, toward the bed.

"To visit my daughter, silly," she said. The room spun. She had always jokingly called Grace her daughter at family events, especially since Grace's mother passed away. Her heart began to warm, and Grace let a small smile form on her lips. She wasn't alone after all. She pushed herself up in bed and reached up to flatten her hair, worried that her natural curls had turned into a bird's nest.

"I'm here to see Jocelyn." Her words slapped the smile off Grace's face.

"Oh," she whispered, barely making a sound.

"Don't act so shocked. We didn't leave on good terms. And now you're here, trying to mess with my daughter all over again."

"What do you mean?" Grace had felt confused before, but this was worse. She wasn't trying to hurt Jocelyn. She wanted to help.

"Oh, Grace, when will you stop pretending?" She

sighed and sat in the chair near the bed. Grace looked down at the chair, wondering how many times it had been launched across the room at a nurse. It looked light-weight enough, yet it didn't seem to have any damage. "You are pretending all the time. Pretending to be rich. Pretending to be Jocelyn's best friend. Pretending to be my daughter. And now, you're pretending to be sick. Such bullshit. When will you ever be you?"

"I'm not pretending anything!" Even as she said it, she knew the words were a lie. She was pretending all the time. She wasn't sure what she was even supposed to really be.

"Bull. Shit," she spat. "Stop it. The doctor told me you are having all the same symptoms as her. Memory loss. Delusions. Next thing you know, you'll be attacking the staff. You are copying her." They must not have told her she had already attacked a nurse. Mrs. Baker glanced at the door and finally back at Grace. Her voice lowered but somehow felt sharper. "So I am here to tell you that you will never be Jocelyn. You are just making yourself look bad. It's disgraceful. Pull yourself together, and I won't file a restraining order on Jocelyn's behalf. Then they'll have to ship you somewhere else. The doctor said the nearest public facility is an hour away. What an inconvenience for you." She unfolded her legs, pulled her purse onto her shoulder, and stood up.

"Mrs. Baker," Grace began, hoping to explain herself, even though she wasn't certain how she could even begin. She wasn't even sure how this had all happened. Mrs. Baker took a step closer to Grace and placed a pointer finger on Grace's lips.

"Don't." She reached into her purse and pulled

something out. She grabbed Grace's hand and placed a small pill bottle in her palm. "Do us all a favor," she hissed before turning on her heel and disappearing out into the hallway.

Grace stared down at the orange bottle in shock. A few white pills shook inside as Grace began to tremble. Jocelyn's name was printed on the label, and just below was the name of her antidepressant. It was a full bottle, just filled at the pharmacy today. She hadn't gotten these for Jocelyn at all. She had come here to give Grace the bottle, to ask her to fix all her problems. And by fixing all her problems, she meant disappear.

Grace stared at the door, thinking the nurse would come rushing in and snatch the pills out of her hand. For someone, anyone, to do something. Instead, she was left staring at pills that could make this all go away. Her mind began racing. *Maybe she's right. You're a problem. All you've done is hurt her and Jocelyn. All you've done is cause pain. You will never be more than a piece of trash. Do it.*

Grace uncapped the bottle and stared down at the little white pills. *Nobody would really miss me,* she thought. The idea bounced back and forth in her brain. But one thought stopped her: Jocelyn needed her. Most importantly, she needed to tell Jocelyn the truth. With the lid screwed back on, Grace shoved the bottle under her mattress. Now not only did she have to tell Jocelyn the truth, but she also had to tell her that she wasn't crazy. The man was real. And he was back. *If he is really here*, Grace thought.

Sitting in silence, she began to study the room. It was the first day it didn't hurt to keep her eyes open or that she was capable of keeping them open. She couldn't hear much noise from the hallway. Whispers started to reach her ears. She frowned. *Maybe I am really losing it.* The voices became stronger, though, and they were familiar. Rising to her feet, she held her breath, trying to hear better. Her eyes scanned the room until she found an air vent nestled behind the chair Mrs. Baker had just occupied. Grace tried to move the chair, but it was heavier than she thought. She wondered if they had made it that way to prevent patients from throwing it. She slid her body between the chair and the wall. With her ear pressed against the cool metal vent, she listened.

"Mom, she didn't do anything. You know that she would never." Jocelyn was speaking. Her voice sounded ragged and labored, as if she was struggling to say anything. She seemed physically sick, not just mentally.

"Jocelyn, you have been blinded by her from the beginning. She has never been looking out for you. She has always been looking out for herself and trying to get ahead. She hopped onto you like a leech and hasn't let go since." Mrs. Baker went silent as Jocelyn began a coughing fit. Grace listened intensely. It almost sounded like bronchitis. *How could she get that sick in a place like this?*

"She isn't like that, I promise. She has always been looking out for me!"

Grace cringed at her words. This time her mother was right.

"Oh really, Jocelyn?" Mrs. Baker challenged. "Where was she the *one* time you really needed her? Where?"

"She was working! She had to work that talent show. She couldn't go to the party because of work!"

It sounded like this conversation had played out between them a million times in the past eight years. Grace felt chills run down her spine thinking of all the times that Mrs. Baker had pretended to be pleasant with her, only to be speaking like this behind her back. How many times had she left a family event just to have Jocelyn and Mrs. Baker fight about her immediately afterward?

"Then why did the cops believe she was a suspect!"

The words seemed to fly through the vent and smack Grace in the face. The cops had questioned her, but they never called her a suspect.

20

July 27, 2011

"Hey, Jocelyn."

Jocelyn spun on her heels and faced Grace. Her brown hair was shiny from being freshly washed that morning in preparation for her evening activities.

"What's up, babe?" Jocelyn chomped on some bubble gum. They were heading to talent show practice with some of the girls. Some of their cabin was planning on doing a dance routine to a mash-up of pop songs from the previous year. Despite their enthusiasm, they weren't great.

"I have a stomachache. Do you mind if I bail for a little? I can meet up with you guys after practice."

Jocelyn made a face and rolled her eyes.

"Gross. See you later." She turned back around without a moment of thought. Grace looked down at her nails. She hadn't even realized she was biting them, but they were almost raw. She wasn't sure if she could do this. Her stomach twisted around itself as she made her way around the corner of the canteen and in the opposite direction of the bathroom.

About fifty yards ahead, she spotted Matt talking to the maintenance man, Carl. She stopped and moved behind a tree. She needed to wait.

Carl disappeared into the maintenance shed. It appeared newly renovated to look like a barn, painted bright red with white trim. The illusion was mostly shattered by the sunlight bouncing off of the solar panels on the roof. Matt glanced around. At first, Grace thought he was nervous, but that didn't quite translate into his posture. Maybe he was just a good actor. Maybe he wasn't nervous at all.

A moment later, Carl reappeared with his toolkit, and both of them set off in the direction of the cabins. The story was that there was a leak in Matt's cabin. He had spilled some bottled water on the ground and was going to distract Carl long enough for Grace to get what they needed. Once the pair was obscured from view, Grace made her move.

Instinctually, she wanted to run. Her legs told her to hurry. But she knew that was suspicious. Instead, she alternated between a normal walk and a half jog as she approached the shed. Her heart drummed against her ribs. Finally, she reached the shed. She forced her head to stay straight ahead rather than look from side to side. She needed to look normal. Matt had told her only bad criminals looked around to see if someone was watching. Good criminals didn't do anything suspicious to begin with. She had asked him how he knew that. He laughed and reminded her his dad was a politician.

Dust fluttered around the shed, causing Grace to cough as she pulled the door shut behind her. Her eyes adjusted and darted around the space.

"If I was a garden tool, where would I be?" she murmured, surveying the space. Behind the riding mower sat a shelf containing grass seed, potting soil, spades, and various other implements. Many shelves remained entirely empty. She maneuvered around the mower until the shelf was directly in front of her. There, she found exactly what she was looking for.

21

November 11, 2019

"She was a suspect only because everyone at camp was!" Jocelyn yelled, her voice cracking at the end of her sentence.

"Jocelyn, I don't think anyone ever told you, but her story didn't add up. The police said she lied in her interviews. They could tell she was hiding something from them. She should have been protecting you! And if she knew that was going on, why did she let you get hurt?" Grace could imagine Mrs. Baker's arms crossed in front of her, staring down at her daughter on the bed. Without realizing it, she had been holding her breath. She glanced back at her own mattress concealing the pills Mrs. Baker had provided. The guilt weighed heavily on her chest.

Just as Grace went to turn her attention back to the vent, she caught a flash of black dart across her door's window. Grace shoved her fist into her mouth before a scream could escape. She recalled the nurse's words about the delusions and her chances of being released. *Is he real? Am I crazy?* She scanned the room. There was nothing to do or to distract herself within the room. Just beige walls and a bed to sleep in for hours and hours. Crazy sounded more and more sensible each moment.

Jocelyn fell into a coughing fit that lasted for what seemed like several minutes. Once the coughs ended, she started gasping for air. Grace grimaced. *It's my fault.* Ever since that night, Jocelyn had issues with her lungs. A few times, it had even turned into pneumonia.

"That damn bitch. She's up to something. That's why she's here. I'm going to get rid of her, one way or another," Mrs. Baker spat. Jocelyn remained silent, apart from her wheezing.

Grace stared at the vent, playing with the edge of the grill. It felt a bit loose, and an idea sprung into her head. This vent could directly connect to Jocelyn's. The idea felt ridiculous and impossible, but she had to let her know the man she was seeing was real.

"Mom, leave her alone. She helped me. She's the one who called the police that night. Besides, she's sick too. Can't she be sick for once?"

Am I the sick one?

"Didn't I tell you about how they found her? She was lying outside her apartment, passed out. Her cat was"—Mrs. Baker cleared her throat—"torn to shreds in front of her. They think she did it. She killed her own cat. Imagine what she would do to you. They say killing animals is a sign someone is a serial killer. She could have been the one there that night."

Grace stood up and stumbled to the bed, tears

blurring her vision. She smashed her toe into the foot of the bed but didn't feel the pain. She collapsed into the bed. The pain in her head was nothing compared to what she felt now.

The image of Harold torn to pieces in the snow replayed in her mind. *How could I have forgotten?* His body was completely in shreds, and his head was missing, and then she passed out. She scrunched her eyes shut to keep the room from spinning. Her breathing became shallow, and she tried to count in her head, but the onslaught of emotion continued. She wanted to scream for help. For a second, she heard someone running down the hallway. Forcing her eyes open, she saw him. At her door. Dressed in black. She tried to make out the face, but before she could, everything went black.

22

July 27, 2011

The talent show was due to begin in about twenty minutes. Some of the campers had already headed out to the stage to get prepared for their performance, while the others who planned to just be in the audience were relaxing in the cabin. Jocelyn was rooting through her vintage trunk.

"I have absolutely nothing to wear tonight," she huffed before approaching Grace's dresser. "What do you have?" She reached for the handle, and Grace quickly jumped in front of her.

"Nothing!' Grace took a sharp breath and tried to play her reaction off as cool. "I'm not letting you back in my stuff after last time." Grace let out a small laugh to smooth over her brash response, and Jocelyn smirked.

"Fair enough."

"Why don't you go see if one of the other female counselors has something? I really only have rags; you wouldn't like them. Plus, they probably wouldn't even fit your tiny frame."

She nodded.

"Good idea." She headed out the door. Grace let out a deep breath before turning around and facing the campers. Most of them were chatting or listening to music. Cell phones were only allowed inside the cabins, so they valued their downtime. Sometimes a bit too much.

"Girls, you should get going to the talent show."

The girls looked around and frowned.

"But it doesn't start for like a half hour," one girl protested. Several others nodded in agreement.

"I realize that, but guess what? All the good seats are going to get taken. You won't even be able to see if you don't get there soon." The girls looked at one another, contemplating the idea. "Come on. I'm not asking, I'm telling you!" The words snapped out of Grace's mouth like something Jocelyn would have said during one of her fits. The girls got to their feet and headed toward the door.

"Jesus, calm down, Grace," one teased as she headed out the door. A few girls gathered by the door, waiting for her to follow after them.

"I'll be right behind you girls. I just have to put my shoes on." The girls spun and headed down the trail to the talent show. She walked to the window and stared out, waiting. Her eyes shifted back to her dresser. When a few minutes had passed, and she couldn't stand staring out the window anymore, she paced back and forth between the front and back of the cabin.

Is it too late to change my mind? What if I just leave now?

Then it's not my fault either way. I'm not responsible. I can still call it off.

The cabin door opened, and in walked Matt.

"Wow, you look nervous," Matt remarked, the smile disappearing from his face.

"And you don't. Somehow, that makes me even more nervous."

Matt approached Grace and put his hands firmly on her shoulders.

"Listen, Grace, it's going to be fine. I've got this. You've already done your part. Right?" he asked, meeting her eyes. She bit her bottom lip and glanced over at the dresser.

"I have a really bad feeling about this. Maybe you shouldn't do it."

Matt kissed her forehead, and she felt butterflies.

"I promise nothing will happen. It will all go perfectly. I have it all planned out."

Grace nodded and moved over to the dresser, pulling open the bottom drawer. Sitting on top of her socks and gym shorts, the garden shears she had stolen earlier were clearly visible. She hadn't even thought to conceal them. *I am not qualified to do something like this,* she thought, her mind flashing images of Jocelyn yanking open the drawer. She had been so close.

Matt wrapped his hands around the garden shears, and Grace released her grip after a moment of hesitation. *It's out of my hands now.* Matt opened and closed the shears. The noise made Grace flinch. When she looked back, Matt was smiling.

"Please be careful."

He nodded and wrapped his free arm around her, rubbing her back.

"I will be so careful. It will all work out. I wouldn't

be doing this if I didn't think so." Matt smiled. "Go on, head over to the talent show. It will all be fine."

Grace released a shaky breath and tried not to let her body shake.

"I'm trusting you."

"I know." He leaned over and kissed her once more on the lips. All Grace really wanted was to stay in that moment. She wanted to stay in the cabin with Matt and ignore everything else: the talent show, Jocelyn, the future. However, none of that was possible.

"Good luck" was the last thing she said to Matt that night. She headed out the door and to the talent show, trying to push the negative thoughts out of mind. With a glance over her shoulder, she saw Matt disappearing into the woods by her cabin. He was dressed in all black and nearly invisible, the glint of the garden shears feeling blinding. She frowned and tried to focus on her job: watch the kids.

I don't need to watch Jocelyn. She's a big girl, Grace told herself. *Everything will be fine.*

23

November 11, 2019

The power was completely out. The hammering of Grace's heart echoed in her ears. Her face was crunched in on itself, her eyes closed so hard it hurt. In the hallways, there was shouting, but over the sound of the blood rushing through her body, Grace couldn't tell if someone was in danger or if it was simply because the power was out. She tried to concentrate on her breathing again, but her chest felt like it was caving in. *You're dying, stupid. This is it. It's over. He's here. He's here. He's . . .*

Thoughts came crashing down over her, racing through everything. Her brain skipped from one thing to the next without slowing down. Jocelyn in the other room and the man in black. The pills under the mattress. The screams. The power outage. The vent. Harold. Her eyes stayed shut; she couldn't see anything with them open anyway. She focused on the air escaping her mouth and desperately trying to pull more in through her nose.

It seemed like hours passed this way. She couldn't judge how long it had taken to calm the panic attack. She finally forced her eyes open. She could make out a few lights through the window, but they were dim. She swung her legs off the bed and groped through the darkness toward the window. She reached the window and stood on her toes to look out. It seemed there was no one in the hallway.

"Help!" Jocelyn's voice rang out. "He's in here! He's here! Help!"

Grace felt chills tickle her spine. She rattled the doorknob but it didn't give. She raced over to the vent and pulled on the grate. With her fingers, she felt blindly around the edges, searching for screws. She could tell there was a flat head screw at the top of the grate and one at the bottom as well. She tried to pry her fingers under the metal and pull. It didn't give. Her fingers felt slick with blood as she continued to yank on the vent. *There has to be something I can use.* She stood and rushed to her bedside, bumping into the chair along the way. Her ankle rolled as she fell to the ground.

"Shit." It escaped from her mouth as barely a breath. She forced herself back up, wincing at the pain. She limped to the bedside and felt the edge of her breakfast tray. Her fingers felt for the plastic fork, blood combining with food on the tray.

"Help! Someone help me!" Jocelyn's screams had become hysterical now. She could hear her labored breathing. Grace's heart ached as she fell to the floor and pulled herself up to the vent.

"Please, God. Please let this work. Please let me get to her." Grace wasn't even certain she could fit through the vent. She would be crazy not to try.

"Stay away!" Jocelyn's voice contorted. He was there and coming for her.

Grace's fingers smudged blood against the surface of the vent as she felt for the screws. She located the bottom one first and tried to line up the fork. The screw was already loose and came off with a few turns.

"Come on. One more." She moved to the top screw, praying it would budge like the first. Instead, the fork snapped in two.

"No!" Tears fell to the floor, mixing with drops of blood. "Please." The noise from Jocelyn's room had stopped. Grace tried to use the broken fork to move the screw, but there wasn't enough leverage now. Sobs racked her body. Her hands rose to cover her face.

"Please, someone help. Someone help her!" As the words flew out of her mouth, the lights turned back on. She moved her hands away from her face and blinked, trying to adjust to the light. She struggled back to her feet, keeping weight off her left ankle, glancing around the room for something new to use for the vent. Her eyes fell upon the armchair just as the door swung open and the doctor entered. Her eyes shifted from the doctor and back to the armchair, where a pair of bloody garden shears sat.

24

July 27, 2011

The final performance was beginning for the talent show. Grace had escaped to the edge of the seating to get away from the noise. She kept checking her watch, waiting for it to read 9:00 p.m. However, once that time passed, rather than her anxiety subsiding, it only increased. At the pause between the campers taking the stage and a remix of "Cotton Eye Joe" beginning, she heard it. The screams. Without thinking, without a moment of hesitation, she turned and ran straight for the abandoned cabins. The screams continued. She couldn't tell, but deep down, she knew it was Jocelyn, and she knew something had gone horribly wrong.

Her legs raced through the woods, the sound of the talent show disappearing behind her. Nobody else had been listening close enough to notice the screams. All eyes had been focused on the stage so nobody even noticed Grace bolt from the crowd. As she flew through the woods, she prayed. *Please let it be inside my head. Please let it just be nothing.* If the plan had gone right, Jocelyn wouldn't still be screaming. *I shouldn't have trusted him.*

"Jocelyn!" Grace roared as she got closer to the old campsite. Each step brought her closer. She couldn't run fast enough. The sounds of the woods echoed around, making Jocelyn seem closer than she was. Finally, there was no sound at all.

Grace stopped and tried to listen. All that she could hear was the blood rushing in her ears. Behind her, she could make out just a little glimmer of light from the talent show, but when she turned back, all she could see was trees. All she knew was that she was moving away from everyone else and closer to Jocelyn.

"Jocelyn!" Grace cried out again, screaming at the top of her lungs. She plunged forward again, trying to close the distance between them. The woods were thinning, and she knew that at any moment, she would be there. All at once, the campsite was before her. Her eyes ran over the scene before her, and her legs wobbled under her weight.

It wasn't just Jocelyn. It seemed like there were half a dozen people lying on the ground. She couldn't make out faces, but she knew Jocelyn had to be one of them. Stopping to look closer, she stood with one leg slightly behind the other, ready to move. Her eyes squinted as she tried to see through the woods. There had been a fire, but it looked like it had just been extinguished, leaving smoke curling through the air.

Behind her, she heard a branch snap. Spinning around, she caught a glimpse of a figure in black disappearing into the trees.

"Matt!" she yelled after him, but he was gone already. A tiny moan responded nearby.

"Oh god, please. Jocelyn?" Grace's breath caught in her throat as the moan came again.

She crouched down next to the body and touched the face. She could make out Jocelyn's silky hair. It was then that she remembered the flashlight she had in her pocket. A camper had thought it was funny to shine it in people's eyes during the talent show, and she had snatched it. She flicked it on and let out a scream.

In Jocelyn's chest sat the garden shears. Sticking straight up. Dark with her blood. Grace flashed it around the scene and tried to count. Seven people were on the ground. Matt had killed seven people. He had left Jocelyn for last. But he didn't finish the job.

"Jocelyn, can you hear me?" Grace moved her face close to Jocelyn's, trying her best to avoid the garden shears. If she looked at them too long, she knew she would pass out. She tried to listen for signs of life.

Nothing. She couldn't hear anything from Jocelyn over the sound of her own heavy breathing. Grace stood up and looked back at the woods. How could she help? There was no cell signal out here, and her phone was back at the cabin anyway. Her brain panicked, trying to figure out what to do. Did she run back for help? That was the only option, until she remembered her trip here with Jocelyn.

The payphone.

Grace raced to the old camp office and pulled the receiver off the hook.

"Please god, please." A dial tone echoed in her ear. "Please work." She jabbed at the buttons in her panic.

Grace tried to dial too quickly and hit eight the first time.

"Come on!" She slammed the hang-up button and typed again, more precisely this time. Her entire body was shaking. *9-1-1*.

"Nine-one-one, what is your emergency?" a man responded. Grace bounced back and forth on her feet, unable to contain her emotions. Relief. Horror. Fear.

"I'm at Camp Willows. There's been an attack. A bunch of people are dead, and my friend is—" The tears hadn't come until now. She felt like she was choking. "She's dying." The words felt like poison in her mouth. Grace almost went on to explain, but the responder spoke before she could.

"Where at the campsite?"

"The old campgrounds."

"How many people were attacked?"

She couldn't remember how many bodies she had counted.

"Too many."

25

"Miss Simmons!" the doctor spat. The bottom of his white coat swayed slightly as he yelled at her. "Step away from the weapon."

Grace held her hands up and backed away slowly. Her mind flipped like a rolodex through the faces in her memory. She didn't remember this doctor, but she also didn't remember a lot.

"I don't understand. How did they get in here? Who—" Grace stopped midquestion. She knew who. "How did he . . ." Grace's breath caught in her chest. When had he gotten in? She tried to run back through the moments of darkness. "It doesn't make sense."

"How did you get these?" the doctor asked, shaking his head in disbelief. Others began to race into the room. "I think we found our culprit."

"Culprit? No, I didn't do anything. Wait, is Jocelyn

okay?" Her breath went from ragged to desperate gasps.

"Miss Simmons, do we have to sedate you again?" Her face darted up from the shears and to the doctor. She couldn't be sedated again. Not now.

"No. Please. No. I will cooperate with anything you ask."

A large male nurse approached the bed, and the doctor nodded.

"Then we are going to strap you onto the bed again. That's happening either way, just so you know," the doctor said as she assessed Grace's face. Grace moved slowly onto the bed in a flat position as the nurse attached the restraints. She could only watch as another nurse grabbed the garden shears delicately. She clenched her hands together tightly, her fingertip stinging. Nobody noticed the cuts, and she wasn't about to make herself look worse. As she glanced over their faces, she didn't see the nurse from earlier. *I wish she was here. She might believe me.* Grace was lying to herself.

Within moments, the room had been cleared and the garden shears had disappeared. Blood remained on the armchair. She counted the droplets as she lay there, over and over. Each time, she came up with a different number. *Did they not see it? The police needed to take samples. It's evidence. My room is a crime scene. He was here, in my room. While I was in it.*

"Grace, focus. You cannot lose control right now." She was trying to convince herself not to spiral. "How could this have happened?" Grace figured he either worked here or he had taken an employee ID card to scan into the room. Regardless of how it had happened, he was more dangerous than she had

145

thought. She couldn't do much strapped to the bed, especially considering Jocelyn was in the next room. *Is she okay over there? Is she even alive?* The staff hadn't said a word. Grace decided she must be; otherwise they would have sedated her without hesitation.

Suddenly, a sharp cough came from the vent. *She's alive!* Grace wanted to cheer. A dark realization quickly overcame her relief. Just because she was alive didn't mean she would be safe for long, though. Grace hadn't realized how tired she was until she had to lay still on the bed. Her eyelids grew heavy. She couldn't do anything more for now. She felt herself drifting off, hoping she would wake up somewhere else entirely.

26

July 28, 2011

"Miss Simmons, can we get you a drink? A soda?" Detective Diaz offered. Grace shook her head and pulled the sleeves of her hoodie down over her hands. There was a chill in the room that she couldn't shake, and the metal chair wasn't helping. "Let me just get you a water then," he suggested before slipping out the door. She glanced at the video camera sitting in the corner of the room. She couldn't remember him turning it on. *Did they turn it on before I came in?* Finally, after a moment, the door reopened, and Detective Diaz re-entered. The harsh light from the lamp above hurt her eyes, and she forced herself to look down instead.

"Here we go," he said, placing the bottle of water in front of her and a second on his side of the silver table. "Let's get started. I'm sure you want to get home."

He was wrong. The last place Grace wanted to go was home. Home was miles away, and she wasn't even sure how she would get there at this point. She hadn't called her parents; she wasn't sure if she was more afraid of her father finding out what had happened last night or him raging about having to make another trip upstate to rescue her.

Last night, after getting checked out by an EMT, she tried to help Marge with damage control. It wasn't like they could pretend nothing had happened when ambulances and cop cars diverged on the camp. Before Grace had left this morning, parents, nannies, and grandparents had all rushed onto the scene to take away their children. Grace thought Marge would be a wreck, but really she seemed in control and focused. As if getting the kids off her hands was a relief.

Snapshots of last night flashed into Grace's brain. She tried to shake them away but they were stuck like an image frozen on a television screen. Regardless, she nodded in response, hoping he would keep talking so she wouldn't have to.

"So, tell me what happened from the beginning." He pulled out his notepad and poised his pen at the top of the page, holding eye contact with Grace the entire time. His skin had the same olive tone as Jocelyn's and the thought made her swallow hard. His biceps tugged on the edges of his gray shirt, the fabric holding on for dear life. If he was trying to be intimidating, it would have worked if Grace wasn't already scared beyond belief. Silence grew between them as tears pooled in her eyes.

Well, Officer, it was all my fault. You see, I set up Jocelyn to be . . . Grace frowned. She couldn't possibly tell him the truth.

"I was working the talent show at camp. They were just about done with the kids' acts. We were wrapping up—"

"And this was on the 27th? Yesterday?" Detective Diaz interrupted. Grace paused and looked down at her lap.

"Yes. The kids were clapping—"

"Miss Simmons, I do not think that is really the beginning of the story."

Her eyes darted toward him. He leaned back against the chair, the metal scraping as he slid away from the table. *He knew.*

"What do you mean?" she asked, hoping her acting skills were as good as they had been the night she told Jocelyn about the party.

"Miss Baker told us something else happened. So why don't you tell me what happened on July 26th?" It was phrased like a question, but it clearly wasn't.

"On the 26th?" He nodded, bouncing his pen against the pad of paper. "I guess it started like a normal day. I was off duty in the evening. I was just hanging out in the cabin. And the girls came back from movie night, and we went to bed."

Diaz nodded and wrote something down on the pad.

"So did you leave the cabin that night? On the 26th?" he asked. His eyes seemed friendly, but the rest of his expression was hard. *Is he acting too?* Grace closed her eyes and hoped it came across as her trying to remember, not trying to come up with a lie.

"Not that I can remember." He scribbled something down onto the notepad. He had it tilted just so that Grace couldn't make out what he was writing. She leaned forward anyway, trying to catch a glimpse.

"Okay, and when Miss Baker arrived back at the cabin, did you two talk?"

Grace clasped her hands together under the table, holding so tightly it made her bones ache. Her mind traveled back to the conversation on the front porch, how Jocelyn had believed Alex was trying to hook up with Grace.

"Of course." Grace had watched enough cop shows to know the less you said, the better. However, she seemed to completely forget the most important part: a lawyer.

"What did you talk about?" he pressed.

Shit! What do I say? Do I tell the truth? Does saying nothing make me look worse?

"We talked about a party that was happening the next night. She said she was going."

Diaz set his pen down and met her eyes once again. Grace looked down to avoid his stare.

"Was there any other discussion about the party?"

"Um . . . I told her I would come after the talent show if I could get away."

"How did Miss Baker find out about this party?" he asked, still trying to look into her eyes.

He knows, he already knows. Grace panicked.

"I told her," she blurted out, the tension growing inside of her. Her hands slid down her legs, attempting to wipe away the sweat on her palms. She couldn't risk lying when the detective had already spoken to Jocelyn. She had surely told him everything. She, unlike Grace, had nothing to hide.

"Okay." He wrote down a note on the paper and looked back up. "How did you find out about the party?"

Images of her kiss with Matt in the woods played in

her mind, intermixed with the carnage he had left behind. When she imagined the kiss, she no longer felt warm or bubbly. He hadn't cared about her. He had played her.

"Matt," she whispered after a moment of silence.

"Matt Snyder?" he asked.

She nodded her head ever so slightly.

"I think so. I never found out his last name." Diaz opened a file folder on the corner of the table and began to pull out photographs. He pulled out one of Matt and showed it to her; his hair was slicked back and he was smiling widely, a tie wrapped around his neck: his school picture.

"Is this him?" Diaz asked. Grace nodded, but rather than replace the photograph back in the folder, he reopened the folder and began to pull out more photographs. These ones were of the crime scene. She closed her eyes tightly, hoping to push away the images in her mind and in real life.

"Miss Simmons, it is really important you tell me everything you can. We have a limited time frame here to catch who did this."

She hung her head. They didn't know it was him yet.

"I understand."

"Do you have any idea who we may be looking for? You came across the scene first."

"Matt. It was him," she whispered, glancing back at his school picture while consciously avoiding the crime scene photographs. If she needed to tell the truth in order to catch Matt for what he did, she would. She didn't think she could live knowing he was still out there, even if it meant she got in trouble. When she looked back up to Diaz, his brow was furrowed.

"Miss Simmons, can you describe to me exactly

what happened the night of the 27th one more time?"

She had done this with the detective the night before, but she had felt so panicked that the details were fuzzy. Forcing her hands back together again, she released a slow breath before starting.

"The talent show was ending, and in between the clapping, I heard screams coming from the old campsite. I started running immediately because I knew that's where the party Jocelyn was going to was." Tears began to fall from her eyes, and she rubbed them away with the sleeve of her hoodie. "I ran as fast as I could, and when I got there, she was there." She gasped for air as her body dissolved into sobs. Diaz grabbed a tissue from the table and handed it to her.

"Go on. It's okay."

"I thought she was dead. There were so many people around. And I looked up, and I saw a man in black clothing running away. It was Matt."

Diaz frowned.

"Did you see his face? How did you know it was Matt?"

"I just knew! It was him."

Diaz had begun writing out diligent notes, and Grace opened her mouth to keep going. To tell the truth. But Diaz pressed on.

"And you saw this man in black running away from the scene?" She nodded. "Then it could not have been Matt Snyder."

"No, it had to be him." She looked directly at Diaz now, her head tilted to the right, feeling as confused as he had looked moments ago.

"Matt Snyder was at the scene when we arrived. He was deceased."

27

November 11, 2019

When Grace awoke, she had no concept of what time it was. Initially, she was even confused at where she was, like one does when they arise from a deep sleep. It didn't take long for it all to come flooding back. The lights had been dimmed in her room and the hallway, so she assumed it was now nighttime. *Maybe it's just nap time for the super psycho ward*, she mused. She reached up and brushed some hair away from her face. It took a moment for her brain to register that she was no longer strapped down to the bed. Hesitantly, she moved her legs; they were free too. She rolled her wrists and ankles, hoping to erase the stiffness in the joints. She sat up in bed and immediately thought of the vent.

She still needed to get to Jocelyn and speak to her. She needed to know that she wasn't crazy. The man dressed in black was out there, and he was more dangerous now than ever. Her plastic fork had gotten lost in the chaos when the lights went out and half the staff had entered her room. Grace's eyes explored the room, searching for something that could be used on the vent. Something thin but sturdy. Finally, her eyes fell upon the nylon foot straps they had used to tie her down. Normally, they would have taken them away once they unstrapped her so she couldn't hang herself with them. But either because of a forgetful or lazy nurse, she now had exactly what she needed. The strap had a metal piece at the center of the buckle that looked to be just the right size.

She stood. Her legs wobbled at first, and she winced as she felt a small shockwave of pain shoot from her ankle as her foot touched the cool tile. Otherwise, she seemed intact. She crept slowly toward the vent, hoping nobody was watching and could tell what she was about to do. She slipped her fingers around the buckle, ignoring the cuts covering her hands. They had mostly scabbed over now. She stretched the buckle over to the vent and lowered herself to the ground. Luckily, it just barely reached. She placed the insert of the buckle into the slit in the screw and pushed down. The metal pressed back into her hand. Her hands were not strong enough to turn the screw.

After a moment, she decided to place one heel on the buckle and press toward the floor. All the flexibility she had built from stretching every morning came into play as she held the buckle in place with one hand and pressed the heel of her foot against it simultaneously. The cool metal pushed into her foot but didn't break the rough, dry skin on her foot. Finally, the screw gave way. She wiped some sweat from her forehead: it was from stress rather than the physicality of the task. She moved her foot away and used her hand to finish undoing the screw, gently placing the metal buckle on the bed when she was done. Her eyes landed back on the door as she watched to see if anyone would notice. Nobody did. With the lights dimmed, they likely thought she was still sleeping and didn't bother to check on her.

Forcing her fingernails between the edge of the vent and the wall, she tugged. Immediately, the vent came loose in her hands. As quietly as she could, she placed the vent under the bed. The vent was bigger than normal, likely due to the age of the building. St. George had been built back when they locked people up for having any mental illness. She took a deep breath and placed her hands on the air duct, testing its strength. Since it was near to the floor, it seemed like there must have been a stud directly beneath it. Slowly, she wiggled her way inside, shimming her shoulders and hips forward.

The duct made it nearly impossible to see how long it was, especially with the outside lights being dimmed. *This seems crazy,* Grace thought. *What I am doing is crazy.* She knew Jocelyn's room couldn't be far, as she had heard her conversation with her mother so clearly. It wasn't. Their rooms appeared to be almost directly next to each other. She could see the soft light filtering through the slits of the vent, and her fingers touched them.

"Jocelyn," she whispered, her mouth pressed close to the vent, listening for anything. The slits in the vent were so tilted that she could not see into the room, particularly with the angle she was at. There was silence.

"Jocelyn!" Her voice was a bit louder this time, like

the frantic whisper a teacher would use during a test. She heard rustling inside the room. It sounded like she was moving to the vent. Seconds later, the light from the vent disappeared. She must have been standing just outside.

"Jocelyn, are you okay? I need to talk to you!" She tried to move her head to see but had no luck. The duct grasped around her body and she could barely move at all. Using her head, she forced the vent open and squirmed her way forward, like a worm desperate to reach grass. She turned her head to look up, pain shooting through her back as she twisted. Her jaw dropped as she blinked, hoping her eyes were lying to her.

"Jocelyn's not here right now," a man's voice declared.

28

July 28, 2011

Matt is dead?" Her voice broke. For the past 12 hours she was envisioning him attacking Jocelyn. The image had replayed in her head over and over.

"Yes. Matt Snyder was found amongst the dead. The coroner's office is still examining the body, but we have confirmation from Senator Snyder that it is his son." Diaz paused and waited for Grace to respond. Tears were pooling in her eyes. She sniffed and wiped at her eyes with the sleeve of her hoodie.

"How did he die?" she asked after a moment of silence. The words fell out of Grace's mouth just as her brain began to put it together.

"As I said, they are still completing the workup on his body. However, it appears that the same weapon that was used on Miss Baker was also used on him."

Tears clouded her vision as she looked at the wall

behind Diaz's head, though she wasn't really seeing anything.

"The garden shears."

Diaz wrote a note on the pad.

"How did you know about the garden shears?"

The question pulled her back into reality. She hadn't even realized she had said it aloud. Panic tossed in her stomach. *Did I just mess up?* She tried to think, but the answer came easily.

"They were there when I found Jocelyn." The memory made her feel sicker than the panic had. "They were—" She grabbed the bottle of water in front of her and took a sip. Her face had grown pale, and she thought for a moment she might pass out. Instead of chills, she now felt like her body was on fire. "They were sticking out of her chest."

Diaz seemed unfazed by this detail. He already knew it. He was just forcing her to retell the story for him, to find details. To catch her in a lie.

"Did you move them?" He asked the question so quickly that it threw her off.

"No. Of course not. They gave us counselors a first aid class, and they said never to remove an object from a wound, so I left them."

"Did you touch Miss Baker?"

She took another small sip of the water, trying to focus on his words and not the bile creeping up her throat.

"Yes. I held her. I thought she was dying." The tears were starting to dry up. It felt like the first time she had stopped crying since last night. You can only cry so much before you can't cry anymore. Grace had felt grateful for the tears. At least the recording would show her terribly upset. That part wasn't an act.

"She was dying, Miss Simmons. If you hadn't found her, she would have most certainly died." Diaz took a drink of his own water now.

The queasiness was fading. Diaz probably thought she would feel relieved to know she had saved Jocelyn, but somehow, she was also the reason she needed saving as well. But none of it made sense. *If Matt wasn't the killer, who was?*

"I know. I'm glad I heard the screams."

"Now, Grace, I want you to think really hard again. You said you didn't touch the garden shears, right? You didn't touch them while they were in her body?"

She bit her bottom lip and gazed up at the lamp above. The blinding light felt like something she deserved now.

"I'm really not sure. Maybe I did when I was checking on her. It's all a blur." Grace knew she couldn't tell the truth now. The truth didn't make sense either, and her story wouldn't help them get any closer to finding the real killer. "When can I see Jocelyn?"

"She is still not in stable condition. I have given your name to her mother, in case she wants to reach out."

She frowned. "I can't see her today?"

"Unfortunately, no. I was with her earlier today and was asking her questions. Unfortunately, her condition"—he stopped and looked to the side, searching for the right words—"worsened after our interview."

"Worsened? Is she going to be okay?"

Diaz stared down at his hands as if he was debating how much he should share.

"Miss Simmons, your friend will never, ever be the same."

159

As soon as the words came out of his mouth, she knew. Grace knew she could never leave Jocelyn's side. She had to make up for all the destruction she caused. Even if it destroyed her.

29

November 12, 2019

"Jocelyn's not here." Grace blinked as she looked around the room, completely lost. Moments before, she had been stuck in the vent with *him* standing before her. Now she was in a small office filled with cozy furniture. A middle-aged man sat in front of her, legs crossed. Time was missing again.

"Wait? Where am I?" Grace's mind raced through the possibilities. Delusions? Schizophrenia? Side effects from sedatives? Time travel? A very vivid dream?

"Grace, you are in my office and we are in the middle of a session. I am Dr. Tyler, a colleague of Dr. Campbell's. What do you remember?"

Grace looked over the man's face. His thick-framed glasses sat low on his nose, revealing his bushy eyebrows. His thick hair was styled meticulously, and he was dressed like he was starring in a high-end whiskey ad. Grace looked down at her hands, tightly grasping the tan leather armrests. Pulling them away to examine them, she saw small cuts still covered them. So something she remembered was real. She just wasn't sure which parts. She cleared her throat before speaking.

"I'm not sure I want to talk about it." One thing rang clear in her head over all the other noise: she could not trust anyone in St. George. That man had access to her, and he was here. She just may not have seen him like she remembered.

"Do you want to talk about the garden shears?"

Grace raised her eyebrows.

"Which ones?" *Was the pair in my room real?*

"You know which ones."

Grace deflated. His answer was vague. The image of them sitting in her room, on that armchair when the lights came on, was burnt into her retinas, but she wasn't certain she could trust that.

"No, I don't want to talk about them."

"Fair enough." He put down his notepad on the glass end table next to his chair and folded his hands in his lap. "Grace, what would you like to talk about?" She stared at the glass table, her mind trying to piece together why there would be glass in a room like this. It seemed like such a huge oversight.

"My job." The words tumbled out of her throat before she even thought about them. Dr. Tyler tilted his head to the side like a curious animal.

"Your job?"

"Yeah, I guess I don't know what's going to happen now. I've been missing from work for . . ." Grace tried to count the days in her head. She came up blank. "I don't even know how long. I'm going to be fired. I probably already have been."

"The staff here have contacted your employer, I'm sure."

Grace shook her head, her hair unmoving in its ponytail. Somebody must have brushed it. "What?"

"It's standard practice when somebody is with us for an extended time that the right people are notified. We took the time to reach out to them."

"Oh." Grace shifted in the chair. She felt more solid on the chair now. The moment of being stuck in the vent had drifted away, and she finally was fully present in the office. She glanced at the clock on the wall. A little after one p.m. *How long have I been sitting here?* Grace didn't bother wasting more brainpower on that thought.

"Now, Grace, if you don't mind, I think it's really important that we go back to the moment that started all this. Normally, I don't do this with patients right away, but we are trying to build up a timeline of events for you."

"Because I don't remember a lot."

"That's right." He offered her an encouraging smile. Despite feeling like a child, she still enjoyed the praise. "So if you are willing to do this with me, I'd love to begin from the start."

Grace looked back down at her hands. Her nails were bitten down so much that it hurt. Cuts were scattered across the fingertips. A red rash spread across her wrists. Grace grimaced. *The man?* She thought. The logical part of her brain immediately responded, *the restraints.* Grace pushed her hands underneath her legs and sat on them. It hurt a little, but it stopped her from thinking about them.

"Let's do it."

He picked up his notebook again and uncrossed his legs. He leaned forward slightly as he spoke. "So it looks like everything began Saturday morning."

Grace blinked. All of this began long before Saturday morning.

"Now I only have so much information, and you will have to help me fill in the gaps where you can."

Grace wanted to laugh. There were a lot of gaps there. She thought about sharing the truth, for just a split second, before the thought from before repeated, *You can't trust anyone here.*

"I can try."

He smiled and nodded before glancing back at the papers. He looked slightly uncomfortable now.

"This part is going to be difficult. I know that and however you feel when we talk about it is perfectly acceptable. Your cat . . ."

Anguish fell over Grace like a cloak. How had she forgotten about Harold again? Somehow the doctor was right—her cat was the start of something. Not the beginning, but at least this chapter.

"I found him dead. On the front stoop of my building."

Dr. Tyler's head bounced up and down like a spring.

"Yes. And he was brutalized significantly. I'm sure that was traumatic to see."

Grace bit her bottom lip and nodded, wiping away a single tear as it fell. Jocelyn had faded away into the background as she finally allowed herself to grieve.

"It was horrible." Her voice cracked.

"What do you think happened that led to that moment?" Grace's eyebrows knitted together, and she met Dr. Tyler's gaze. "It's okay. You can share."

"Share what?" Grace asked, trying to decode what he wanted her to say. Did he know about the man? Did he know who had slaughtered her cat?

"Grace, this may be hard to answer, but what happened to your cat?"

Silence nestled into the room as Grace stared at him. *He thinks I did this.*

"My cat got out and was slaughtered."

"By whom?"

Grace felt anger burst throughout her body.

"Not by me, if that's what you're suggesting," she spat. She thought about standing up and walking out. Then she remembered this wasn't just some routine therapy appointment. She was in St. George, basically their prisoner.

"I was just trying to fill in the blanks." He sighed. "It just doesn't look good, what happened. Why would somebody do that? Only somebody who is extremely upset." He locked eyes with Grace. "You have shown signs of that."

"I am not some serial killer experimenting on animals before the real thing! The man who has been following me did it. He's who you should be psychoanalyzing, not me." Grace shifted in the seat and glanced at the door. Could she get up and leave? Was that an option?

"A hunting knife was found in your apartment. The police say it was likely what was used on your cat."

Grace felt the room spiral and swirl around her.

"What? No, that doesn't make sense."

"After EMTs arrived on the scene, they called the police because of your cat. The police asked your landlord for entry into your apartment. The knife was one of the first things they found."

Grace tried to control her breathing but she couldn't.

"I didn't kill my cat." Her voice nearly wobbled but she kept it steady. She closed her eyes and tried to think back to that morning. There had to be something there she could remember. That she could hold onto.

"I understand it's painful to—"

"My apartment. He broke into my apartment. He put the knife there." The words stopped the psychiatrist in his tracks. *Did Dr. Campbell tell him about this?* She remembered telling the doctor about her apartment being broken into when she was first taken to the hospital.

"The man. The one you keep seeing?"

Grace tried to fight down the urge to say nothing. What she was describing sounded a lot more like paranoia than reality.

"Yes. He broke into my apartment. A couple times I think."

"How do you know that?" Grace thought back to the fear when she woke up that Saturday morning and the window was open. She remembered waking up from a nap and her front door being ajar.

"My window was open and my door one time too. Right before my cat was murdered."

"And you didn't call the police. Why was that?"

Grace knew how bad that looked. Either she was paranoid and imagining all this, or she was lying about it all because she murdered her cat.

"I called my father about it. I was scared, but I didn't know if I was overreacting."

"You called your father." Dr. Tyler was interested now. Before, he had made it seem like this was just a routine conversation he would have with any psych patient about why they murdered a beloved pet. Now, he was paying attention. *Must be some Freud shit*, Grace thought.

"Yes. And he told me I was just being dramatic and that everything was fine. I figured I had just left them open or—" Dr. Tyler looked as if he was about to leap out of his chair. "What?"

"That doesn't make sense."

Grace frowned and looked down at the ground. *Yeah, I know*, she thought.

"I just didn't want to be in trouble if I was wrong."

Dr. Tyler shook his head and put down his notepad once more.

"That part I understand." He hesitated a moment before continuing, sitting there with his mouth hanging slightly ajar. "But, Grace, what I don't understand is this phone conversation. Your father is dead."

30

August 3, 2011

"It's my fault," Grace whispered as she sat at her parent's secondhand kitchen table. They had been in the middle of a silent meal. Since she had returned from camp a few days ago, her mother had insisted that they all eat together. At least for dinner. It was an unpleasant experience for all involved.

"Oh sweetie, please stop saying that. There's this *thing*. I read an article about it once. Oh Lord, what is it called?" Her mother tapped her fork against her chicken as she thought. The dried-out breast didn't move. "Some kind of guilt. When you survive an attack. You feel awful because you wonder why it was you who lived or why didn't you stop it. I'm sure Jocelyn probably has it too."

Her father seemed to grunt in agreement.

"Happened with 9/11."

Grace looked up at her father, his white shirt already speckled with some ketchup. His eyes stared down at his plate, but he was obviously paying attention. Psychology was not something he really believed in. When her mother had suffered from postpartum depression, she had to go live with Grace's grandmother for a month because her father couldn't (or wouldn't) help her with that "hokey stuff." Her mother's blue eyes blinked in surprise, but she forged on.

"You had no idea all that stuff was going to happen."

Grace almost choked on her water as her mother said that. Her mother reached over and rubbed her back as Grace coughed.

"I am trying to tell you something. You need to listen." Grace's voice took on a more demanding tone. She had spent the past few days locked up in her room, only coming out for meals. She had sobbed. She had tried to journal what she was feeling, but writing it down in no way lessened the guilt. It only made it feel stronger. Now she made direct eye contact with her father, who put down his fork and stared back. Her mother pursed her lips as she waited.

"I *am* the reason this happened to her. It's *my* fault she went to that party because—"

Her father's fist smashed into the tabletop. Both Grace and her mother jumped. Silverware clattered against Corelle plates. Grace's mouth hung open as she stopped speaking, unsure what her father was going to do. He had never physically harmed her, or her mother for that matter, but he could be equally cruel with his words. Mostly, he was neglectful.

He rose from his chair and strode around the table.

169

Grace leaned back against her chair, trying to compensate for his approach. He closed the distance between them in seconds and wrapped his calloused hands around her shoulders. Grace felt fear for a brief moment at his large frame so close to hers. His grasp was firm but not painful. Kneeling down, he stared directly into Grace's face. She tried to look away.

"Look at me, damn it!" Spittle flew from his mouth onto her face. Grace flinched and turned her gaze to her father. She expected to see rage, but instead, his wide brown eyes had softened. She didn't recognize the look on her father's face.

"You can sit here and say it was your fault all you want. But I'll be damned if my daughter lives her whole life thinking she's got to make up for some damn rich person's mistake. This is why I told you we don't associate with them. They only hurt us, again and again and again." He pulled in a deep breath and tried to refocus. "You're old enough to do whatever you want. I don't want to know what you did, and frankly, I don't give a shit. If you wanna live your life trying to make up for it, be my guest. But no matter what, you don't tell nobody about it. Not the cops, not a teacher, and especially not that Jocelyn girl. You are not throwing your life away because of it. Nobody needs to know. You're still a kid, and I don't want to see you following in my footsteps just because you feel guilty. You understand me?"

Grace nodded, her eyes wide. This was the most honest conversation he had ever had with his daughter. They both felt vulnerable and uncertain. Grace wasn't sure if she was supposed to speak or what she would even say given the circumstances.

"Good. Now whether I like it or not, I know you

went to that camp because you want something better than what we got here. I respect that. You deserve that. You're smart. Keep chasing after that. Pay your dues if you have to clear your conscience, but don't let none of this stop you."

Grace bit her bottom lip.

"I won't," she whispered as her father's eyes began to water. She had only seen the man cry when he was drunk. Her own eyes pricked with tears, and she breathed in and out deeply, trying to calm herself

"Maybe someday you'll make something of yourself, and you'll become one of those rich snobs I hate." He forced a chuckle to try to disguise his emotions. He pulled Grace forward into a hug, her arms pinned under his. Her frame pushed against his despite not quite fitting together. For the first time in years, she felt love for her dad.

31

November 12, 2019

"No, no, that can't be right. We talked. I called him. He said he was going to Tony's to watch the game—" A pit in Grace's stomach swallowed the rest of her words. Her brain seemed to split in half as she tried to remember. Her fingers came to her temples as her mind erupted into pain. *Did I talk to him? Am I making it up?* She honestly couldn't remember. All she knew was that something felt very, very wrong.

"Grace, please remain calm." Her eyes darted back up to the doctor. He had his palms raised as if he was afraid she would attack. Her eyes narrowed.

"I am calm." The words rattled inside her mouth like dice. She needed to at least pretend that she was calm. She couldn't let herself be sedated again since she was positive that was what was causing her confusion. The drugs had scrambled her brain, blurring the lines between reality and fiction. She pulled her hands away from her head and stared at the fading cuts. *This is real,* she told herself. *I saw him. I was in the vent. This is real.*

"Grace, if you don't calm down, I will have no choice but to sedate you." Grace's eyebrows knit together as she listened to Dr. Tyler's voice, raised as if he was calling for help. She hadn't moved from her spot. There was no threat to him.

"What?" Grace wondered if she was hearing things too. Maybe she was imagining his voice. Despite this thought, something deep in her gut told her that this was real.

"I need assistance!" Dr. Tyler shouted as he rushed at Grace. His hands wrapped around her wrists. She didn't struggle as she focused on trying to remain calm. Her instinct was to yell and shout that she was calm and no threat. *That's exactly what he wants me to do,* she thought. His grip around her wrists tightened as he forced them to move around as if she was fighting. *He's setting me up.* Grace wasn't sure how she could get out of this, but she knew it was an act. Dr. Tyler wasn't there to help her. Either she was truly crazy or he was there to make things worse.

A man built like a linebacker rushed into the room with a needle ready. Everything was happening so fast her vision was blurred. It was like trying to make out an action sequence on a dark movie screen. Grace tried to stay still but her body instinctively tried to move away. Dr. Tyler's hands stayed tight around her wrists as he pinned his body weight against her on the chair. She knew it was only a matter of seconds before she would be out cold.

I need to remember this. Her eyes flicked across the office, trying to focus on small details because the whole picture was too fuzzy. She remembered learning in a psych class that images helped with memory, so she tried to study objects throughout the room. His faded leather armchair. The rims of his glasses. The leather-bound bookshelf. A small fishbowl with a blue betta fish. The fish was the last thing she tried to memorize before the world slipped away.

PART TWO

32

November 14, 2019

"Wake up, Einstein!" Grace tried to pry her eyes open but grogginess fell over her. She reached out and rubbed her lids, trying to force herself awake. *Einstein*, she thought. Only one person ever called her that. Her eyes flicked open and fell upon Jocelyn, who was staring back at her from above with her intense green eyes.

"Jocelyn." Grace's voice sounded strange in her own ears. It was as if she was suffering from a cold or recovering from having a breathing tube in. Jocelyn's cackle filled Grace's ears and the corners of her mouth upturned. It felt like a thousand pounds had lifted from her chest at the noise of her old friend laughing.

"In the flesh." She gestured to herself like she was a prize on a game show. Grace shut her eyes and let out a deep breath that felt like she had been holding onto for far too long. She propped her elbows underneath her and hoisted herself into an upright position. Scanning the room, her eyebrows furrowed. Posters covered the walls. Half-empty water bottles covered every open surface. Laundry piled up in the corner. She wasn't in St. George anymore. She was somewhere else entirely.

"We're at your house?" Grace asked, trying to flick through her memories to find how this had happened.

"Where else would we be?" Jocelyn asked, perching herself on the window seat of her bedroom. She cracked open her window and pulled a pack of cigarettes out of the pocket of her jeans. She lit one and took a long, slow drag as if it had been her first one in a while. Settling in now, she had one leg bent up against her chest, the other dangled over the edge of the seat, swinging like a pendulum.

"St. George. We were both at St. George."

Jocelyn nodded firmly as she exhaled smoke out the open window.

"I guess Einstein's back at it again! Good job."

Grace frowned as she listened to Jocelyn. She felt like she was toying with her, trying to purposely mislead her. Thoughts of Jocelyn's true self invaded Grace's mind. She wasn't a good friend. She never really had been, but Grace had forgotten all that since she had been on the hunt to save her.

"Whoa, wait. Then, it was real. The guy?"

Jocelyn stared at Grace as she took another drag, waiting to answer.

"Guess you aren't as bright as I thought." She chuckled and flicked ash from the cigarette out the window. "He wasn't real. You were sick. I mean, I was too, so I don't really blame you."

"Oh." Grace forced herself completely upright and tried to brush away the shame of being mentally unwell. She didn't judge Jocelyn, so why would she judge herself? *Because it's my own fault,* Grace told herself. Glancing down at her hands, she saw her battle wounds were nearly invisible. So much so it was like they hadn't existed at all.

Jocelyn turned her attention back out the window. Shades of pink spread mixed with purple as the sun set. Grace had no concept of time apart from that. St. George felt like it was years ago.

"Yeah." Jocelyn bit her lip. "Kind of strange that we both imagined the exact same thing. I didn't believe it at first. I thought it had to be real, but I hadn't seen him in a while. And he wouldn't exactly just leave me alone suddenly only to come back later, would he?"

Grace played with the throw blanket that had been spread across her while she slept. She methodically twisted and untwisted a frayed edge.

"He could be toying with you," Grace whispered.

Jocelyn's head snapped back to Grace. Just moments ago, she had considered Jocelyn was doing the same thing to her, so it wasn't so far-fetched. However, there seemed to be genuine concern in Jocelyn's face that dissuaded Grace's doubts.

"Toying with me?"

"It's like the whole predator-prey thing. Obviously, if it's the same guy, he's like a serial killer, right? Maybe he gets a kick out of watching you suffer. Watching *us* suffer." Grace paused as she changed her phrasing. The man wasn't just exclusively after Jocelyn, after all. He had targeted Grace just as much, if not more.

"I mean, I guess that makes sense. From a psychological perspective." Jocelyn snapped closed the window, and Grace flinched. "Sorry," she murmured.

"You're the one that got away, right? So maybe this whole thing is meant to punish you for that."

Jocelyn stared down at her socks.

"I mean, I guess. But why me?" Jocelyn asked.

Grace sucked on her cheek as she let her eyes wander around Jocelyn's room. She didn't want to say why because she had a pretty good idea it was her fault. After a silent moment, Jocelyn continued. "I get the theory, but I just don't think it's true. He's not back. And I mean, it's not the first time I've seen him. The doctor says it's pretty common to have the same hallucinations if it stems from trauma or whatever."

Grace's brain stuttered. Jocelyn had never told Grace about her sightings of the killer from that night.

"You've been seeing him all along?"

Jocelyn looked up at Grace and gave a tiny nod. The pit in Grace's stomach swallowed her breath. Grace had always thought it was just her. The cigarette dangled from her hand, and Grace stared nervously, waiting for ash to fall down onto the wood floor.

"Pretty much since the cops stopped investigating. I mean, they got literally nowhere with the case, and the guy is probably still out there. I guess my subconscious just started seeing him because I was scared. Because it was a possibility."

Grace felt the terror of her words deep inside her bones. Once she found out that Matt had been a victim, her mind had raced. Who could have been the killer? It didn't make any sense. All of the counselors were cleared, but the police must not have done a great job since they still didn't know about Grace's true involvement that night. It was like some random man came out of nowhere, stumbled upon the party, and slaughtered everyone. That had never been the plan. They just wanted to scare Jocelyn a bit. Embarrass her. Not scar her for life.

"But you're positive it's not real. Just pretend?" Grace stared into Jocelyn's eyes. Determination spread across her friend's face.

"Positive. It's all up here." Jocelyn tapped her temple, the cigarette nearly touching her hair. Grace didn't know how to feel, but she certainly didn't feel relieved.

33

July 18, 2011

He was lurking through the woods when he heard voices up ahead. He had been planning on making his way home, but this gave him pause. Straining to hear, he attempted to identify the voices. Two females. Fifty yards ahead. The woods were dark, but his eyes had already adapted. Carefully, he approached, avoiding branches and piles of leaves. Young girls scare easily. That he knew very well.

Laughter bounced through the trees, and he grimaced. He closed the distance within a minute, searching for cover nearby. He could nearly hear their voices. Edging around the clearing, he finally was within range.

"She's the most annoying one of them all."

"You only think that because she is exactly like you!" Once again, the pair of girls began laughing, and he scowled under the cover of his hood. A low chuckle escaped his own lips. He recognized the voices now.

Navigating delicately, he moved behind one of the cabins. The cover of night protected him from being seen, as long as nobody was really looking. He didn't care if he was seen. He could take down both of them if he really needed to. But he didn't want to—yet.

It didn't take long before the girls became vulnerable. At least emotionally. His ears had a distant ringing noise in them that prevented him from making it all out, but he could sense the tone of their voices. Playful, but still scared. It would be easy enough to spring into action and end it now. He licked his lips and turned away from the cabin. Even though he didn't want to, he knew waiting would make it even better.

34

November 14, 2019

Jocelyn pranced back into her bedroom carrying a pizza box she had ordered from the local place down the road. After their conversation, Grace hadn't felt too hungry. Her stomach acid felt like it was boiling inside her. Jocelyn, on the other hand, seemed hungrier than ever. She set the box down on her paisley comforter and passed a Kate Spade plate to Grace.

"I would have gotten paper plates, but you know how my mother is."

Grace took the plate and stared down as a slice was placed on it. She swallowed hard as her mind looped back to St. George and Mrs. Baker.

"This might sound weird, but how did we end up here? Like obviously it makes sense you are here, but why am I?"

"Oh, you mean because Claire totally hates you

now?" Jocelyn raised an eyebrow and shoved a slice in her mouth, grease coating the corners. Grace had forgotten that Jocelyn frequently called her parents by their first names. It always threw her off.

"Yeah, because of that." Grace lifted a slice to her own mouth and took a tiny bite. It still felt like she was choking as she swallowed.

"She was pissed at you, but I told her that if she treated me the way she was treating you, it would be messed up. You can't just blame somebody for somebody else's mental problems. Especially if they have their own."

Grace thought for a moment the bite of pizza might tumble back up her throat. She coughed at the taste of bile and put her plate to the side. The room felt like it was spinning. Jocelyn's hand wrapped around Grace's shoulder.

"You okay?"

"Yeah, it's nothing. Food just went down the wrong way." Grace rubbed her chest with an open hand, the fabric of her t-shirt wrinkling, and stared down at the hardwood floor. "Did she sign me out or something?"

"I guess they had you on one of those involuntary holds, but then I made my mom raise hell. I told her otherwise I wouldn't stay home with her." She grinned. "They agreed, especially since they couldn't hold you much longer without a judge or somebody signing off on it. I guess they didn't want more work."

Grace bit her bottom lip and nodded. That made sense. "So what day is it?"

Jocelyn took a look at her lock screen.

"Thursday, apparently. Wow, who knew?" She shrugged her shoulders and grabbed a second slice from the box. The smell almost made Grace sick again.

"Thursday? Shit!" She scrambled to her feet, though they wobbled beneath her.

"Calm down. Where do you think you're going?"

"I need to go to work. I need to see if I still have a job."

Jocelyn reached over and grabbed her hand, wrapping their fingers together.

"Your boss is probably already home. It's dark outside." She gestured to the window. Grace hadn't even thought about that. A tear ran down her cheek. A whole week had passed since she had been in the office. She was screwed. "You can go first thing tomorrow. Get his dumb coffee ready or whatever it is you do and suck up to him. Maybe offer something he can't refuse."

Grace grimaced.

"Jocelyn, I can't do that . . ."

Jocelyn rolled her eyes. "If it's good enough for me—"

"No. No. I can't do that."

"It's your own funeral." Jocelyn sighed and climbed off the bed. "You can stay the night if you want. I figured you would want to because you know . . ." She didn't have to finish the thought. Grace settled back down onto the end of the bed. Her chest felt tight, but not like she expected. She knew she was going to screw up this job sooner or later. It was almost a relief to know it had finally happened.

"Thanks," she whispered.

"You can stay in here too. Don't want my mom sneaking into your room at night!" Jocelyn let out a belly laugh that caused Grace to shiver. *Was that real? The pills?* Jocelyn sure made it sound like it was.

"Thanks. I'm just gonna go to the bathroom."

Jocelyn picked up her phone and unlocked it before starting to scroll endlessly. She didn't respond as Grace turned and headed toward the door. Her hand shook as she reached for the knob. *Please don't let her be out here. Please. Please. Please.*

The hallway was empty.

Grace let out the breath she didn't know she had been holding. Jocelyn's home wasn't updated like she had always envisioned it would be. The walls had dark wood panels and high ceilings. There wasn't the clichéd open-floor plan like so many homes had now. The hallway had zero windows. Grace used to think it was cozy, like a cabin. Now, it made her feel constricted, like a coffin.

Her feet padded along the floor to the bathroom. Socks muffled her steps on the polished hardwood. *Small miracles*, she thought. As she listened to the house, she heard nothing. *Is anybody else even here?* There was no sound other than her own. Maybe they were asleep. Maybe they were out somewhere. Regardless, Grace did not waste the opportunity by contemplating the idea too long. She found her way to the bathroom, two doors down, exactly where she remembered it was. Inside, she used the toilet and stood in front of the sink, the bright light fixtures casting harsh light on her face.

"Jesus Christ," she whispered as she studied herself in the mirror. She turned the water as cold as it would go and splashed it against her face, especially rubbing her eyes, which had dark circles. If she was Jocelyn, she would be scheduling an appointment for a facial. But she wasn't Jocelyn. And she was pretty sure now she could never have a life like hers.

She snatched the hand towel and wrapped her face

in it. The urge to cry overwhelmed her. Biting her bottom lip until it hurt, she pushed down the feeling. With her face dry, her eyes flicked back to the mirror, and the black shape lurking behind her.

35

July 19, 2011

His angular face was framed in the window, staring down into the cabin. Never before had he been so close to Jocelyn. Her chest rose and fell slowly. He drummed his fingers against the glass lightly, barely audible. Jocelyn didn't wake, but she tossed over on the bed, her face scrunched up before him. In the moonlight, he could only get a few details, but for now, it was enough.

But that wouldn't last for long. He licked his lips, his breath beginning to fog up the window. The cabin porch creaked as he turned and left her behind, untouched.

36

November 14, 2019

"Grace!" Jocelyn broke into the bathroom, nearly hitting Grace with the door. She had crumpled to the warm tile floor like a forgotten receipt. The screams had stopped now, but the panic hadn't. Jocelyn fell to the floor next to her and pulled her friend to her chest.

"What happened?" Jocelyn sounded hesitant.

Grace opened her mouth to speak, but no words came out. Her body shook as she cried. It was a matter of seconds before she was hyperventilating. Jocelyn held her tightly.

"Deep breath in, and out. You are okay. I am here." Jocelyn's voice was soft and nurturing. Later, Grace would wonder where that softness came from. She had never seen her friend care for anyone else. Empathy wasn't a part of her vocabulary. But at the same time, she had never let her friend see her like this. After a few minutes, her heartbeat had regulated, but she still gasped for air whenever a sob escaped her throat.

"He was behind me. I felt him breathing against my neck."

"Shhhhhhh." Her friend pushed Grace's hair off her face and touched her cheek softly, her fingertips cool.

"He was here. Right there. So close."

"It's okay. He wasn't really here. You imagined it. We have a security system. It would have gone off. And I didn't see anyone. I didn't hear the door open after you went in."

Grace's eyes darted around the small bathroom. The glass shower was empty. The window was frosted and way too small for anyone to get through. Jocelyn was right. He couldn't have been real.

"It felt real." Her words were so faint she almost couldn't hear herself.

"Let's get you in bed. Do you want something to help you sleep? Your brain needs rest." Jocelyn helped Grace to her feet, grabbing onto her shoulders when she wobbled.

"Yes." For the first time in several days, that was all she wanted.

* * *

The cab drove her to the city. Jocelyn had insisted she pay for it to take her to the office directly. Mostly, it was because she didn't want Grace using public transit and getting confused. After last night, she had to agree.

She had borrowed some of Jocelyn's clothes from when she had her last office job. It had only lasted a week, not long enough for her to even go through the whole wardrobe Mrs. Baker had paid for. Grace ran her fingers over the silk red shirt. It felt like butter against her skin.

"Ma'am. Ma'am!" Her attention snapped back to the cab driver in front of her. "We're here."

She nodded and passed him the cash Jocelyn had shoved in her hand.

Grace opened the door to the lobby of her building. She forced herself to stand up as straight as possible. Jocelyn's Valentino heels clicked loudly throughout the first floor. The marbling of the floor made Grace feel queasy if she stared at it too long. If she was going to do this, she needed to channel as much Mrs. Baker as possible. That woman had more audacity than anyone had a right to. And that was exactly what Grace needed to keep her job.

Just before the elevator door shut, a hand reached out to stop it. Grace held her breath, waiting for the man to appear. It was only Kate. Grace almost laughed at the relief she felt. Just a week ago, she would have felt dread at being stuck in the elevator with Kate, who wouldn't shut up no matter how little you engaged. Now, it was better than the alternative her mind supplied.

"Grace! You're here!" Kate's voice sounded exorbitantly cheerful. She wrapped her arms around Grace. Grace's eyebrows furrowed together. *Was she always this friendly?* Grace had always assumed she was nosy, not kind. The physical touch unsettled Grace.

"In the flesh," she choked out before realizing she had mimicked Jocelyn.

Kate pulled away and looked her up and down, biting her bottom lip.

"Are you okay? What happened?"

Grace bit her bottom lip.

"Just had an itty bitty breakdown." She tried to laugh it off.

Kate nodded intensely.

"That happens a lot around here. You'd be surprised honestly." Based on how competitive the office was, Grace didn't doubt it.

"How mad is he?"

"Mr. Harris?"

Grace nodded, glancing at the elevator display. They were only a few floors away.

"Do you want the truth?" Kate asked, hesitant.

"I think that tells me enough." She made a conscious effort to stop her hands from shaking. Grace looked down at her outfit. She looked ridiculous. Mr. Harris would take one look at her and feel zero sympathy. She knew he would. The elevator doors opened, and Kate reached out and gave Grace's hand a squeeze.

"Good luck." Her encouragement was hollow though. They both knew how this was likely to end.

Grace straightened herself up and marched across the blue carpet toward Mr. Harris's office in the far corner of the open floor. She could feel eyes on her as she approached. There was no doubt that Harris had thrown a public temper tantrum in her absence. She was likely his scapegoat for anything and everything that had gone wrong the past week.

As she weaved through the cubicles, her eyes finally fell upon Harris's office. He was at his desk, squinting at his computer screen. Her anxiety vibrated inside her as she moved to the door. He looked up before she could knock. Their eyes locked, and he motioned for her to come in.

"Well, I'll be damned. Didn't think you would have the balls to show up here again." Grace swallowed the lump in her throat and opened her mouth to start speaking. She had heard him speak this way before, but never to her. He threw an open hand into the air with a wicked smile. "Wait, no, let me guess, I have a bet on this. Did you have a great-aunt die?"

She bit back tears and crossed her arms around her body.

"No sir." She knew better than to say more, and she wasn't sure if she could anyway.

"Shit. I'm going to tell people that's what it was anyway." A smirk played upon his lips. For just a second, Grace felt hopeful. His demeanor was far more playful than angry.

"I can't even begin to say how sorry I—"

"Shut it. You leave for one day off and take five?"

Grace couldn't meet his eyes, so instead she focused on a crumb on the carpet beneath his desk.

She opened her mouth to speak again before remembering he had told her to be quiet.

"I think you already know what I'm going to say, Grace. I thought you were better than this. To give absolutely no notice and not show up? That would get you fired for just one day, let alone five."

Mr. Harris touched the frame of his glasses to adjust them. Grace's brain felt something click deep within. Somebody had told her they had contacted her employer.

"Nobody reached out to you?" She looked up at him. He huffed and glanced down at his watch before replying.

"No, your people didn't get in touch with my people. Because you were my people, Grace!"

Dr. Tyler was the one who had told her about reaching out to work. Short visions sparked inside her head of their session, but only fragments and feelings. She could tell it just felt very wrong. Jocelyn's voice echoed in her head, telling her it wasn't real. She believed her.

"Grace, hello." Harris was snapping his fingers to get her attention. She flinched at the gesture, but her vision cleared and she stared back at him, uncertain what had just happened. She had disappeared inside her head, but it seemed like it was only a second. "There weren't any personal effects on your desk, so you can go now."

Her legs felt too heavy to turn around and walk out of the office.

Mr. Harris let out a dramatic sigh and picked up his phone. "James, we need you up here." The words sounded like she was underwater. This couldn't be happening. This job was all she had.

"No, please," she choked out. "I can't be fired." Harris rolled his eyes and spoke back into the phone.

"Hurry." Grace devolved into tears and crumpled to the carpeted floor. Harris glanced out to the rest of the office and saw his employees staring at the scene.

Harris brushed by her as he hung out his office door, the glass window quivering as he grabbed onto the door. "Get back to work! Unless anybody else wants to be fired." He didn't have the authority to fire all of them, just the ones on his team, but the fear was enough for them to pry their eyes away from Grace.

When security entered, Grace was pushed up against the wall, unable to speak. She was hyperventilating. Harris didn't come back after he had left her.

"Ma'am," an urgent voice said. She glanced up to see two men standing before her. A scream almost escaped her throat before the illusion disappeared. For just a split second, she had seen him, two of him. And then, he was gone.

37

July 21, 2011

From the treeline, he saw one of the girls dart toward the woods. His teeth flashed a grin as he watched her run. Just seeing someone move with that amount of urgency made his adrenaline spike. Since daylight was still lingering, he could make out her features now. Her strongest feature was the hardness to her face. Something bad had happened. He grinned and glanced back at the office.

Keeping enough distance that she wouldn't notice, he pursued her. He was surprised by her speed. Her pace was easy for him, but he could see her legs pumping faster than was typical for a girl her size. *Small*, he thought. Her body was frail, almost like she was malnourished but not quite. He never understood why girls strove for that look. It wasn't attractive. Notably, she was much shorter than average. He couldn't make out by how much, but it was a few inches. Enough to make a difference.

By the time she reached the clearing, her breath was ragged. She hoisted herself onto the picnic table. He kept his distance behind her. Was she crying? He couldn't tell, but he hoped so. That would make this even better. He stood and waited. Everything was going exactly to plan.

38

November 14, 2019

Grace sat on her bed, staring through the living room to the front door of her apartment. Without the lights on in the living room, she could just see the glint of the doorknob and chain lock. Jocelyn was sorting through her drawers at the foot of the bed and pulling out pieces of clothing to pack into one of the suitcases Grace's mother had bought all those years ago.

"This will be good for you. Good for both of us."

Grace wasn't so sure. After going into the office and being forcibly removed, she had called Jocelyn. She didn't know what else to do. More than anything, she felt numb.

"I don't know." She thought back to unpacking her things when she first arrived at camp, and packing them at the end, alone. A shiver ran through her body and she stared down at her lap.

Jocelyn knelt down to Grace's face. Her eyes hardened and she gave a small shake of her head. "Stop being a shit. I want company. You need company. It'll be good for us."

Grace forced a small smile. It was a good idea. If that man was real, and Jocelyn was wrong about him being a delusion, then it was better they were together. They could watch out for one another.

"Fair enough." She stood up and started to help load up her bag, retrieving the same kind of underwear she had unpacked with Jocelyn before. Jocelyn's eyes darted over to the granny panties for a moment before looking away. When she didn't comment, Grace thought about how much had changed.

"Can you cover rent?" They had never talked too much about money, except for that summer. It just was something unspoken between them.

"What?" Grace had done the math. She had enough money to cover a month's rent. If she didn't eat.

"I'm just asking because I can help you out. It's not a big deal. Don't make it one." Jocelyn lifted her eyebrow, challenging Grace to say something. Grace just nodded and focused on packing.

"It'll be just like old times." Her tone was an attempt at cheerfulness, but the words were haunting.

"Yeah, just like before." Grace couldn't help feeling like this was a mistake.

* * *

The town car pulled up to the Baker estate. Even though Grace had just left it this morning, it felt entirely different. Jocelyn was on her phone, lighting up the dark interior of the car. Grace stared up at the house's enormity. Trees framed the edges of the house, casting shadows against the dark stone exterior of the home.

"It looks like something straight out of a horror movie, right?"

Grace's eyes darted to Jocelyn. She hadn't even realized she was watching her.

"Honestly, yeah."

Jocelyn let out a little laugh.

"I've always thought that. Claire gets offended by it. I usually say it to piss her off." She paused. "You might not want to, though. You're already in deep shit."

"Are you sure they are okay with me staying here with you?"

Jocelyn waved her hand, dismissing Grace's concern.

"What are they going to do? Say no? It'll probably take them a week to even notice you."

"Even with our recent . . ." Grace wasn't sure how to put it delicately.

"Hospitalizations? Yeah, I mean, Claire seems to think that once I get sprung, I am a picture of health." Jocelyn let out a short and sharp laugh, but her eyes darkened. The town car had stopped, and they climbed out. The driver unloaded their bags and carried them into the house as Jocelyn led the way.

The foyer of the house had an echo when you spoke too loudly. To the left was a sitting room that was exclusively used for parties. To the right was a large dining room that sat more people than Grace would ever feel comfortable inviting to her own home. Two staircases that met in the middle were before them, leading to the second floor. Dark wood covered all these rooms, including the staircases. If she had to describe the house, apart from being wealthy, she would say it looked foreboding. Jocelyn was right about the horror-movie comment.

"It feels so empty in here," Grace commented, glancing around the side rooms. "Nobody is around."

"Yeah, I guess you mostly came around when we had parties and stuff. Don't worry, I'm sure my parents have something elaborate planned soon. The holidays are on their way." Jocelyn moved through the arch under the staircase and into the kitchen. The darkness of the wood made it look more like a tunnel than a doorway. Grace glanced back at her bags, sitting alone at the door, before following.

"Speaking of your parents, where are they?" As Grace made her way into the modernized kitchen, Jocelyn let out a muffled sob. She was holding a piece of paper. "What's wrong?"

Jocelyn swiped at the tears and rolled her eyes, completely ineffective at pretending she didn't care.

"My parents have decided to take a last-minute trip to Colorado. Skiing, apparently." She sat down at the island and stared out the window to the backyard. Grace put her hand on her back and rubbed in gentle circles.

"They didn't tell you before?"

Jocelyn turned around to glare at Grace. *Obviously not,* Grace thought.

"Marie!" Jocelyn shouted out. The name echoed off the high ceilings. Grace remembered the house manager, Marie, and how poorly she was treated by Mrs. Baker. Back then, Grace had wanted to imitate that, despite all the values her father had tried to instill.

"And it looks like they told everyone else to take the week off too. It really is just like before, huh?" Jocelyn let out a dry laugh. "At camp. I got there early because they abandoned me." Grace had never thought it was so dramatic before, but now, her parents really had abandoned her days after she was being treated in a mental hospital. Grace's stomach bottomed out as she added up the similarities in her head. It was almost like it was choreographed. It was too close.

"They couldn't even be bothered to leave the note themselves. They must have had one of those maids write it or something." She tossed the note into the trash can without a second glance.

"I don't like this," Grace whispered, staring at the back window too. "This is a big house to be all alone in."

"Try growing up here."

The sound of Grace's phone caused them both to jump. She scrambled to her feet and headed back out to the foyer to retrieve it from her purse. When she glanced at the caller ID, memories flashed back into her head. Memories of pain. Of grief. And now, confusion.

Her father was calling.

"Dad?" she whispered as she picked up the phone. There was silence on the line, and she could hear breathing. Her father didn't ever call her. Something must be wrong.

"Hi, honey."

She cringed and glanced down at her feet. He wasn't a pet-name type of dad.

"Are you okay?" Her memory wandered back to someone telling her that her father had died. It was unclear what was made up or real. She could visualize a funeral. Her dressed in black, but not crying. But here he was, talking to her.

"Yeah, I'm okay. I wanted to check on you." She thought back to the last conversation they supposedly had, telling him about the potential break-in at her apartment. She had been led to believe it never happened. Her body leaned forward, trying to help herself focus on just this conversation, without all the rest of it.

"Check on me? Why?" More than anything, Grace sounded suspicious. Suspicious of her father. Suspicious of the doctors. Suspicious of even herself.

"Well, that hospital up there called me and told me you were sick. That they were keeping you for a few days. I just tried to call them to check on you. I worry sometimes about you being like your mother."

Grace suddenly felt hot. She moved over to the staircase and sat on the second step, afraid she may faint. Her eyes stared at the latch of one of the large front windows.

"Like mom?" She remembered the postpartum depression her mother had suffered. But Grace wasn't pregnant, let alone postpartum.

"Yeah, she always had problems with that stuff. I thought you knew." This conversation was sending Grace tumbling into an abyss. First, her father calls. Now, he is asking about her mental health. They hadn't spoken a word about this since she came back from camp and he told her not to blame herself. Her stomach somersaulted into an alternate reality.

"I mean, I knew some of it."

"Grace, maybe I should tell you more." There was silence on the line. She felt sick and leaned her forehead against the cool wood of the staircase. He didn't wait for her to respond. "Your mother never had cancer."

"Of course, she had cancer. Dad, are you drunk right now?" she asked, but she knew he wasn't. His words were perfectly clear.

"I am not drunk." The way the words came out sounded more like himself than anything else he had said so far. "She never had cancer, but she thought she did. She was convinced it was killing her. I took her to a couple doctors, but none of them found a thing." Grace remembered hearing them talk about getting second opinions, but she thought that was just routine. She thought they were just verifying the diagnosis, not searching for it.

"Did you take her to a psychiatrist?"

Her father huffed.

"I should have. She didn't want to go, and I didn't believe in it either. But that's what killed her."

"You okay?" Jocelyn called from the other room. Grace moved the phone away from her face.

"All good," she croaked out, feeling for a moment she might actually faint, or throw up, or both at the same time.

"What do you mean that's what killed her? The cancer, right? Nobody found it in time." She was trying to put the puzzle pieces together, but they didn't match up.

"No. There was no cancer. She killed herself."

39

July 27, 2011

He had been following her all day. She had a nervous energy that he feasted on. He knew what was coming, and his skin tingled in anticipation. It was almost like approaching an orgasm. Earlier, he had almost revealed himself as he watched her attempt to sneak up to the maintenance shed. She had desperately searched around to make sure nobody was watching her. She completely missed him. He wondered what it would be like to touch her, to hold her. He had shaken his head to try to remove the thoughts, but they kept creeping up on him. Maybe, depending how things went, he could act on those desires.

The day had dragged on, minutes feeling like hours as he counted down to the beginning of the party. He hadn't been invited, but he would be the guest of honor.

He would be lying if he wasn't a little nervous. He had never done something like this before. Despite his excitement, he was filled with doubt. Not about what he was going to do, but if it was the best way. There was no room for doubt. Only action.

40

November 14, 2019

Grace reached down to pick up her phone. There was a high-pitched ringing in her ears that stopped her from hearing her father calling her name through the speaker. Her fingers wrapped around the phone, but she couldn't lift it to her ears.

"No, no, no," she murmured, her other hand rubbing her face clumsily. "This doesn't make any sense." Her thoughts flew by her like a train careening off the tracks. *She died from suicide, not cancer.* Grace shivered. *That doesn't make any sense. And dad. He's on the phone. He's talking to me. But I thought he was dead. They told me that. They told me he was dead.* She couldn't argue with the fact that she was on the phone with him. He clearly was alive. Considering he was a ghost was not even an option. She could be imagining him, but she wasn't on anything anymore. *But I am still seeing him . . .*

"Grace!"

Finally, she lifted the phone back up to her ear.

"I'm here."

"I'm sorry you had to find out this way. I guess I thought you needed to know all along, but I was too scared. I didn't want it to affect you."

Grace swallowed hard. She opened her mouth to tell him she understood and that it was okay, but it wasn't. He had hidden this from her. A major part of her life.

"Why now?" There was an edge to her voice now. Her father cleared his voice before responding.

"Well, it's affecting you. Hiding it from you didn't stop anything, huh?" He let out a sad chuckle. Awkwardness spread across the line. "What I'm trying to say is you are a lot like her. And I wanted to let you know the truth and that I want to help." Grace scoffed through her tears. Her father felt disheartened by her response but trudged on. "I am sorry. You are going through a lot. I should have listened to you earlier about it. I shouldn't have brushed it off, like I did with your mother."

Grace stared out one of the front windows to the grass lawn and empty stone drive. Her face felt hot with embarrassment from her father trying to intertwine himself with such a personal part of herself. This was new territory and she wanted to keep him out. It felt too intimate. He didn't deserve to get that close to her.

"Please let me help you. Why don't you come home? I don't want you staying alone. I can cover your rent if you need me to for a few weeks. It would be a little tight but—"

"I'm not staying alone."

Her father waited for her to elaborate. When she didn't, he took a guess.

"Jocelyn?"

"Yeah, so I'm good."

Her father released a deep sigh. It wasn't from relief.

"No, I think staying with her is the exact opposite of being good. I can come up to you and—" His voice cut off as Grace pressed the end call button. Her hand shook as she set her phone down on the stair next to her. She wrapped her face in her hands and focused on not crying. Her mother had been so sick in the last few months. It had never been from cancer; it was from her mind. She thought of how Jocelyn had seemed so sick while they were in St. George. Grace had heard it in her voice. Goosebumps covered her arms, but her face felt hot. Sweat spread across the small of her back.

Jocelyn's footsteps fell softly on the floor behind her. She could hear her caution as she approached. She didn't bother lifting her head.

"You alright?" She reached out and touched Grace's elbow. Her skin burned from the touch. Grace swallowed hard and rose to her feet.

"I just need to be alone." That was the furthest thing from the truth. Was she supposed to say the truth? Her mother had been so sick she killed herself, and Grace probably had inherited all those stellar genes? Or that her father had now just decided to care because he probably felt guilty?

He must blame himself, she thought. *He didn't do enough and his wife died. Now his daughter is heading down the same path.*

If she was alone, she would have laughed. It was so ironic that he decided to care now. When it was nearly too late.

"Are you sure?" Jocelyn stared at Grace, not with a look of concern but one of desire. She wanted to know what was wrong. Grace's eyes shifted up to the ceiling, trying to stop any tears that might fall. For a moment, she wondered if Jocelyn enjoyed hearing about other people's pain. Grace decided she probably did. After what Jocelyn had gone through, it seemed fair.

"I'm sure." She focused all her energy on making sure her voice stayed even. Before she could change her mind or Jocelyn could convince her otherwise, she turned around and headed upstairs to hide away in one of the guest bedrooms.

41

July 27, 2011

In the distance, he could hear the talent show. Closer by, he could hear people gathering. One thing surprised him. Dumb and Dumber didn't know it would be an actual party. They thought it was just a part of the lie the roommate had made up, but he found great joy in making it real. More people would make her feel more humiliated, which was the goal. The two masterminds should have thought of that.

The boy, Matt, was lurking nearby. On that night, he laid out the plan for the roommate like he had been thinking about it for a while. He seemed chomping at the bit to do it. Now, he could almost feel the nervous energy buzzing off him. He had listened to most of their plan, but he had to walk away after a certain point. *So childish*, he thought. *They don't know the first thing about revenge.* Their plan revolved around embarrassing

Jocelyn. Scaring her a little bit. Nothing more than a prank. He felt disgusted. But that was okay; he would take it on himself.

He could see Matt and followed behind him, but he was moving so slowly it would take a while before he reached the party. Matt had nearly walked right past him a few moments ago, without even noticing. He was oblivious.

"Come on, you can do this." He was startled by the sound of Matt's voice. He could make out Matt's shadow against the trees practicing jumping out and brandishing the garden shears. He wanted to laugh but restrained himself.

"Alright, here we go." He was an amateur. He hadn't even checked to see if Jocelyn had arrived yet. She had, of course, but that didn't matter. He wasn't going to get that far. Matt started to take a step forward before hesitating. He bounced back and forth on his toes, trying to hype himself up.

A baseball bat smashed down on Matt's head. He crumpled to the ground like nothing. He resisted the urge to spit on Matt. Instead, he lifted up the garden shears before placing the blades on either side of Matt's neck. The crunch made him feel light-headed with pleasure. He was only getting started.

42

November 15, 2019

There was a soft rapping on the door that made Grace jump. She hadn't even heard footsteps approach the room, and this house creaked across every inch. Hesitant, Grace pulled the handmade quilt from the king bed further over her, as if it would offer any protection. She couldn't force herself to speak.

"Grace." Jocelyn's voice sounded like a raspy whisper through the door, but it was there. Relief momentarily coursed through Grace's veins. At least it was only Jocelyn, even though Grave wasn't sure she wanted to see her right now anyway.

When there was no response, Jocelyn turned the doorknob anyway, and slowly, the door swung inward.

"Oh, you're awake. I thought maybe you were asleep when you didn't answer." Tension hung in the air between them. It was nothing Jocelyn had done, but

Grace wasn't able to feel anything at the moment. Jocelyn was carrying a box of tissues in one hand and a bottle of water in the other. "I just thought I'd bring you some supplies."

Grace's face and neck had large splotches of red spread across them. Her eyes had swollen and her eyelashes still appeared wet. At the sight of the tissues, Grace involuntarily sniffled.

"Thanks," she managed. Jocelyn set the tissues down on the bed next to Grace and passed over the water. She reached down and plucked a piece of lint from her cotton pajama set. Grace took the chilled bottle and pressed it against her forehead. Her head had begun pounding about an hour ago, when she had first started crying. Now her sinuses were clogged, and she could feel the dull throb of a migraine coming on.

Jocelyn spread herself out on the opposite side of the bed, facing Grace and the wall head-on. She let her eyes wander around the room as if she was avoiding acknowledging how upset Grace was. That was fine by Grace. She didn't want to talk anyway.

"This room is so crusty."

Grace let out a small laugh as she followed Jocelyn's gaze around the room. The bedspread was an embroidered floral piece, the kind that was more aesthetic than functional. It felt scratchy to the touch. She hadn't really noticed before. She pointed to the bookshelf in the corner. Most of the shelves were lined with first edition novels, but the center one, at eye level from the bed, held something Grace hadn't seen for years.

"Your mom's angel collection?" Grace snorted as she stared. Snot started to dribble out her nostril, and she fumbled to grab a tissue.

"Jesus, yeah." Jocelyn rose and walked over to it. "Claire has always had a thing for these. They are so tacky." The porcelain pieces resembled a variety of cherubs in different poses or environments. One was gardening. Another held a cross to its chest.

"I guess your dad had sense enough to force them in here, away from the public eye."

"They do seem nightmare-inducing. My mother isn't even religious. I've always thought they were so dumb."

Grace shrugged and blew her nose again.

"I mean, people have statues of things they don't think are real all the time. Like garden gnomes. She must just really like them."

"Well, if she likes these for their decorative value, maybe she needs a visit to St. George." Jocelyn let out a dry laugh before a glimmer appeared in her eye. "Want to do something bad?"

Grace felt a pang of electricity surge through her body that almost made her gasp. Doing something bad with Jocelyn had gotten her into enough trouble for a lifetime. Jocelyn could read the expression on Grace's face and frowned.

"Oh, come on, it's nothing illegal or anything." While this was meant to comfort her, there was still a huge host of things they could do that weren't technically illegal, but that would still spell trouble. Grace knew that firsthand.

"What?" She almost said she wasn't interested. However, her curiosity got the better of her. Plus, whatever it was, she didn't want Jocelyn to do it alone.

Jocelyn tapped her finger on her lips playfully as she stared back down at the collection of angels before selecting one holding an even smaller angel. She turned back to Grace and grinned. She tossed the figurine into the air and caught it, her eyes challenging Grace.

"Oh, no, no, no, no. We can't destroy them. First of all, that's like bad karma. Breaking angel statues on purpose? Second of all, your mom would be so pissed."

Jocelyn shrugged and picked up a second angel.

"Suit yourself. But I think smashing these babies with a baseball bat could count as therapy. And I think we both need some." Jocelyn spun on her heels and floated out of the room. Before she made it too far down the hall, she peeked back into the guest room.

"You coming?" Grace sighed and threw the covers off her body, revealing her yoga pants and t-shirt. "Thought so," Jocelyn called as she headed back down the hall.

* * *

In the backyard, by the edge of the woods outside the home, just past the pool, Jocelyn spread her legs and adjusted her stance. They had dug out two dusty pairs of ski goggles out of the garage for safety purposes. Jocelyn swung the bat in a graceful arch, preparing for the first hit. Grace stood a few yards away, holding the angel with the cross. She bounced back and forth on her feet, nerves pumping through her body.

"This is honestly so messed up." Grace stared down at the angel. "I think it's looking into my soul."

Jocelyn's laugh echoed through the backyard. Her laugh made Grace smile the smallest bit. The cloud of pain that had overwhelmed her earlier had receded into the background and had been replaced with anxiety over what they were about to do. Plus, a sprinkle of excitement.

217

"In order for it to do that, you would have to have a soul first." Jocelyn's smirk made Grace feel uneasy as her conscience weighed her down. She shrugged her shoulders and warmed up to throw.

"Ready?"

"I've been ready to do this for *years*." Jocelyn held the aluminum bat behind her shoulders, swaying her hips in a way that baseball players would mock.

Grace wound up and tossed the figurine underhand toward Jocelyn. She worried that she wouldn't be able to do it well enough for Jocelyn to hit, but the loud crack proved otherwise. Fragments of porcelain and dust sprayed through the air, and Jocelyn cheered.

"Hell yeah!" Jocelyn did a small victory dance before picking up the largest chunk left from the figurine: the head. She tossed it up in the air herself and smashed it again, leaving nothing discernible left. Grace offered a nervous smile as Jocelyn met her eyes.

"Good job, pitcher. Hit me again," she jeered, taking her stance once more. Grace plucked another figurine from the ground by her feet. Adrenaline was already racing through her body. Even with the guilt, this felt exhilarating.

"Ball two!" Grace threw the second figurine at Jocelyn, who missed this time. The angel tumbled to the ground, a piece of its wing breaking off.

"Damn it." Jocelyn picked up the piece and tossed it back toward Grace. She fumbled to catch it, the ceramic wet from the grass, but eventually held it firmly in her grasp. They both were silent as they prepared for another hit. Grace ran her thumb over the broken spot where the wing used to be and felt overwhelming sadness. Tears were gathering in the corner of her eyes, even though she couldn't quite explain why.

"I'm ready." Jocelyn jolted Grace out of her own reality. She blinked away the tears before launching the angel through the air a second time. Another satisfying crack spread through the air. Grace was watching as the dust dissipated when movement caught her eye. Dusk was approaching, but there was still a decent amount of light. But there he was, clear as day, at the tree line. Grace opened her mouth to speak but nothing came out. Instead, she just pointed.

"What, what is it?" Jocelyn asked, spinning on her heels as the man disappeared into the trees. "Grace?" she asked, a nervousness spreading into her voice.

"Him. He was . . ."

Jocelyn stared back at Grace before tightening her grip on the bat.

"You saw him? There?" Now, Jocelyn was pointing too. Grace nodded. "You think it was real?"

Grace shut her eyes tightly and tried to think. It felt real. She could almost make out the features of his face, but his hood cast just the right amount of shadow to stop her.

"Yes," she finally whispered. Jocelyn nodded and sprinted off to the trees.

"Come here, motherfucker!" she yelled and pulled the bat up above her head, ready to swing.

"Jocelyn, no!" Grace yelled, her legs feeling like lead. She watched as Jocelyn disappeared before deciding she had no choice. She had to follow her.

43

July 27, 2011

Matt hadn't made a sound. In a way, that was disheartening. But he reassured himself that the rest wouldn't be that way. Near the end of the clearing that made up the old campsite, he assessed the other camp counselors from behind a large bush. A few seemed drunk, which removed a bit of the challenge of tackling so many at once. But at the same time, he craved the challenge. He dropped the baseball bat down by Matt's body, a few old leaves fluttering up in the air. He couldn't carry it along with the garden shears. They were the most important part, especially if he wanted to get away with this. He placed them at his feet and swung his rifle around to aim into the clearing. Jocelyn slipped into one of the cabins with another counselor. He grinned.

"Perfect," he whispered. Now, he took aim. *Pick off*

the fastest ones first, he thought. If a few escaped, it wasn't a big deal, as long as they didn't see him first. And as long as Jocelyn wasn't one of them.

He fired off four shots before it registered to the group what was happening. His training had paid off. At least his military tour got him something other than nightmares. The fifth counselor spun on her heels to run. She had partaken in a few drinks and stumbled over a tree root near the edge of the camp. He picked her off easily.

The cabin door swung open and the boy Jocelyn had disappeared with materialized. His pants were only halfway on. The boy opened his mouth to speak, but shock had taken root. What do you say to a shooter when he is coming right for you? Nothing.

"J-Jocelyn, run," the boy said, but he was blocking the doorway. She pushed him out of the way just in time for her low-cut white tank to get splattered with blood from the other's gunshot wound. Blood coated the dangling part of the office sign. She screamed and stumbled over his body, panic swallowing her as she saw the others.

She squinted at the shooter, but he knew she couldn't make anything out through his ski mask.

"Why are you doing this?" she yelled, trying to walk backwards, away from him. She knew better than to turn her back and run. That hadn't worked out for the others. He had underestimated her awareness.

"Because of you."

Jocelyn tripped over a body, and another scream flew from her lips. He closed the distance between them within seconds. She had twisted her ankle when she fell, and as she tried to get up, she fell again.

"What did I do? What did I do?" She panicked as

she saw him get closer. She dragged herself backwards across the dirt, staring up at him with huge eyes.

"Everything." He smashed her head with the butt of the rifle. The time had finally arrived.

44

November 15, 2019

"Jocelyn!" Grace had managed to get her legs to race into the woods, but they felt tight and unprepared. She had neglected her normal morning stretches the past few days. There was too much going on. Her legs were not ready for chasing boogeymen into the woods.

"I see you!" Jocelyn's voice cried out in the woods. Goosebumps spread across Grace's skin. She pried the ski goggles off her face as she stumbled through underbrush toward her friend's voice.

"Jocelyn!" Her voice cracked this time, her breath ragged. Her nose began to run from crying earlier. It felt like a few minutes went by without a sound from Jocelyn. Grace wobbled to a stop, sliding on dead leaves. Shivers played across her spine like fingers on a piano. Déjà vu fogged her brain. She held still, trying to listen. There was not any noise. That was a bad sign.

"Where are you!" Grace began running again, trying to move in the same direction as she had heard Jocelyn yell from. A moment later, Jocelyn called out.

"Over here!" Grace was mostly heading in the right direction, but turned to the left a little to get closer. She forced herself into a sprint before she found Jocelyn standing with her back to Grace.

"Hey, are you alright?" She jogged over to Jocelyn and placed a hand on her shoulder. The trees had thinned out a bit, but they were still surrounded by woods. Jocelyn stepped to the side, the bat still in her hand. Before her lay a body. His body.

"Jesus Christ!" Grace stepped back, staring at him. He was face down, but he didn't appear to be moving. His frame was so large, Grace couldn't understand how Jocelyn had knocked him down.

"I just panicked. He turned around and came toward me, so I just hit him. I had no other choice."

Grace's body was shaking, but Jocelyn appeared stock still. She must have been in shock.

"It's okay. You had to. He was coming for you," Grace reassured her, the words coming quickly. "Holy shit, he's real. He's real." She stared down at her tormentor before looking back to Jocelyn. She almost wanted to cheer because she wasn't crazy after all.

"You were right." She swallowed hard and closed her eyes. "He's real. And he was in the hospital. He was there. He was going to kill us."

"Joce, you had to do it. You saved us."

"Do you think he's dead?" she whispered, opening her eyes to stare at Grace.

"I'm not sure." Nervous energy spilled out of her. Her heart was pumping so hard it almost felt like it wasn't moving at all. Her chest ached.

"Who is he?" Jocelyn took a step forward, but Grace grabbed her shoulder.

"Don't. What if he's alive?" They both stepped back and stared. "What do we do?"

"We can't tell anyone."

Grace's eyes whipped from the body to Jocelyn.

"Of course, we have to tell people. I am not going down for this piece of shit."

Jocelyn raised the bat above her head and moved toward the figure's head.

"Wait! We should at least see who it is. I need to know what he looks like."

Jocelyn stared over her shoulder at Grace. She wasn't sure what to do. She couldn't stand by and let Jocelyn murder a man, even if he might be dead already. Even if he deserved it. At least, that was what she told herself as she moved closer to the body. Jocelyn paused and let the bat rest at her side once again.

"Be my guest. But after, I'm smashing his face in." Jocelyn's hand moved to her stomach, touching the raised scar through her shirt. "This has been a long time coming."

Grace released a shaky breath and closed the distance between her and her tormentor. "Alright," she whispered, bending down. She placed her hands on the shoulder of the man, and counted aloud. "One . . . two . . . three . . ."

Using all her strength, she hoisted the body up and over. His eyes were shut. Grace stayed close, studying his face. He had a buzz cut and a defined jawline. His face looked gaunt, almost like he was malnourished, but his frame was large and muscular. Parts of his jeans were caked with mud and leaves.

"I don't know him," Grace murmured, turning around to look at Jocelyn. "Do you?"

"Yeah," she whispered. "He's my brother."

Grace felt panic spread through her. Alarm bells screeched in her head just before she felt something smash against her head.

45

July 27, 2011

He stared down at Jocelyn's body, her hair obscuring her face and he cringed at the ringing in his ears. She was unconscious, but he felt like he was the one under attack. He stood frozen, lost in his own thoughts. A sound launched him back into reality.

"Jocelyn!"

He let out a low growl at the sound. It was the other girl. The one she had befriended. And then, betrayed. The rifle was swung around his back, and the garden shears dangled from his left hand. He didn't have time to do this right. Unless he killed the other one too. But that wasn't part of the plan. She needed to be around to confuse the police. To lead them astray long enough for him to get away. He was pretty sure she would flake under pressure and reveal her pathetic plan, but even if she didn't, the police would at least suspect her for a time. She had a motive. And she would look guilty as hell.

He listened to her yells getting closer. It wasn't supposed to be like this. There was meant to be more time. After briefly debating picking Jocelyn up and carrying her away, he decided he couldn't. This would have to be good enough.

With both hands wrapped around the garden shears, he plunged them into Jocelyn's stomach. He had meant to aim higher, but his judgment was clouded. The plan was ruined. Footsteps were approaching from behind him. Jocelyn was still breathing, but it was shallow.

"Fuck you," he whispered. It wasn't clear to whom his words were directed. There was a long list of people he could have meant. With one last look, he tried to memorize the moment. Here he was, standing over her, just as he imagined. Deep down, he did feel better. A weight had been lifted from his mind. For the first time in years, he felt free.

With his newfound energy, he sprinted out of the clearing just as the girl approached. He stood in the distance and watched her for a moment. A grin spread over his face as he saw her panic. Somehow, the panic made him more satisfied than anything else.

46

Grace was beginning to think that waking up to her head pounding was normal. It was happening more than ever before. Rather than open her eyes, she closed them tighter as she awoke, trying to keep the light out. She heard hushed voices, but they sounded miles away. A distinct ringing in her ears covered everything as she tried to remember what had happened. When she opened her eyes, the memories slammed her brain against her skull.

Before her stood Jocelyn and the man. She had called him her brother, but Grace didn't understand. Jocelyn didn't have any siblings. She was an only child, just like her.

Grace was spread across a stone floor, and she had half lifted herself off the floor where she had been lying. Dried blood was crusted to her forehead. They were in a cellar of some kind, but it looked more like something that had been abandoned. Cobwebs and dust coated the shelves around her. A dead spider was curled up a foot away. She couldn't remember if Jocelyn's parents had a wine cellar, but if they did, she struggled to believe this was what it looked like. Jocelyn's words flashed back in her head. *It looks like something straight out of a horror movie, right?* Maybe this wine cellar was all a part of it.

Her brain lagged behind in processing. Before she realized the danger she was in, the man in black was standing right in front of her. His black boots were still caked with mud from outside. Words bubbled up in her throat. Her instinct was to yell out to Jocelyn. To tell her to be careful. But Jocelyn knew who he was. Rather than looking afraid, Jocelyn leaned against one of the shelves, one leg crossed casually over the other.

"Hey there, Einstein," Jocelyn spat the old pet name with venom. Disgust overwhelmed her facial expression as she stared down at Grace. The man stood there with his arms crossed. His hoodie was finally down. His eyes looked down at her with an intensity that made Grace look away.

"What is—"

"Shhhhhhh." Jocelyn smirked. "Don't hurt yourself trying to figure it out now. Jesus. You are so predictable. It's pathetic."

Grace flinched at the words. *Predictable,* she thought. *What did I do?*

"Your brother?" Grace asked.

Jocelyn gestured to the man beside her.

"Meet Noah."

"You don't have a brother." Grace shook her head. He stood there staring down at her, not speaking a word. His face was expressionless. Somehow seeing it was more terrifying than not.

"Au contraire, mon frère." She chuckled and elbowed Noah. "See what I did there?" His expression was unchanged.

"Anyway, he's my half-brother. Apparently, while my parents were engaged, my dad got a little frisky with another woman. And you know how my parents like to handle things. So they made him disappear." She shrugged as if this was normal. Grace stared at them blankly, her brain trying to turn Jocelyn's words into something logical.

"Your brother tried to kill you?" Grace asked, her head spinning. Jocelyn laughed so hard she nearly fell to the ground.

"Fuck, no. Jesus. He just helped me with this little bit. You see, we got reunited a month ago or so. And we talked and talked. And I told him all about what happened at camp. He told me how my dad gave his mom hush money. It was quite the family reunion."

Grace exhaled.

"He's not the guy." It was fake. Jocelyn was doing exactly to her what she had done.

"He is *not* the guy. But, Grace, sweetie, aren't you going to ask? Why, Jocelyn? Why are you doing this?" She did a poor imitation of Grace's voice. Her eyes narrowed as she stared at Jocelyn.

"You know . . ." Grace's voice was a whisper. She tried to use her hands to push herself up, but the muscles in her arms felt useless. Instead, she just stared down at her hands, smudged with dirt.

Jocelyn flashed a large smile and pulled out a blue journal from behind her back.

"Next time, don't write it down."

Grace shut her eyes and exhaled heavily. It could be worse, she told herself. She was fine. They were safe. But she really pissed off Jocelyn. The whole point was to tell her what had happened that summer. She wanted to tell her the truth, but not this way.

"Wait—" Grace's brain began to race through her memories. Her apartment being broken into. Her journal must have come from there. He had tortured her. Maybe not physically, but mentally. Jocelyn had pretended she was a victim too. Grace felt her blood boil as she got to the final thought.

"You butchered my cat!" Adrenaline hit her bloodstream and she sprung to her feet and lunged toward Noah. He pulled out a hunting knife from a sheath. He didn't even need to move forward. She stumbled backwards, crashing into one of the shelves, a bottle of wine crashing to the ground. Jocelyn looked over. Surprise passed over her face for just a moment, but she concealed it quickly.

"Grace, you still haven't asked the right question." Jocelyn brushed her hair behind her shoulder. Turning her head to the side, she cupped her ear with her hand. She leaned forward, away from Noah and closer to Grace. "Let me hear it. Please. I'm dying to tell you."

Grace frowned. She wasn't going to give her the satisfaction after what this creep had done. But finally, a real question popped into her head. Jocelyn had the journal, which was evidence, but she didn't have that until after Noah had broken in.

"How did you know? Beforehand."

She gestured to the journal. Finally, Noah spoke.

"She told me what happened at the camp. I told her it seemed kinda fishy about the party. How you told her about it. How that guy—what's his name?"

"Alex," Jocelyn reminded him.

"How Alex *told* you about the party, but he wasn't even there." Noah smirked at Jocelyn, and Grace wondered if they had rehearsed this conversation.

"So, I made a phone call to our buddy Alex. He's doing great by the way. Two kids and only one divorce. And sure enough, Alex never told you about a party. He didn't even know what was happening until it was over."

"I knew as soon as she told me you were a dirty little liar."

Jocelyn moved between her brother and Grace.

"So my dear brother here said, hey, she had something to do with it. Imagine my surprise, when he breaks into your apartment, steals your journal, and I find out it was a *fucking* prank!" She let out a sour laugh. "You couldn't even do that right, huh?"

Grace exhaled slowly. Redness spread across her cheeks from embarrassment and anger.

"He killed my cat," she whispered, a tear falling down her cheek.

"Well, you almost got me killed, so I think we're even."

Grace looked up at Jocelyn.

"So this was all just to scare me? To get back at me? That is so childish."

"Really? Because it sounds an awful lot like what you did." Jocelyn smirked and stepped back. "So you and Matt were going to just scare me. He was going to jump out from the bushes and scream with a pair of garden shears?"

Grace cringed. The plan had been beyond stupid, but it was supposed to be harmless.

"I was upset."

"I bet you were surprised, huh? When some psycho showed up instead?" Jocelyn tilted her head to the side, intrigued, as if Grace hadn't almost caused her death.

"I thought Matt snapped."

Jocelyn nodded in an exaggerated manner. Noah's eyes wandered around the room, and he yawned. The knife was still in his hand.

"Apparently not." She paused and studied her fingernails like she hadn't just terrorized someone for two weeks. "See, I had to do the same thing to you. I wasn't going to hurt you, and I'm still not going to, seeing as your journal told me what you really wanted to do. I just wanted to scare you a bit." She shrugged. "Game over. I win. It was fun while it lasted."

"That's it?" Grace asked. It was meant to sound grateful, but it nearly came out like a challenge. Jocelyn's eyes narrowed. "I mean, it's over?"

Jocelyn nodded and sighed.

"Yep, it's all done."

"I could go to the cops, you know."

"And they'll believe a recently released psych patient who sliced up her own cat?" Jocelyn scoffed.

Grace felt nothing. No anger. No sadness. There was nothing left.

"Fair point."

"Noah, can you go get all her things together so she can get the hell away from me?" Noah nodded and mounted the steps up the cellar. His footfalls were heavy and echoed off the walls. Finally, when the door slammed shut, Grace forced herself to speak.

"I'm sorry, Jocelyn. You know I didn't mean to hurt you."

"Yes you did," she snapped, her hair flying into her face as she yelled. She took a deep breath and straightened herself, returning to her casual position against the wall. "Maybe not physically, but you wanted to hurt me. That was the whole point. And now, we are more than even. Maybe next time you should try a little harder. If you want to scare somebody out of their mind, I have a couple tips."

Grace swallowed and frowned. The cellar door reopened, but Noah didn't reappear.

"Noah?" Jocelyn called. "Are you done?" She moved toward the steps, but the door slammed shut once more. Something bounced down the stairs that looked like a grenade, but smoke filtered out of it.

"What's happening?" Grace asked, coughing. Jocelyn ran up the steps, Grace following behind, beginning to feel light-headed. She jiggled the bronze door handle, but it didn't give.

"I don't know," Jocelyn whispered as smoke filled the air.

47

October 14, 2019

He sat in the high-end café sipping on his coffee. The smell filled his nose and made him feel dizzy for a moment. His stepfather always reeked of coffee. He only drank it when absolutely necessary, and meeting Jocelyn at a café made it feel necessary. The café was made worse by the fact that everything on the menu boards sounded foreign to him. What was he going to get? A hot tea? He found something deeply repulsive about men drinking tea.

She adjusted herself in her seat as he stared across the table at her. The small round table made them sit closer than he was really comfortable with. He could smell her perfume when she sat down, sporting a pair of ripped jeans and a striped sweater. There were moments where her facade dropped, and he could see her discomfort. Perhaps even guilt.

"So what was it like for you growing up?" she asked, trying to make small talk. He wasn't sure if she cared or was just trying to be polite.

"I mean, pretty normal. The money from your dad helped." He couldn't reveal the truth. The money wasn't much, but his mother had signed a nondisclosure agreement when she was pregnant. After time had passed, and she realized how much she could have gotten, she regretted settling. Instead of asking for more money when she lost her job, she did the only other thing she could: find a husband. She picked the first guy who had a stable job and a pension and jumped aboard. Literally.

One of the few things Noah was grateful for in his life was that his mother couldn't get pregnant again. She had complications from his birth. If she had been able to get pregnant, Noah would have tried to kill the baby.

"Did your mom remarry?"

Noah wanted to laugh. There was no "remarry." It wasn't like her father had ever been married to his mother.

"No. It was just us." He told her the same lie he told himself every night when he woke up in a cold sweat. He tried to pretend his stepfather had never existed. He certainly had made sure he didn't exist anymore, but that didn't make the memories disappear. The pain washed over him for a moment, forcing him to close his eyes. His eyebrows furrowed and deep creases appeared on his forehead.

He remembered the first time it ever happened. The way the light from the hallway filtered into his bedroom. His stepfather's large shadow blocking the doorway. His rough hands that grasped him so tightly he had to bite his lip to stop himself from crying out.

"If you tell your mother, she will be so sad. You don't want to make your mommy sad, right?"

Noah remembered thinking at the time that it was strange. How his stepfather's voice sounded. It was almost like he cared. He knew now that was just an act.

The rest of the nights blended together in flashes of flesh and sweat. The cologne that his mother had bought for Christmas. The heavy breathing.

He flinched when he felt a hand on his arm.

"Are you okay?" Jocelyn asked. Instead of being concerned, she looked uncomfortable. He needed to change that.

"Yes, sorry. Just remembering my childhood can be difficult." He gently ran his thumb over her small hand before pulling away. Was that too intimate? Her smile told him it was okay. He cleared his throat before continuing. "I bet you're wondering how I found you."

She nodded, staring directly at him. She looked unsure, as if she was trying to prepare in case things went bad fast. Her eyes darted to the side door and the exit sign above the kitchen's entrance. He did the same thing whenever he was out. You always needed to have an escape plan because people could never be trusted.

"I was doing some research for a paper I was writing. True-crime-type stuff. I'm a journalism major. I got a little bit of a late start, but I'm working on it." Jocelyn offered an encouraging smile. "And so I was going through the digital archives of the local paper, and I just got this sudden urge. Like almost divine intervention or something. Not that I believe in that." While the last part was true, he was only saying it to appeal to Jocelyn's anti-religious views.

"I wanted to look up my dad. I knew his name. It

was in some paperwork my mom had. So I googled his name, and bam—" He clapped his hands together loudly. Jocelyn jumped a little at his enthusiasm. "Sorry. It's just exciting.

"It's okay. I get it."

"An article came up. About that awful camp massacre. They had interviewed your dad while you were in the hospital. And I thought, wow, I have a sister. There was a lot to unpack there, but that was the main thought: I have a sister."

Jocelyn took a sip of her latte and smiled.

"And that sister is me."

Noah nodded emphatically.

"I just am at the point in my life where I don't have a whole lot. My mom moved away, and it's just me." She didn't move away. She died. Of completely natural causes. "So finding you was amazing." Noah stared into her eyes. He knew he had her. Hook, line, and sinker.

"It is definitely amazing." Her voice was soft. It was so different from the last time he had heard it, eight years ago.

48

November 16, 2019

"You have got to be kidding me!" A loud thud forced Grace to open her eyes. This time, she was draped over a leather armchair and Jocelyn was standing by a large wooden door. By the look of it, she had made a futile attempt to kick it down.

"Locked?" Grace asked.

Jocelyn turned to look at her directly so she could see her roll her eyes.

"This is all your fault."

"My fault?" Grace's jaw dropped.

"Yeah, you must have like pissed him off extra or something."

They were locked in a room together, and Jocelyn was thinking Grace had done something wrong.

"Then why did he lock you in here?"

Jocelyn pressed her back against the door and sank

down to the hardwood floor. "It doesn't make any sense." Desperation dripped from her words.

Grace sighed and scanned the room. Getting locked in a room was becoming too familiar for her.

"Wait." She stood up and closed her eyes. "No." She reopened her eyes, but the room was still the same. Leather books lined the shelves. On the coffee table before her sat a fishbowl with a dead blue betta fish.

When Grace didn't continue, Jocelyn looked up at her.

"What? What is it?"

Grace shook her head as the memories raced back. Dr. Tyler. That was her last memory from St. George. He had told her that her father was dead. Then, he pretended she was out of control just so she would be sedated. She was given such a strong sedative that she had dismissed the whole thing as imagined. She had believed it was just a combination of the stress and the pills. But now that Noah was real, and he had been put on a mission to torment her, that changed her perspective. Some of it had to be real, but how much?

"I was in this room. With a doctor."

Jocelyn shook her head.

"This is my dad's study. You weren't here. There was no doctor."

Grace paused and stared down at her friend.

"Honestly?" Grace questioned, raising an eyebrow. They stared at each other, but neither backed down. "It's the last thing I remember from St. George."

Jocelyn frowned and stood up, moving toward Grace.

"Well this is my parent's house, so I don't know what to tell you."

"How did I get here from St. George?" Grace

asked, her brain trying to unravel her past. It was sloppy and messy, but she had to make some sense out of it.

"My mom signed you out, and she brought you here. You were pretty out of it still. I was with you."

"And I remember waking up in your bedroom. Was Noah here in between that?"

Jocelyn shook her head.

"No, because my parents were here. At least, they were before you woke up. The next morning is when they left for wherever they went skiing or snowboarding or whatever the hell it was."

"Well, I'm telling you, I was here and a doctor told me my dad was dead and then he had me sedated."

"Wait, back up." Jocelyn sat down on the couch and put her hands on her knees. "Tell me everything you remember."

Grace went through the story, finishing off with the details about the fish and books.

"That's so weird." Jocelyn frowned, trying to piece it together. Their focus had been so strong that Grace had nearly forgotten what Jocelyn had done to her. Or what Noah had.

"Yeah, and then, this big guy came in and injected me while the doctor held me down, even though I wasn't struggling." The memory flashed before her eyes. She had been horrified but somehow not surprised. "He was really big," Grace murmured, trying to concentrate on the memory.

"The guy who came in?" Jocelyn asked.

Grace nodded, but she couldn't pull up the man's face in her memory.

"I don't know for sure, but I think it might have been Noah."

"Grace, I promise you, that was not part of the plan."

Grace gestured toward the locked door to the study.

"I think it was. Just not your plan."

49

October 16, 2019

Noah's phone clattered against his desk, the vibrations nearly echoing off the walls, informing him that Jocelyn was calling. He stared down at it, an excitement building within him. *She is calling me. She wants to talk to me.* For a moment, he stood, contemplating. He shouldn't be getting so excited about the call, or taking it personally.

"She doesn't even know me," he murmured. After all, who Jocelyn met two days ago was an entirely different person than who her brother truly was. He waited until the call was just about to go to voicemail before jabbing the answer button with his finger.

"Hello?" he asked as if he hadn't bothered to check who was calling.

"Noah, hi, it's me!" The amount of faith it took for someone to say "it's me" versus their actual name was promising to him. She was already starting to trust him.

"Hey, sis!" He cringed at himself and bit his fist to stop himself from gagging. While she was his sister, he only wanted to be close to her for one reason.

"Hi." Her voice sounded as if she was a teenage girl whose crush had just picked up the phone. There was a brief moment of awkwardness. Noah wondered if that ran in the family. "So I was just calling to see how you were doing . . ."

"I'm good. Just still trying to process how crazy it is that we met." That part was at least mostly true. He couldn't believe he had gotten so close to her once again. When he had left the café, his skin felt like it was vibrating. She had no idea who he was. There had been a split second in the café where he was certain she had recognized him. That she knew he almost killed her. But it passed.

"Same. Hey, I was wondering if we could meet up? I know it's kind of short notice, but are you free now?" Noah's brow furrowed. Sudden changes in plans were how mistakes got made. However, this could work to his advantage if he played it right. There was a small hint of worry in her voice. If he could prey upon that worry . . .

"Um, yeah." He kept his enthusiasm in check. It seemed like his whole timeline had just moved up.

* * *

"I'll get the bacon omelet with wheat toast."

The waitress nodded and turned toward Jocelyn. The woman was squat but sturdy. She had a mole on her chin that Noah felt the urge to slice off. *Would she scream?* He grabbed his water and took a sip.

"Could I just have the buttermilk pancakes? No syrup but extra butter please."

"You got it, honey."

She took the menus and disappeared behind the counter.

"Did you see the size of that thing?" Jocelyn asked. Noah stared up at her, confused. Jocelyn let out a small laugh. "I think it was staring at me." *The mole!* Noah let out a loud belly laugh. They were more similar than he thought.

"I thought the same thing." He allowed his disgust to show on his face. "I wanted to chop it off."

Jocelyn giggled as if the comment was good-natured.

"Anyway, I really wanted to get together because I've had a lot on my mind."

Noah couldn't help himself from leaning forward in the booth, eager for her to continue but restraining himself. Under the table, he was wringing his hands, trying to release his nervous excitement.

"What's going on? I noticed you sounded a little worried on the phone."

She bit her bottom lip and glanced around the diner. Finally, after a deep breath, she forged on.

"So you know how you brought up the camp thing when we met?" Noah gave one short nod. "Well, you probably read the articles. You know what happened to me?"

He used all his willpower to make sure he didn't smile.

"Yeah. I mean, I don't know everything. But I read a couple articles. I was curious." Noah had read the articles when they had initially been published. He even attended a few of the funerals of the other victims. It helped temper his disappointment that his plan hadn't been executed as flawlessly as he had hoped.

"Ever since, I haven't been quite right," said Jocelyn. Noah tilted his head to the side, imitating thoughtfulness. "In the head, I mean."

You and me, both, Noah thought. It wasn't completely true. Noah hadn't been quite right since the first time his stepfather came into his bedroom at night.

"What do you mean?" Inside his head, his fingers were crossed and he was chanting *please have flashbacks* over and over. If he had to relive his worst moments, so should she.

Jocelyn scratched her head and stared down at her lap. After a moment of hesitation, Noah reached across the black-and-white checkerboard table and lightly touched her arm, just for a moment.

"Hey, it's alright. You can talk to me. I won't judge you."

She gave him a sad smile.

"I mean, I have some issues with that night coming back to me."

Noah 2–Jocelyn 0.

Except that wasn't an entirely fair way to keep tally when she started off with every single advantage in life.

"But that's not the biggest thing. Something has always felt kind of off. Like they never caught the guy. And like, did he ever do it again? I don't even know because maybe he did, and it was just completely different that time."

Noah forced himself to frown and nod. He reached across the table once more and squeezed her hand quickly. The physical contact was electric for him. He was so close.

"They really have no idea?"

"Nope. And because of that, it's almost like it never happened."

Noah was confused. How could it have not happened? Especially when she relived it from time to time. Jocelyn saw his expression and sighed.

"I know it happened. Obviously. But I was the only one who made it out and saw what happened. I'm the only one who can remember it."

No, I remember, he wanted to say.

"I get it. That has to be hard." He knew it was hard never getting recognized for all his hard work. And most people thought it was just some random guy who stumbled across the scene. That it was sloppy and unplanned. It was insulting, honestly. But he knew better than to try to correct the public perception, even anonymously.

"So you think about it a lot?"

Jocelyn shook her head and tried to play it off.

"Not like, a lot, a lot. Just occasionally." Her right eye twitched. She was lying.

"Do you ever wonder if they got it wrong?"

Her eyes darted up to his. Either she had or was wondering why he was.

"What do you mean?" Her voice was barely audible now. There was fear in her eyes. Not of him, but of the possibility of someone like him.

"Maybe it wasn't some random guy. Maybe somebody planned it." He put his hand on his thigh to stop it from bouncing. Sitting here talking about it with her was almost too much for him to handle.

"Not really. I mean that makes it a whole lot scarier, right?"

Noah thought back to Grace's conversation with Matt. "Definitely."

50

November 16, 2019

"Do you think he's going to just leave us here to starve?" Jocelyn asked. They had spread out on the floor of the study after finding some fleece blankets in a chest of drawers.

"Maybe." Silence fell heavily over them. They stared at one another, lying on their sides. Grace found herself working up the courage to come right out and ask, but she was afraid of the answer. "Um . . ."

Jocelyn dragged her eyes up from the floor to Grace. "What? Do you have an idea of how to get out?"

Grace shook her head and frowned.

"What then?" Jocelyn spat.

"Do you think he was the one . . ."

Jocelyn's eyes narrowed. Grace had already asked this question earlier when they had been in the cellar.

"He had to be the guy." Grace felt the words get caught in her throat. She thought back to her dad's words. *People don't wait eight years to finish something like that.*

"But why now?"

"I don't know, okay?" Grace sighed. Jocelyn blinked back tears and avoided looking back at Grace. For the first time in a while, Grace swallowed all her emotions and pushed them deep down.

"Look. We are never going to get out of here alive if we blame each other or ourselves. We both messed up. Bad. I'm sorry. I'm sure being stuck in this room makes you feel sorry, too." Grace felt the resentment coming off Jocelyn in waves and let out a deep sigh. "If he was the one who did this, it wouldn't have mattered what I did. He would have found you, and he would have hurt you." She choked back the tears that tried to fall. This was not the time to fall apart. "I just made it easier for him."

"Me too, I guess." Jocelyn rolled her eyes.

"So let's operate under the assumption that it was him before. Why come back now?"

Jocelyn put her head in her hands.

"I don't know!" she shouted, exasperated.

Grace flinched and looked around the room. She inched closer to Jocelyn, who looked at her with confusion.

"What are you doing? I don't want a hug if that's what you're thinking."

Grace slid in against Jocelyn.

"What if he's watching? Listening?" she whispered into Jocelyn's ear.

"So what?" Jocelyn refused to play along, speaking at a normal volume.

"What if he put us in here just so he could watch?"

Jocelyn's face contorted with disgust. "Watch us? Like this is *Saw* or some shit?" she was whispering now, as well.

"Basically." They both stared straight ahead, too afraid to look around for a camera, partially because it would confirm their fears but also because it would reveal what they knew to Noah.

"This is even more screwed up than the first time."

Grace turned her head to the side, considering Jocelyn's words, her eyes glancing toward the small crack between the wooden door and the floorboards.

"Maybe that's the point? To make it worse? Maybe the first time wasn't bad enough—" Jocelyn gave her an evil look. "For him, I mean."

"But that doesn't answer your question. Why now?"

"He doesn't want to get caught?" Grace offered. They both knew it was a shitty answer.

"Maybe he thought the first time was enough." Jocelyn glanced at the door to the study. "But after a while, it wasn't." Grace stood up and paced the room. The why didn't really matter; it didn't change their situation.

"Can you not do that? It's making me queasy."

"Yeah, the fact that I'm walking around is what is making you feel sick." Grace resisted the urge to roll her eyes. She reminded herself of her own advice. They had to put everything aside and focus. She sat back down next to Jocelyn.

"We need a plan."

Jocelyn nodded in agreement.

"Where do we start?"

"Well, I guess it's kind of like an active shooter situation?" Grace asked. It was at least the closest thing either of them could think of. "So we can't run because we're locked in here. Hiding isn't an option."

"Did you, like, memorize the presentation?"

"That was kind of the whole point, Jocelyn. Now focus. So our only option is to fight back." Grace scanned the room for things that could be used as weapons. "Your dad's paperweight. It could really do some damage, right?"

The blue glass crab sat on the desk, staring toward the window. Claire probably thought it was tacky and hated it, even though it made her a hypocrite.

"Yeah."

The room almost seemed like it had been scrubbed of anything else they could use. Grace rose and checked the fishbowl. It was plastic. Not very useful. Finally, she wrapped her fingers around the crab. It had a lot of weight to it. She turned it over in her hand and frowned.

"What?" Jocelyn asked, rising to her feet now. If there were cameras, they were drawing a lot of attention to themselves.

"Check the door."

"What? Why?"

Grace stared down at the bottom of the crab. Written in black permanent marker in all caps was RUN. She turned it so Jocelyn could see.

"The fuck?" Jocelyn approached the door.

"Wait, wait, what if it's a trap? It's got to be. He did this." Grace's forehead pinched together in thought. Jocelyn stopped and turned toward Grace.

"Well, do you want me to check the door or not?"

Grace bounced on the balls of her feet, her own stomach beginning to feel sick.

"I'm not sure. Maybe we should—"

Jocelyn put her hand on the door anyway. Grace stood still, suddenly feeling light-headed. This was all too much.

"I think we need to reevaluate the plan," Jocelyn whispered. Grace moved to join her at the door. "It's unlocked."

51

November 11, 2019

"Suckers," Noah hissed under his breath as he peeked through the security window.

He had gotten a job as a CNA about three weeks ago, right after his conversation with Jocelyn at the diner. He knew it would come in handy soon enough. The job was easy to get. St. George was desperate and paid like shit. The job was basically his when he showed up for the interview sober and wearing clothes.

That morning, he had brought in donuts for the security staff, laced with a sedative he had stolen from a patient's meds. It was easy enough. And the people who worked security got the job the same way he had, so it wasn't like they were highly qualified. Within an hour, both men were completely passed out against the security desk, and Noah had returned to shut down the power.

"Hello?" he called from the doorway, feigning innocence. Neither man responded. He moved toward Roy, the bigger of the two, and lifted his arm. It immediately slumped back down onto the desk in front of the monitors when he let go. "Oh no, I sure hope nothing bad happens . . ." He grinned devilishly as he reached for the main power breaker. "Oops." The lights in the room went dark and were replaced by the dull backup generator.

Before leaving the office, he used a small hammer he had concealed in his scrubs to smash the interior doorknob, leaving the men stranded but also preventing others from getting in. Even though the door had an updated lock system, the way these old doors worked, both sides needed to be intact. Until somebody got their hands on a screwdriver, the men were stranded, along with the power switch.

Already the floor was in chaos. Nurses ushered patients from the dayroom into their individual rooms. One man, who had been relatively stable thus far, was raving about how the aliens were finally coming to get him. Noah was pretty sure it was his sedative that he had stolen. He hadn't bothered to learn any names since he was already on a first-name basis with the two most important people around.

Nobody even batted an eye at him. Everyone was so focused on making sure that the patients were okay that they didn't even think about delegating a task to him.

"Guess I better check on my patients." He smiled as he thought back to his locker, where he had concealed the garden shears. A small droplet of sweat raced down his back, giving him shivers as he anticipated what was to come next.

52

November 17, 2019

"It's a trap, right? It's got to be a trap." Now, Jocelyn was the one pacing across the room, her eyes flashing back to the door that stood ajar. Grace flexed her fingers around the crab paperweight.

"I mean, unless we aren't the only ones in the house . . ."

Jocelyn almost tripped as Grace spoke.

"I mean it's my dad's study. You don't think—" Jocelyn forced herself to stop midsentence. The possibility was too much to bear.

"You said they left on a trip. They are skiing or whatever. They are completely safe. We would have heard them if they were locked up in a different section of the house. We know that he's been in this room: I know he has because he put us here and this is where he had that fake therapy session with me." Grace frowned. She couldn't quite pull together the timeline in a way that made sense. The therapy session happened before she remembered waking up in Jocelyn's house. But how could he have pulled it off with everyone there? She swallowed hard and set down the paperweight.

"So we need to run. You said yourself that's the first thing you should do. Let's go. We're burning daylight." Grace's face scrunched up as she struggled to formulate a thought. Noah was a psychopath. Or at least, close enough to one. He wanted to watch them suffer.

"Let's go. But we need to stay together. Are there any guns in the house?" Grace's father had taken her shooting once, after the incident at camp. He said she should know how to protect herself just in case. She never thought she would need to prepare for the exact same situation as before.

"Um, I think my mom might have one in the bedroom. Dad hates them, but she wanted to have one for when he was traveling for work." Jocelyn hesitated. "It's small."

"Small is better than nothing. Come on." Grace led the way into the hallway, taking a quick glance in both directions for Noah. The house was silent.

"I feel sick," Jocelyn whispered as she followed behind Grace, their sneakers making small noises as they moved.

Grace felt the same way. Her brain darted a million places. Maybe he rigged the hallway with the same gas that had made them pass out before. Maybe he was waiting in the bedroom with the gun himself. There were so many variables that Grace felt the stress press against her lungs.

Grace stopped just before she turned the corner to the hallway. Jocelyn bumped into her but stopped herself from shoving Grace to the floor. She could hear her blood pumping in her ears as she exhaled carefully. She forced her head around the corner, going against every instinct in her body.

It was empty.

"Come on," she whispered. Jocelyn nodded, and the pair crept down the hall, prioritizing stealth over speed.

"Are we playing hide and seek?" Noah called. Grace felt coldness run down the length of her entire body. "Come out, come out, wherever you are!" Noah's voice was playful. Both of them were stuck to the floor in the middle of the hall, paralyzed by his call. The doors around them were all shut, and Grace felt utterly lost.

"He's not close," Jocelyn hissed. Grace shook her head. It was too much. She felt herself trembling. Her body temperature seemed to be flipped from hot to cold so fast she couldn't keep track. Any bravery she had earlier had dissolved.

"Let's keep going," Jocelyn whispered. Despite her best efforts, Grace didn't budge. "I am not dying today." Jocelyn pushed past Grace and into her parents' bedroom. The fear had entirely disappeared from her as Grace looked on in awe.

"After this, let's play freeze tag. I'm it, and you freeze." His cackle echoed off the cavernous walls. He could see her. She knew it. How, she wasn't sure. But then again, she didn't know how he did a lot of things.

Left, right. Left, right. Grace had to force her feet to shuffle forward. Noah was laughing again, and this time he sounded closer. There had to be cameras because he was nowhere in sight, and his voice had started far away.

It felt like an hour before Grace finally crossed into the master bedroom. Like most of the house, this room remained authentic: wood floors, wood trim accenting dark walls. Jocelyn spun around, her body tense, but she relaxed when she saw it was Grace. Wrapped in her fingers was a small handgun, one that could be easily concealed in a purse.

"Do you know how to shoot?" Grace asked, moving around the bed to Jocelyn's side. Seeing a gun felt so foreign to Grace. She hadn't seen one, let alone held one, in over five years. A look of panic flashed over Jocelyn's eyes. Threatening someone with a gun was one thing. Shooting them was entirely different.

"No." Her voice was nearly a whisper. Grace slowly reached out and wrapped her fingers around the barrel, careful to aim the gun away from them, and Jocelyn released it. "Do you?"

"My dad showed me a while ago. The gun wasn't this tiny though. It's so light." Grace wrapped her hand around the grip and lined up the sight with the open door. "I wasn't a great shot," she admitted.

"Marco . . ." Noah's voice echoed in the hallway. Jocelyn stepped toward the door but stopped when she realized Grace had the gun.

"I guess I should go first." Grace frowned as she stepped forward. "Do I shoot him in the leg or—"

"The chest. He deserves to die. He's a murderer."

Grace wanted to respond that would make her a murderer, too, but she didn't bother.

Grace stepped into the hallway, her eyes darting left to right. Nothing but potted plants in various states of dehydration.

"Boo!"

Grace's head whipped around. Noah had sounded like he was right behind her, but he wasn't.

"It's the intercoms." Jocelyn gestured to the small box below the light switch. "He must be controlling which one it plays from." While it was a relief to know he wasn't close, she knew it meant he was watching them.

"Do your parents have security cameras?"

Jocelyn bit her bottom lip.

"Yeah. I forgot about them. I don't think they are everywhere." Their eyes fell upon the gun. If he could see them, he knew.

"All we need to do is get out. I'm sure he already took out the phone line." Grace wasn't even sure if Jocelyn's parents had a landline. Not many people did. "We will use this if we need to, but getting away is most important."

Jocelyn gritted her teeth. She didn't agree, but fear kept her from speaking up.

"The nearest neighbor is about a half mile away from the other side of the house." That didn't sound like a lot, but when you were stuck with a psychopath, it was like a marathon.

"Which door should we use?" Grace asked. "He knows our every move."

"The front door. It has a couple exits nearby if he is there. It's safest," she whispered.

"Let's go." Grace tightened her grip on the gun and plunged into the hallway.

53

November 11, 2019

The sight of Grace Simmons sticking halfway out of an air vent almost made Noah break out laughing. She was just slim enough for it to work. When he saw her scrambling with the vent earlier, before he pumped some gas into her room to make her pass out long enough that he could place the garden shears, he thought there was no way she would be able to make it over to Jocelyn's room. Now, she lay knocked out on the floor, spilling out of the vent like melted ice cream.

Time to get to work, he thought. He pocketed the tape recorder that contained Jocelyn's screams. He recorded them during one of her previous freak-outs, knowing it would come in handy eventually. Jocelyn's room was now vacant: her mother checked her out earlier that day. He pulled out his phone and texted her.

Is your mom coming to get her?

Night had fallen over the unit and he was one of only a few nurses working. When he saw Grace was making her move through the vent, he had arranged for the others to go on break, convincing them that he could handle it. After all, they were just one floor down if he needed them. But he wouldn't need them. They all agreed after the panic from the power outage.

His phone buzzed in his hand.

First thing in the morning.

He gave Grace's limp figure a smile.

"Perfect," he whispered as he leaned over and moved some hair out of her face. "I'd like to say that you are just an innocent pawn in all of this, but honestly . . ." He stood back up and pulled over the wheelchair he had ready. He forced his hands under Grace's body and hoisted her into the chair, reaching around and strapping her in so she wouldn't fall.

"Honestly," he grunted. "You are pretty damn entertaining on your own."

Noah opened the door to Jocelyn's room, cautious to make sure nobody was walking past. He had pizza brought into the break room just to be safe. It clearly had worked.

"People are so damn gullible," he murmured as he pushed Grace into the hall. "And you, I mean, wow. I thought it would be hard to trick you, but you are so suggestible. I just made you a little paranoid, gave you a few drugs." He whispered the last part under his breath. "And voilà! You started seeing me even when I wasn't there. I'm not gonna lie, Grace. That surprised even me."

He unlocked Grace's room and pushed her inside, guiding the chair to her bed.

"I hate this part though." He unstrapped her and

forced her back into the bed. "So damn   heavy . . ." She wasn't really heavy, but she was deadweight. When she had made her way out of the vent, which he had unscrewed earlier, just in case, he had let her scream once or twice before injecting her with a slow-release sedative that he was *pretty* sure wouldn't kill her. He hadn't thought about how heavy it would make her, but it was good practice for what was ahead. Besides, he needed something strong enough she wouldn't remember being checked out of St. George. Even though Jocelyn was his main target, he figured there was no harm in having a little extra fun along the way.

"Lots of heavy lifting coming my way," he reasoned as he pulled the scratchy blankets over her body, tucking the length of it under her sides. To any outsider, he looked like he was tucking in a patient lovingly. Instead, he was fantasizing about what he could do to make her scream.

"I will see you tomorrow." He ran his fingers across her pale cheek. "Sweet dreams," he hissed, grinning the whole time.

54

November 17, 2019

"Jocelyn!" A shriek echoed through the halls, so loud it reverberated off every surface. Grace's hands flew to her ears instinctively, the gun pointing to the ceiling.

"Mom?" Jocelyn called. She almost broke straight into a run, but Grace snatched her wrist, pulled her back. "Let go! It's my mom! She's in trouble."

Grace shook her head.

"He's messing with you. I know it." Grace swallowed hard. "I think he did the same thing with me, but with you. Maybe it's a recording."

Jocelyn shook her head.

"But it was her voice."

"Maybe it was, but she's not here. Remember?"

They both thought back to the spontaneous ski trip. It made sense for her parents to run off without warning. It happened all the time.

"How did he get her voice?" Jocelyn spat, her eyes meeting Grace's with a new intensity.

"I don't know. A home video? It was loud and kind of staticky, I think." She wasn't actually sure if she had heard any static, but it didn't help to have Jocelyn panic. "Let's just focus on one step at a time. We need to get out. Then, you can call your parents. We need to get to the front door."

Jocelyn couldn't bring herself to speak, so she just nodded. Grace slipped her hand off Jocelyn's wrist but reached down and gave her hand a quick squeeze before letting go entirely. The pit of her stomach churned, but she couldn't let fear get in the way.

"Let's go," she whispered before adjusting her grip on the gun, her palm sweat making her grip shaky.

The intercom had gone silent. Grace wasn't sure what was worse: Noah taunting them or the silence. At least when he was busy messing with the intercom, Grace was pretty sure he wasn't nearby. Now, he could be anywhere.

"Do you think he has a gun too?" Jocelyn asked. The sweat that ran down Grace's back felt like ice.

They reached the top of the stairs, and as far as they could see from the left staircase, the foyer below was clear. The entryway table had mail scattered across it that Grace hadn't noticed before.

"I think he must."

At the realization, Grace's heart seemed to have stopped entirely. For a second, it crossed her mind that Jocelyn might still be in on this. Maybe they were both messing with her. Double-teaming. But when she thought back to the fear in Jocelyn's eyes when they heard her mother scream, she knew she was wrong. Jocelyn was terrified too.

"Why do you think that?" Jocelyn asked. Grace froze and turned to look at her.

"He knows this house. Like seems to really know it. The paperweight, the intercom, the security cameras." Grace gestured to emphasize the point before remembering she was holding a gun. Her father had taught her all about proper gun safety, but her instincts fought against her, especially with how light this one was.

"He must have known about that gun. He wouldn't have left it there if he didn't already have one."

"You're right." Grace bit her bottom lip.

"Just be careful," Jocelyn whispered before pointing to the stairs. "He's unpredictable."

Grace tried to swallow the lump in her throat. "No shit." Nausea crashed over her, but she tried to swallow it down. She couldn't vomit. Not now. Grace forced herself to start down the stairs, holding the gun in one hand while gripping the railing with the other. She knew she should be ready to fire, but she was too afraid she would get light-headed and tumble down the stairs.

The foyer was silent, and Grace eyed the front door and the afternoon light dimly shining through the front windows. They were so close to getting out. But something broke the silence.

"Jocelyn!" Claire Baker's screech seemed to be coming from the kitchen, and Jocelyn jolted forward. Grace grabbed her arm to hold her back.

"What if it's a trap?" Grace asked, even though the voice had been crystal clear this time. Grace was sure there was no static.

"It's my *mom*, Grace!"

"Let me just peek around before you run in like some hero."

Grace stepped off the stairs and turned the corner. The kitchen looked empty, but all they could see was the stainless steel of the fridge and range as well as one of the island stools. The backdoor was just on the other side of the island.

"We just need to check the kitchen. If she's not in there, we'll just keep going straight out the back door," Jocelyn argued, and Grace had to agree. If it was her mother, she would want to do the same. On a silent count of three, they took off.

They both still had shoes on from when they had gone out back to break the angel figurines, so Grace thought they had a good chance to get far. At least a better chance than if they were barefoot.

As she ran, she had tunnel vision, telling herself over and over to just focus on the door. There was hope as long as Claire wasn't in the kitchen. But she was.

Jocelyn's screams pulled her focus away from the door, and she tried to skid to a halt. Instead, she crashed to the floor, palms and knees scraping against the ground. The gun fell and clattered against the hardwood.

"No! No! Mom! Dad!"

Grace's vision blurred as she tried to assess the scene, but finally it came into focus. Hanging from the ceiling, with newly installed hooks, were Mr. and Mrs. Baker. Jocelyn scrambled to the island and grabbed a kitchen knife. She climbed onto the kitchen table, desperate to cut down her parents, but they weren't moving. Their bodies almost had a blue tinge and their forms were shriveled, deforming their facial features. But the more Grace thought about it, the more they lacked any color at all. They had been dead for a while.

Noah had just now taken the time to string them up.

"Jocelyn, stop." Grace climbed to her feet and rushed to her friend, trying to pull her down from the table. "They're gone. You can't save them." Jocelyn fell to her knees on the table and wrapped her arms around her mother's dangling legs.

"Looks like you give a shit about them after all," Noah remarked, leaning casually against the doorway of the kitchen.

55

November 12, 2019

The house was silent. Three hours earlier, Noah had distracted the maid by breaking a vase on the opposite side of the house. He had slipped in through the open garage door. While she was busy cleaning it, he slipped some crushed-up sedatives into the soup she was making. It worked like clockwork. Unless there was something that made people suspicious, they trusted the world absolutely.

Grace, of course, hadn't been awake to eat. She was still heavily drugged by the medication he had given her yesterday evening. She came in and out of it, but he was confident he could make it work.

You ready? The text popped onto his screen. He replied with a thumbs up. A minute later, there was a quiet tap on the kitchen door. A man in a suit entered when Noah pulled open the door.

"I just have to get her set up, and then we are good to go. You studied all the key points, right?"

The man rolled his eyes.

"I'm not an amateur. You paid me for a reason." Noah nodded and let out a slow sigh. He was beginning to feel anxiety creep up. The foreign feeling made him increasingly uncomfortable. This part of the plan was risky, but he thought it would be worth it. Messing with Grace took his plan to a whole new level. Especially with what he was going to do next. Hiring somebody else to do his dirty work from the internet needed to be worth it.

"Can you help me get her situated?" The man grunted and followed after Noah as he led his way toward the back stairs for the servants. "I just have to inject her with something small, and then we can move her. It should wear off within a half hour."

Noah cracked open the door to Jocelyn's room. Jocelyn was passed out on a chaise while Grace was sprawled across the canopy bed. Noah took a moment to contemplate her position. Normally, she slept crunched up, like she was trying to make herself as small as possible.

She hadn't really spent much time conscious since she left St. George, apart from when she was brought here. Noah had made sure to give her a spiked water bottle when she left to help sedate her on the way home. Noah crept up to Grace while Jocelyn snored. The sleeping pills seemed to amplify Jocelyn's normal snore.

He uncapped a syringe from his pocket. He had already drawn a very small dosage of the sedative. Just enough to ensure they could move her without her jolting awake. He pulled back the sheet and injected it into her arm. After a few moments, he could see her body physically relax. Noah motioned for the man from the door to come help. He grabbed her under the armpits while the other took her feet.

"We have to stop meeting like this," he whispered quietly enough so that the man couldn't hear what he was saying. Together, they carried her to the study. Noah propped her against the couch and turned to the man. He had settled into an armchair and slid on a pair of glasses.

"How do I look?" he smirked, and Noah smiled.

"Almost perfect. Here, take this." He snatched a notepad off the desk and passed it to him. "Now you look like Dr. Tyler. She should wake up within a minute of this one. Don't fuck this up." Noah pulled out a second syringe and prepared to wake Grace up.

"Chill."

"Oh, and play this. Just for a minute. Make sure you stop it as soon as she starts to wake up." He nodded and took the small tape recorder. Noah headed out the door just as Dr. Tyler hit play. He closed the door as the recording played Jocelyn's screams.

56

November 17, 2019

"You're a fucking murderer!" Jocelyn yelled, lunging off the table and toward Noah with the chef's knife. The blade shone in the light coming from the windows as Grace looked on in shock. Jocelyn fell short, tripping over herself. She crumpled into a heap in front of Noah, the knife still in her hand.

Noah stepped forward and put his foot over the flat edge of the blade, using his weight to stop Jocelyn from withdrawing it.

"Well, duh," he spat, staring down at her with a level of disgust that neither had seen before. His face had contorted from the normal features earlier to a new person entirely. Rage seemed to ooze out of his every pore. Grace tried to swallow her fear, but the lump was caught in her throat. Some small part of her had still hoped that Jocelyn was joking. That this was all an act.

But now, her parents were hanging in the kitchen, and Noah looked like a wolf searching for its next meal.

Jocelyn was sobbing now, her body trembling against the floor.

"Pathetic. You don't even give a shit about them on a normal day. You hated them. You said so yourself."

Jocelyn's eyes darted up at this. "Shut up! I *loved* them."

"No, you loved their money, bitch. You got a dreamy lifestyle with your own parents. Nobody came around and hurt you. Nobody! You just hurt your own damn self." Noah spat on Jocelyn. She collapsed back into sobs.

Grace tried to shake herself into reality. *The gun! Get the gun!* Her eyes searched the room before finally finding it near the island. If she moved, she was certain Noah would be on top of her in seconds. She tried to use her foot to slide the gun over to her, but it was out of reach.

Grace looked back up at Jocelyn. She was crumpled on the ground, shaking and crying, but she had propped herself up so she was almost in a tabletop pose. Her forearms were flat against the ground, and her back was arched so that her face was visible underneath her body. She was staring directly at Grace, mouthing something.

All of a sudden, Jocelyn sprang to her feet and rushed at Noah. He was caught off guard, but responded instinctually. He shoved her backwards as she closed the distance, and they both tumbled backwards. She fell, but he managed to stay upright.

Grace used the opportunity to crawl over to the gun. She gripped it tightly in her hand and rose to her feet. She tried not to look at the bodies dangling from the ceiling. She tried not to think about the fact that she could miss. She tried to focus.

Noah was already staring at her like he knew what was coming next. Her arm quivered as she lifted the gun toward him. She thought back to what her father had always taught her. Shoot to kill. There was no time to hesitate. She pulled the trigger.

57

November 14, 2019

Noah sat on the street across from the Baker residence. It made it easier since what they proclaimed to be an estate was gated. He saw everyone go in and out. A town car pulled into the driveway, and he pulled out his binoculars.

"Who do we have here?" he mused, staring across the lawn. Jocelyn was coming out of the house, designer bag in hand, cell phone pressed against her ear. Noah despised the fact that he shared DNA with this woman. She was like every rich stereotype rolled into one. She climbed into the car, and it made its way back down the driveway. Just after the gate closed, Noah got out of his beat-up Ford and shut the door carefully. He walked up the street as if he was going to someone else's home, but made a sharp turn at the tree line. While the front of the property was gated, the forest around it was so immense the Bakers had never bothered to do the whole lot. He took one backwards glance at the car and hoped the signal jammer would work. This is where things got serious, like they had all those years ago. Instead of feeling nervous, Noah felt excitement tingling throughout his body.

Through the tree line, he could see the kitchen doors. He wished it was summer so that they might be out by the pool. Cleaning up after them in the house could be messy, depending on how this went down.

He reached down and double-checked that his handgun was still in its holster. As he began moving toward the back doors, his face shifted completely under the cover of his black hoodie. His eyes seemed to glaze over, with a fire burning just under the surface. A grimace spread across his features. He had considered putting on a mask, but he was confident nobody would be left to identify him.

From his back pocket, he retrieved his lock-picking kit. He edged over to the door, peeking into the kitchen through the glass door. Claire Baker was at the island near the fridge, pouring some red wine, her hair in a low ponytail and she wore a tight button-up blouse. From the angle Noah was at, he could see between a pair of buttons to her white bra underneath. A large glass. Noah grinned as he waited for her to head into a different room. Instead, she gulped down half the wine and refilled it. Noah rolled his eyes. This was the woman his father had decided to be with? A drunk. His stepfather had been a drunk too. It was the only way he could explain away the things he did to Noah.

Finally, she headed into the foyer and, Noah guessed, into the front room. He slipped over to the door and tested the lock. For a moment, he debated just shooting the door open, but he resisted the urge. With his toolkit, he made quick work of the lock. Sliding glass doors were never difficult to get open when the secondary lock wasn't engaged.

"Time for the games to begin." He stepped inside as a sickly smile spread across his lips, never quite touching his eyes.

In what they undoubtedly called the "sitting room," Mrs. Baker was draped across the white couch, staring straight ahead at the wall. In one hand, she scrolled mindlessly through her phone, while in the other she nursed her wine. As Noah stood in the doorway, he could hear the faint noise of talking. He assumed she must be listening to something through headphones, but he couldn't make out quite what it was. If Noah had to guess, it was likely some true-crime podcast. White women ate that shit up.

Noah approached her from behind the couch. As he got closer, he could hear what she was listening to. Not true crime. Some trashy podcast where women talk about sex. He rolled his eyes as he heard the word "cock." He had assumed that the woman his father decided to stay with was better than that. But then again, maybe the sex is exactly why he had stayed.

It happened fast. Within seconds, a plastic bag went over her head. The wine spilled and her arms flailed. Noah grimaced as he saw the wine splatter over the white upholstery. Stains like that triggered something deep inside him. Regardless, he kept a tight grip on the bag, using his elbows to hold her down against the couch. In a minute, her body went limp. He didn't bother keeping the bag on until her heart stopped completely. There were some plans he had with her before it was all said and done.

He used his free hand to pause the podcast on the phone. Quiet fell like a heavy blanket over the room, leaving him feeling unsettled. Noah focused, trying to listen for movement upstairs. There was none. This was easy, he thought. He frowned as he contemplated this. He didn't want easy. He wanted a challenge. He reassured himself with the hope that he could get one soon enough.

PART THREE

58

November 17, 2019

The gun didn't fire. Grace stared at the gun in shock, confused. In her mind, a little flag that read "BANG" unfurled from the end of the barrel. She attempted to pull the trigger again, but nothing. Her eyes darted to Noah, who smiled deviously from the other side of the island, next to the fridge.

"Aw, look. No bullets."

Grace thought back to how light the gun had felt. Checking for ammunition had never crossed her mind. Blood rushed to her head as anger filled her. Noah had known there was a gun, and he had unloaded it.

Jocelyn stumbled back to her feet, colliding with her father's body as she did so. She released a scream that startled them both.

Neither of the girls knew what to say. The gun had been their only hope besides running. Apart from the knife on the ground, there appeared to be no weapon on Noah. Yet, they both seemed frozen in place. Finally, words crawled up Grace's throat and out of her mouth.

"Run!" Grace turned on the spot and bolted for the sliding glass door. Just before she reached it, another scream rang out. This time from herself. The glass on the door rippled and cracked before her. Her ears rang, and it took her a few minutes to realize what had happened.

Spinning around slowly, she discovered Noah standing with a gun of his own. A hunting rifle. Whether it had been strapped to his back or hidden out of sight in the kitchen, she wasn't sure. Inside, she cursed herself for not thinking to look closer.

"I wouldn't do that if I were you," he taunted, gesturing toward the door with his gun. Grace felt bile climb up her throat. She swallowed it down and instinctively held her hands out in front of her. In the corner of her eye, she could see Jocelyn doing the same.

"Please. You don't have to do—"

"Shut the fuck up!" Spittle flew from Noah's mouth as his expression shifted from a devious smile to pure rage. "You don't get to tell me what to do! Nobody gets to tell me what to do."

Grace flinched away from him, feeling fear race through her veins. A small part of her brain told her to accept this. There was nothing she could do.

"Drop the gun," Noah instructed. Grace bent down and set it carefully on the hardwood floor. "Kick it over here." Grace did as he asked and watched the handgun slide across the floor, spinning as it went. "Now, I'm going to give you a choice here, Grace. Are you ready?"

She nodded her head slightly as her eyes moved between him and Jocelyn. Jocelyn sat in a heap against the kitchen table, visibly shaking. Her mother's body swung like a pendulum overhead. Her dad's weight held him mostly still.

"Wonderful." A grotesque smile blossomed across his face, giving Grace chills. His emotions had bounced so quickly between rage and happiness that she had whiplash. "So why don't you tell us the story of what happened that night?"

"That night . . ." Grace bit her bottom lip. Immediately, her consciousness flashed scenes from the campground. The bodies. The blood. Jocelyn's screams fading into nothing. The garden shears.

"You fucking know what happened! Say it."

Grace flinched and opened her mouth to speak, but nothing came out.

"I know what happened, Noah. I read the journal." Jocelyn's voice seemed to have a comforting tone. As if she was trying to soothe a wild animal.

"I'm not asking her for your sake, you dumb bitch." Noah kept the gun pointed at Jocelyn but turned his attention to Grace. "Go on."

"Matt and I had planned to scare Jocelyn. We had stolen some garden shears from the maintenance shed. I had told her there was a party."

Noah was hanging onto each word with an intensity that made her question herself. Jocelyn stared straight ahead toward the stainless-steel refrigerator, but she was listening too.

"There was a party though, right?" Noah asked, the corners of his mouth turned upward.

"Yes. I didn't know that."

"You're welcome." Noah shrugged, licking his lips.

"Wait. You invited the others?" Grace felt like the room was spinning. She had known he was involved, but not how much.

"Wow. I thought you were smarter than this. Of course, I did. It wouldn't be nearly as much fun if it was just Jocelyn and Matt. A little text from Jocelyn's phone spread the word quickly. Sneaking into the cabin while you were sleeping was the easy part." He cleared away the smile on his face like a dirty plate. His expression turned vacant as he continued. "Why did you invite Jocelyn there?"

"To scare her a little. Embarrass her, I guess."

"Embarrass her even though she would be the only one there? Other than Matt." He clicked his tongue to shame her. "Amateur."

Grace's stomach swirled. He was right. They hadn't thought the plan through. The most it would do was piss Jocelyn off. It wasn't revenge. It was just dumb.

"You're right."

A glimmer sparkled in Noah's eye. Finally, the recognition he thought he deserved.

"Want to know what I would have done?" Noah had lowered the gun slightly, now more relaxed. Jocelyn's gaze was distant. Grace wasn't even sure she was listening anymore. In all likelihood, she was somewhere else entirely.

"Sure."

Noah barked out a laugh. "I would have invited her to a party. A real party. And I would have made her watch as I killed every last person there. Then finally, when she's the only one left, I would take my time with her, real slow."

Grace's mind flashed to the sexual undertones of what he was saying. She thought about the fact that

284

they were half-siblings and tried not to let a reaction pass over her face. *Are they even actually related?* she wondered.

"Then, I would listen to her scream."

"That's exactly what you did." Jocelyn's voice came out of nowhere. She was now staring straight at Noah, her eyes dead.

"No, it's not." He admonished her like a child. "Your little friend, if you could even call her that, pranced in and ruined the party before it was over. She ruined everything."

Grace stared down at her feet. Even knowing how horrible Noah was, how despicable he acted toward Jocelyn, she felt disgusted by herself. He was a monster, but in a way, so was she.

"Grace." Jocelyn's voice was soft again. Noah opened his mouth to quiet her, but hesitated. "It's okay. It's not your fault."

Grace tried to speak but she could feel her heart caught in her throat.

"How sweet." Noah tucked the gun under his arm so he could clap, the noise reverberating off the walls. Grace looked on in horror as the gun bounced with each movement he made. "Now, here comes the choice. Are you sure you're ready?"

Grace didn't move her body in any way. She was too terrified to make a sound. Instead, she focused on trying to hide the fact that her entire body was trembling.

"I'll take that as a yes. Since I'm such a nice guy, I'll let you decide. Would you like to stay here with me or would you like Jocelyn to?"

Grace tried to blink away the confusion. Jocelyn appeared unfazed.

"You're asking me to choose which one of us you let go?" The words felt sour on her tongue.

"Basically. You get to choose if you live or if she does."

59

November 17, 2019

All of his calls within the past five hours had gone immediately to voicemail. Grace's phone was either off or dead. He stared at the gates with the house lurking beyond.

"Fucking looks like a horror set." Harry Simmons stared back down at his daughter's contact info. He had sent texts to her, but no dice. He'd even hunted down Jocelyn's Facebook to send her a message. He was skeptical it would work anyway, considering her profile picture was from 2016. When nobody had answered, he got in his Dodge truck and drove.

He didn't know where Grace lived, let alone Jocelyn, and he spent most of the drive beating himself up for not being a better father. Grace had never really had friends. The closest person to her was Jocelyn, and Harry always had a nagging feeling that she didn't even really like her that much. Not that Jocelyn seemed to truly appreciate Grace either.

He thought back to the anxiety in his daughter's voice when he had talked to her just a week ago. He should have believed her. Something was definitely wrong. And it was more than just an apartment robbery.

When he made it into the city, he found the nearest phone store and demanded they locate his daughter. Of course, they were useless. But then he remembered the app his daughter had mentioned once before. When she first went away to college, she had downloaded it for him on his phone.

"Just in case I go missing." She had sounded so solemn when she said it. Ever since that summer, she had carried around the knowledge that bad things did happen. And they could happen to her. He had just grunted and put the app in a folder without ever looking at it. Now, it showed her location as a big blue dot. It had last been updated a few days ago (much to his frustration, it didn't say how many). He assumed she had been without her phone since then. Whether it was broken or dead, he couldn't be sure. But it was better than nothing.

The large gated entrance to their home intimidated him. Security cameras were mounted periodically across the wrought iron gate. It made his skin crawl thinking about Jocelyn's parents sitting in their home, sipping five-hundred-dollar wine and mocking him. He was sporting jeans and a Hanes t-shirt, which was plain apart from the stains that speckled it. *What the hell was I thinking?* Once again, he blamed who he had been two hours ago, not who he was now. Because at least now, he was trying.

Harry shuffled over to the intercom and pressed the small white button. Nothing happened.

He pressed once again, leaning forward in case the feedback was quiet. Finally, it burst to life, spitting out sharp static.

"Can I help you?"

Harry swallowed the urge to mock them. No shit, he could help him. Why the hell else would he be there?

"Yes, hello." He cleared his throat, his awkwardness causing red to spread across his face. "I'm looking for my daughter. Grace."

There was a long pause where it was only static. Harry fiddled with a loose hangnail on his thumb.

The static disappeared. Harry wondered if maybe they had blown him off. Instead, the gate's motor began whirring as it struggled to pull the heavy gate open. He let out a slow breath and unconsciously crossed his fingers. If he had been a religious man, he would have said a prayer.

The driveway felt long to him, despite the reality. He forced one foot in front of the other, dreading having to speak to Jocelyn or her parents. He had met them once or twice before. Each time, he had walked away feeling like a member of their staff. He squinted as he attempted to recall what had been said to make him feel that way but came up empty. The longer he focused on it, the more he questioned whether he really had spoken to Jocelyn's mother or if it was the maid.

He ran through what to say when he reached the door. Did he speak kindly? Did he engage in pleasantries? His gut told him no. He needed to demand to see Grace immediately. Rich people weren't used to being on the receiving end of demands. They wouldn't know how to react.

Finally, he approached the tall brown doors. He wasn't sure what to do. Knock? They had those large iron Victorian-era door knockers staring down at him. The engraved lions looked fearless. The Bakers knew he was coming. Why hadn't they greeted him at the door? For a moment, he felt his stomach turn and debated using a nearby planter as a trash can. When the feeling passed, he grabbed the knocker and hit it against the door twice.

"Nothing?" he whispered when a moment passed. He reached for the door handle. "Should I?" He bit his bottom lip. If they opened the gate for him, was going inside trespassing? He knew he would definitely end up serving time for something so stupid as that. Regardless, he pressed down the latch and pushed. It was unlocked.

60

November 17, 2019

Noah stared directly into Grace's soul, waiting for a response. He seemed to salivate at the idea of her having to choose between herself and Jocelyn. Grace shifted her weight from side to side, tiny glass from the door crackling under her shoes, unable to bring herself to speak. Her brain was like a high-speed train jumping from thought to thought. She bit her bottom lip and closed her eyes, unable to handle the intensity of Noah's gaze.

"I have spent the last eight years trying to fix the mistake I made. To make up for how I hurt you, Jocelyn."

When Grace opened her eyes, she stared at Jocelyn cowering below her parents' bodies. Tears had stained her t-shirt, but she appeared to no longer be crying. Instead, her expression had hardened. She clearly didn't want to give Noah any satisfaction. She didn't respond.

"Isn't that nice?" Noah mocked, cocking his head to the side. "So you choose yourself? You're going to let her go free?" Eagerness spread across Noah's face as he raised his rifle once more, turning the barrel toward Grace.

"No. I'm not saying that." Hesitation echoed through her words. She tried to swallow, but she felt like she was choking. Like her windpipe was being crushed. "I can't spend the rest of my life doing this." Grace felt like she was just talking aloud. She didn't mean anything one way or the other. She couldn't live with herself if she let Jocelyn die. But she didn't want to keep making sacrifices for a girl who nearly got her killed too.

"So you are choosing Jocelyn?" He slowly turned the gun away from Grace, his smirk growing larger. A small voice in the back of her head told Grace it didn't matter. He was going to kill them both anyway.

"I think we're even. I think we hurt each other equally." Grace was trying to apologize to Jocelyn, but she wouldn't meet her gaze. "Your blood isn't on my hands. It's on his hands. It's *always* been on his."

Noah widened his stance and propped the stock of the rifle against his shoulder.

"Any last words, dear sister?"

Grace closed her eyes. She couldn't watch this. For a moment, she regretted the choice. If he really was going to kill them both, she wished she would die first, just so she wouldn't have to see this.

"Fuck you both," Jocelyn spat.

"Right back at ya."

Grace felt her whole body clench as she waited for

the gunshot. When the house's intercom system buzzed instead, signaling a visitor at the gate, she nearly jumped out of her skin. She forced her eyes open. All of them were staring toward the foyer. Noah hadn't lowered his gun, and Grace debated for a moment if she could disarm him while he was distracted. Eventually, she decided it was a good way for them both to get shot.

"Don't move. I'm not done with either of you," he taunted as he shuffled sideways toward the nearest wall intercom. It was a complicated screen built directly into the wall's infrastructure. His body ended up blocking the screen.

"Can I help you?" Noah glanced behind him to check that nobody had shifted.

Grace felt goosebumps crawl up the base of her spine as she heard the voice on the other end of the intercom. Her father was here.

61

November 17, 2019

"Hello?" Harry's voice hesitated. If he thought the outside of the house had been frightening, the silence within was even worse. His palms felt sweaty, and he swiped them across his jeans. The bottom of his stomach seemed to be spreading into his chest.

Ahead, he heard the floorboards squeak, but there was still no reply to his call. A small voice nagged in his head. *Turn around. This is stupid. This might even be trespassing.* Harry reasoned that they had unlocked the gate. And the front door.

"Grace?" he called, forcing his feet forward. The sun had begun setting and the lighting cast long shadows over the hardwood floor of the foyer. He wasn't sure he had ever been in a house worth this much. Maybe even one worth half as much.

His head pivoted as he heard movement again.

Muffled voices. His tongue turned to cotton inside his mouth.

"Grace!" His voice held more urgency this time. More conviction.

"Da—"

Harry broke into a run now. He may not have seen his daughter in a while, but he knew her voice. The feeling in his gut told him something was very wrong.

He stumbled into the scene, his eyes scanning the kitchen. Immediately, they landed on the bodies dangling from the ceiling. Vomit rose into his mouth, but he swallowed it down. Jocelyn was huddled in the corner of the kitchen, partially hidden behind an island. Grace wasn't there.

"Jocelyn?" He hesitated as he approached her. She wasn't meeting his eyes. In fact, she looked almost dead. She was so still. "What's happened?" He had to force himself to speak. Her appearance nearly left him in shock.

Her mouth opened but just hung there.

"Dad, watch out!" Harry heard Grace call out from behind him as he spun on his feet just in time to see the gun.

62

November 17, 2019

Noah had not anticipated Harry's arrival. Even with the hundred scenarios he had run through in his head for the past several years, Harry had never been a part of it. Initially, he thought this could add to the excitement of his final moments with Grace and Jocelyn. Neither was going to live. It was fun to see Grace try to reason why she should be the one to live, though. He was pretty sure Jocelyn knew it was a farce.

As Harry entered the house, Noah tried to come up with a plan. He was always methodical, and surprises were never his strong suit. He knew Jocelyn was broken. Her parents were dead. She knew both she and Grace were dead. She was not a threat. Besides, it wasn't like Harry Simmons was there to save her.

With the gun to her back, Noah forced Grace out of the kitchen and into the walk-in pantry to the right of it. The first time he had snuck into the house, he had spent several minutes mesmerized by the quantity of food kept there. When he was younger, he didn't know when his next meal would be, while his sister got to live like this. He had dragged his fingertips over the clear canisters, daydreaming of the life he could have had. The pantry had solidified it for him. There was no other way to finish this. Jocelyn had to be eliminated.

"Keep your mouth shut," he hissed, spit landing inside Grace's ear. Grace's body shook against the gun barrel. She needed to stop this. She needed to get her dad out of here. Her mind darted back and forth between sacrificing herself and hoping he could save her. In reality, she was sure they would both die.

She heard her father calling her name and closed her eyes. In a moment of courage, she tried to respond.

"Fucking bitch." Noah forced his hand over her mouth, muffling the words. They both listened to his footsteps. "Showtime," Noah murmured before forcing her out of the pantry. Harry's back was to them both as he stared at Jocelyn. Noah released his grip and stepped forward, the gun beginning to rise toward Harry.

"Dad, watch out!"

Harry spun on his heels just fast enough to see the gun pointed toward him. Instinctively, Noah turned to point the gun at Grace before he could stop himself. He made it halfway before Harry lunged for the gun.

The two hit the floor as Grace stumbled backwards. The room was silent except for the struggle between the two. Grace and Jocelyn stared onwards in disbelief. It was difficult to tell what was happening and who had more control over the fight. Grace's brain finally clicked into gear as she moved into the kitchen, pulling a butcher knife from the block. With her fingers wrapped tightly around the handle, it felt awkward and clumsy. Her brain briefly considered why so many horror movies showed the killer holding a knife this way when it felt so unnatural.

Turning to the wrestling pair, she tried to focus, trying to get her brain to slow down the men rolling on the floor.

"Get off me!" her father yelped as Noah tried to force him flat onto the floor.

Grace tried to locate the gun, but it was all happening too fast. All she knew was Noah was pinning her father down. She channeled every piece of hate and fear from the last two weeks into her arms as she drove the knife down into Noah's back. As he let out a scream, another noise rippled through the air. A gunshot.

Grace stumbled backwards away from the noise. The knife was no longer in her hand. The ringing in her ears overtook everything else. Her eyes blurred as well. So much seemed to be happening, but it all felt like slow motion at the same time.

"Dad!" she called out, but she couldn't even make out the sound of her own voice. Her throat felt raw as she realized she was screaming out over and over again. Finally, her vision cleared. Before her sat a lump of bodies. Her father's body. Noah's body. Tangled together with blood intermixing between the two. She could barely see her father's brown eyes over the side of Noah's shoulder. They stared straight up at the ceiling, unblinking.

"No . . . no," she was whispering over and over again. Arms enveloped her, and she tried to rip her body away. Jocelyn's arms held on firmly, forcing her to stay still. She felt the cool tile floor underneath her. She didn't remember collapsing to the ground.

"It's okay," Jocelyn was muttering through a few tears of her own. Grace looked at her. *She's not crying enough. She doesn't understand. My father is dead,* she thought. But that wasn't entirely true. Jocelyn had lost both her parents today. The grief had affected Grace's judgment, though. There was no way for her to reconcile her feelings with reality. But eventually, another thought struck her too.

"He's dead?" Grace whispered, lifting a shaking finger toward Noah's figure.

"I'll check." Jocelyn stumbled to her feet like a newborn foal, waving from side to side as she moved. Grace winced and eventually looked away while Jocelyn touched Noah's neck. The room was filled with heavy silence as they both waited. Slowly, Jocelyn pulled back her hand.

"He's gone. At least, in my not-so-professional opinion."

Grace let out a breath she didn't know she had been holding.

"Are you sure?"

Jocelyn sighed. "As far as I can tell. You're welcome to check if you want."

Grace thought about approaching her father's body and shook her head vehemently.

"No."

They both looked around the room, struggling for words to say. Jocelyn's eyes fixed on her parents' forms dangling a few feet from the floor.

"We need to call the police," Grace whispered. Jocelyn nodded in agreement but neither moved. "Do you have your phone?"

"If I had my phone, do you think any of this would have happened?" Grace shook her head at her own ignorance. Jocelyn was right, and Grace wasn't thinking straight.

"My dad . . . He probably has his phone on him. Or maybe Noah." Grace stared at Jocelyn, begging her to move and check.

"I can't do it. I already checked for a pulse." Jocelyn did already look quite queasy, and she had been rather unsteady on her feet. Grace slid her hands under her and pressed herself up on the cool tile floor. She could feel her pulse thumping in her ears as she struggled forward. Weights felt like they were attached to her feet as she got closer, inch by inch. Finally, she was within reach of the bodies.

"Be careful! You shouldn't move them," Jocelyn urged.

Grace frowned.

"How do I check for a phone without moving them?"

Jocelyn looked away. She didn't have an answer either. "I guess you have to."

Grace forced her hands downward and touched Noah's body. She gave it a small push, but he didn't move. His body was draped across her father's. Eventually, she gave him a shove, and he slid to the side, landing like a broken doll. Grace avoided looking at her father's face, though every instinct in her body told her to. She, instead, focused on his pockets. She could see the outline of the phone. With one eye shut and the other squinting, she forced her fingers into his pocket and retrieved the phone. She ignored the blood pooling by her feet.

She fumbled with the phone, nearly dropping it to

the ground. She backed away quickly, as if from a bomb, and flattened herself against the kitchen island. Her father's phone stared at her, demanding a password. It took her a moment to realize she didn't need it. She hit the emergency button and hit call. She pushed the phone up against her ear and waited.

"9-1-1, what's your emergency?"

Grace felt the blood drain out of her face as she tried to respond.

"We need . . ." Her world went black as she collapsed under the weight of reality.

63

November 18, 2019

The sheets felt scratchy against her skin. They were certainly better than the ones she had dealt with at St. George, but they still weren't soft. Grace reached over to the table next to the bed, relieved by the fact there were no restraints. Her hand paused as she stared down, appreciating the fact that it was over. The nightmare had ended. Even though parts of it had been real.

She grabbed the ice chips and spooned a few onto her tongue. She crunched down almost immediately, feeling the chips shatter in her mouth. An IV hung out of the crook of her elbow, pumping in fluids. A large window displayed the parking lot, and Grace watched longingly as visitors came and went. It didn't really seem like it was necessary, but after she had passed out, EMTs assessed her and determined she was severely dehydrated. It made a lot of sense. She wasn't even sure how long she had been held up by Noah, but fluids hadn't been her number one priority for a while.

"How are you feeling?" A young nurse strode through the doorway and to her bedside. She was examining the monitor and not looking directly at Grace.

"Okay, I think."

"Great!" She paused and stared directly at her for a moment. It felt like forced eye contact. Grace wondered how much they had told the hospital staff.

"Is everything okay?" Grace asked after a moment of awkward silence. The nurse swallowed and looked back at the monitor for just a moment.

"The doctor wanted me to ask how you were feeling. Mentally, I mean. They were wondering if you would like to meet with a psychiatrist, given your medical history."

Grace was now the one staring. She hadn't thought about the fact that now her medical records would forever label her as a difficult patient. A person who attacks hospital staff. She tried to push away the bitter thoughts forming in her mind.

"Do I have to?" Grace forced the words out, hoping she didn't sound like an indignant child.

"Of course not. It's not mandated. They were just thinking that since you just went through a pretty traumatic experience, that it might be beneficial."

Grace felt like she had to agree with the woman. Therapy was a good idea. For everyone. But the idea of sitting in someone's office while they poked around inside her psyche terrified her now.

"Can I think about it?"

The nurse bit her bottom lip.

"They were planning on releasing you soon, so you kind of need to decide now. We can always provide you with the information to go somewhere later?" she offered. The idea of freedom dangled on the edge of Grace's mind. Last time, the hospital hadn't been so willing to let her go.

Grace nodded and flattened the hospital sheet across her stomach.

"That works. If you could give me the info, that would be great."

"Okay, I'll be right back." She sauntered out of the room, unfazed.

Grace wondered how many people the nurse dealt with like her on a daily basis. *Does she judge me? Does she think I'm pathetic?* Grace shook her head in an effort to dispel the negative thoughts. She closed her eyes and forced her breathing to slow. The mere thought of going to another psychiatrist terrified her. She didn't think she could trust one.

She grabbed her cell phone. Luckily, the cops had recovered it from the scene after investigating. It took a few hours, but eventually, it made its way back to her. Jocelyn had swung by with it early this morning, hoping to use it as a reason to check on her. She had been treated for some injuries as well, but she hadn't gone into detail with Grace, and she had been too caught up in her own thoughts to push.

"You doing okay?" Jocelyn had asked. Grace hadn't thought about her response before her mouth opened.

"No." She shrugged and offered a sad smile. "You?"

"I'll probably never be okay again. But at least we have each other, right?" Grace remembered nodding and feeling tears pooling in her eyes.

"We're each other's family now," Jocelyn added, giving Grace's hand a squeeze.

She stared down at her hand now and wondered where Jocelyn was. Was she going to see a therapist? She probably needed just as much counseling now.

The nurse returned with a small business card. "Dr. Roberts. She is the person we work with most frequently for outpatient therapy."

"Perfect. Thank you." Grace stared as the nurse began to pull out the IV and unhook her from the machines. There was a sense of freedom that overwhelmed her. But with that freedom came fear. She had seen Noah dead with her own eyes. She could imagine him being stuffed into a body bag. Even though her logical mind knew all these things to be true, she couldn't help but feel uneasy. She brushed it off as she swung her legs over the side of the bed. *I am safe. Everything is fine,* she repeated to herself, over and over again. Maybe if she thought it enough, it would feel true.

64

November 22, 2019

Grace felt better once she saw the inside of the therapist's office. It wasn't like the ones she had been in before, or the fake one either. It had large windows and felt airy, not stuffy like Mr. Baker's study was. There were no fish tanks or books lining the walls. Only plants accompanied by a few pieces of abstract art.

"I like the paintings," Grace commented as she settled down onto the small purple sofa. Small talk made her uncomfortable, so she always tried to take the initiative.

"Thank you. A few were made by patients." The therapist's cropped hair swung as she sat onto a floral armchair by the window, facing Grace. "So as you already know, my name is Dr. Roberts, but you can just call me Sarah. There's no point in trying to make my ego any bigger than it already is." She let out a small laugh, and Grace smiled. She could tell it was a joke the young woman told each patient. By her calculation, Sarah couldn't be more than a few years older than herself.

"Thanks for seeing me." Grace glanced down at a loose strand on her knitted sweater. She forced herself to leave it alone.

"Of course. So why don't you start by telling me why you are here?"

Grace had run through this question a million times. She had thought about what she should tell the therapist. Eventually, she decided the whole truth was the best option. There was no harm in telling the truth. Jocelyn knew everything she had done, all the mistakes she had made years ago. Her eyes fell onto her hands, sitting neatly in her lap, and she exhaled.

"Eight years ago, I made a mistake that got blown out of proportion."

Sarah tilted her head to the side as Grace spoke, curious. Her body was perched to one side of the armchair, leaning against the right armrest.

"What was the mistake?" she asked after Grace had paused for far too long.

"I tried to scare my best friend." Grace had thought about using that title for Jocelyn for a long time. It hadn't felt right until they had sat on her hospital bed together, talking about how they were family now. There was nobody else in Grace's life. It was just her and Jocelyn. She dug some dirt out from under her thumbnail.

"Scaring your friend doesn't seem like a big mistake. It seems harmless. And you must have been a teenager, right?" Sarah crossed her legs and tapped her foot to an invisible beat. Grace wondered if she had ADHD. She considered whether that would be a troublesome disability for a therapist to have.

"Yes, but it wasn't really harmless. I did want to hurt her, because she had hurt me. But she ended up being attacked." Grace expected surprise to cross Sarah's blank face. None did. "She was almost murdered. I was just trying to scare her, and someone else came along and took advantage. But I think it was all planned. The man who did it had been planning to hurt her for a long time." Grace ran through the story, surprised by how heavy the weight in her chest had felt only now that she noticed its absence. As she told more and more of the details, she realized how silly it all had been. How childish she had been to ever think it was her fault. She settled into the couch, allowing her body to relax a little now that the truth was out there.

"And now, this friend," Sarah began. Grace had intentionally not mentioned Jocelyn's name. "She is friendly with you? After everything that happened?"

Grace frowned. She had tried not to linger on the idea that Jocelyn had gone to such intense lengths to get back at her. But at the same time, it seemed like maybe Noah had taken it further than Jocelyn had ever intended. If she thought about it for too long, her stomach felt sick.

"Yes. She is my only friend."

Sarah nodded, a sad smile spreading across her face.

They carried on like that for a few more minutes. Grace explained how Noah had made her believe she was crazy, though Grace wasn't sure if that was true. Had she ever doubted her own sanity? Mostly, she just believed everyone around her was missing the obvious.

As the session wrapped up, Grace did find herself

feeling better. Sarah tried to push more about the idea of Grace befriending Jocelyn even after all the pain Jocelyn had caused, but Grace dodged those questions. It wasn't a topic she was willing to address. There were some facts of life that simply needed to be accepted.

65

November 23, 2019

Grace had settled onto the couch when the melodic doorbell rang through the house. When she had gotten back from her therapy appointment yesterday, Jocelyn had been surprisingly absent from her home. Grace had sent a text, asking when she would be home. Jocelyn, just as she would before the events of the past few weeks, blew her off. Something about a rooftop party and a cute boy.

Grace had felt strange spending the evening alone in the house. Wherever she walked, she felt like ghosts were watching her. She kept the lights on just so she could avoid seeing shadows lurking throughout the rooms. Unable to sleep, she spent most of the night watching videos on her phone, mindlessly scrolling until the sun rose. It wasn't until then that she felt comfortable enough to sleep.

Now, the doorbell echoed through the rooms, the sound bouncing off the walls. An eyebrow raised, Grace snuck toward the front window of the sitting room, hoping that there were no reporters desperate for a story scoping out the house. She wasn't sure what you were supposed to say when you were a witness to multiple murders. When you were staying at a dead couple's home. A cop car sat in the driveway, but Grace felt no relief.

The doorbell was ringing again by the time she made it to the front door. She opened it and stepped back, planning to invite the police inside. That was what they always did in the TV shows. She didn't have anything to hide. He flashed his badge as he began to speak.

"Grace Simmons?" the cop asked, though she was fairly certain he already knew he had the right person.

"Yes? Jocelyn's not home right now, if you are looking for her?"

The officer shook his head. He was a stout man with a belt wrapped tightly just under his stomach, forcing the button on his dress shirt to strain. His right hand rested on the edge of his belt.

"No, ma'am. We were looking for you."

Grace's brow furrowed.

"Me? Wait, is everything okay with Jocelyn?" Images flashed through Grace's mind. Rape. Parties. Drugs. Overdoses. Death. Every possible scenario rushed through her head so quickly she stumbled backwards. It only made sense at this point for something bad to happen to Jocelyn too. Something worse than what she had already gone through.

"Miss Baker is safe down at the station. I'm here—"

"At the station? So something did happen?" Grace's words smashed together violently as she spoke. She could feel her legs struggling to hold her up. It was happening all over again.

"I'm sorry, but I can't share any more details with you. I'm just here to bring you down to the station."

"Yeah, of course." Grace only hesitated as she moved through the door because she was uncertain if she would pass out or not. His refusal to tell her anything made her believe the worst-case scenario.

In the back of the car, Grace sat silently, watching the dead trees as they flew by. Static came across the radio before a man's voice began speaking. Inside, her anxiety fluttered in her stomach.

"Torres, did you locate her?" Grace looked up front to the officer as he grabbed the radio to respond.

"Driving her in right now." The static made the hairs rise on her arms. A pit was forming in her stomach. Something did not feel right.

"Rogers said you can use room four."

"Got it," Torres replied. Grace rested her head against the cool glass window as she felt her head begin to pound. She felt nauseous, but she couldn't remember the last time she had eaten. The night before, she had planned on ordering takeout with Jocelyn, but after her text, Grace had just decided to go to bed. She took a few deep breaths to keep herself from vomiting.

"You alright back there?"

Grace's head shot up as she looked at the officer. He was staring at her in the rearview mirror as they sat at a stoplight.

"Yes. I just don't feel well."

Torres made a grunting sound. He didn't seem to

care either way, but something about the way he kept glancing nervously into the rearview mirror told Grace he was watching her closely, even when his eyes weren't on her. *Does he think I'm unstable? How much does he know about me,* she wondered, avoiding looking in the mirror now. Every time she glanced back up, it seemed like he was watching her.

Torres pulled into the station and parked directly by the entrance. He had to come around and open the door for her, as the backs of police cars weren't built to open from the inside.

"Can I see Jocelyn now?" she inquired, moving toward the station doors after he gestured to them. He followed closely behind her, one hand resting on his pistol.

"We just have a few questions for you, if you don't mind."

A frown spread across Grace's face. She spun on her heels to look Torres in the eyes.

"I thought I was coming down here to see Jocelyn. Is she not here?" Grace bit her bottom lip, realizing he had never really explained what he was doing at the house.

"We can discuss Jocelyn inside the station. Please." He placed a hand on her arm and gestured to the doors. Grace felt a shiver race down her spine as she complied. It wasn't a request, even if he did ask politely.

The station entrance was bustling. Grace tried not to make eye contact with anyone. Her mind flickered back to all those years ago when she was being interviewed about the attack at camp. She remembered thinking Matt had been the killer. Believing that she herself was responsible. She remembered the emotions that had crashed over her when she discovered that Matt was dead.

Is Jocelyn dead? The thought shot through her mind before disappearing. *No. They wouldn't bring me here just to tell me that.*

She debated with herself about what they could want to know.

Torres led her into an interview room with dim lighting and cool air. "Take a seat. I'll be right back with my partner."

Days ago, an officer had stopped by the hospital and asked her a few questions. They had told her they had already spoken to Jocelyn, and they just wanted to verify a few details with her. It had seemed routine. Like an open and shut case. She couldn't remember if that was the cops' words or her own. They didn't ask about their background or the motivation for Noah or even why Jocelyn allowed Grace to be attacked. Her brain tried to replay the conversation as she rubbed her hands across her jeans. *Did they ask about that? Did they know?* Grace couldn't be sure. Her thoughts had still been jumbled from the dehydration and the shock of it all.

A knock echoed throughout the room before the door swung open. It made Grace feel as though she was in a doctor's office. Why would a police officer knock? It wasn't as if she could hide anything in here.

Torres glanced up at the camera in the corner and gave it a small wave. The other detective, a small and thin man, let out a sigh as he sat down in one of the metal chairs across from Grace.

"I'm Detective Rogers, nice to meet you." He had a file folder open in front of him, not bothering to make eye contact or shake her hand. Torres settled in next to

Detective Rogers, shifting his chair farther away so he could have the space he required.

"Why are you recording? Am I in some kind of trouble?" Grace felt the headache blooming in the back of her head. It only added to her discomfort.

"It's just standard procedure, ma'am," Rogers explained. Still, he made no eye contact.

Grace couldn't remember ever being called ma'am before, and it felt quite intentional.

"You said you had some questions?" Grace looked to Torres, who gave a small nod. He opened his mouth to speak, but Rogers began instead.

"We just have some details we need to clarify from the events the other day. Before we begin, since we are recording, I just have to make you aware of your rights. I'm sure you're a smart girl. You have the right to remain silent. Anything you say can and will be used against you in a court of law. You have the right to an attorney. If you cannot afford an attorney, one will be provided for you. Do you understand the rights I have just read to you? With these rights in mind, do you wish to speak to me?"

Grace's mouth formed a tight line. She tried to remember if they had said this before. Her mind blurred, and she told herself that they must have. They probably did it before every interview. That was the lie she decided to tell herself.

"Am I under arrest?"

"No. But we need to make sure you know what you are saying here can be used as evidence," Torres chimed in.

"Evidence against who? Noah is dead. My father is dead."

"I suppose we could use it as evidence against

anyone. The case hasn't been completely closed yet, which is why we need your side of the story." Torres opened his mouth to carry on where Rogers left off, but Rogers made a small hand gesture to stop him. "The entire story." The silence grew in the room. Torres stared at the table, clearly uncomfortable in the silence, while Rogers seemed to enjoy each second. Finally, Grace spoke.

"What do you mean?" She swallowed the lump that was forming in her throat.

"Why don't you start with what happened in the kitchen?" Rogers suggested, the words flowing out smoothly as if he had practiced it before.

Grace's mind mentally flipped through the images she could remember. Each one made her want to flinch.

"Jocelyn and I were running. We were trying to get out of the house. When we got to the kitchen . . ." Grace swallowed hard before continuing. "Her parents were hanging from the ceiling. They were already dead."

Torres was avoiding eye contact, but Rogers was nodding eagerly like he found the story enthralling. Sweat had formed on his upper lip, and he licked it away. Grace forced her eyes off his face and down to a loose strand on her sweater. If she didn't fix it, soon the whole thing would unravel.

"Then, Noah walked in. He had a gun. He told us that I could decide which one of us got to live, but I was pretty sure he was just messing with us." Grace envisioned the betrayal on Jocelyn's face when she had chosen herself. The two of them were the final girls, and Grace had mentally prepared to be the only one left.

Her eyes glanced nervously to the camera. Could it register the guilt on her face?

"So when Noah entered the kitchen, he had a gun? He had it aimed at you?" Rogers's eyes narrowed as he focused on Grace. Grace hesitated before responding. While his words themselves were not aggressive, his expressions made it feel more and more like an interrogation.

"Yes, he had a gun. He pointed it at me and Jocelyn. Then, before he could do anything more, my father showed up. He was at the gate and buzzed the intercom. Noah answered and let him in."

"Why would he let him in?" Torres was the one who asked this. There was genuine confusion spread across his face. Rogers threw a look at Torres, but he didn't say anything.

"I wondered that myself." She adjusted uncomfortably in her seat. It was something that had crossed her mind a lot, especially since her therapy session. If Noah hadn't let her father in, what would have happened? Would she be alive? Would her father? She cleared her throat before continuing. "I guess he was cocky. Maybe he thought it would be more fun if my dad was there to watch?"

"Are you guessing or do you know?" Rogers was leaning back in his chair, smugness spreading across his face.

"I'm just assuming," Grace sputtered. "I'm sorry, but should I have a lawyer?"

"You can request a lawyer if you would like, Miss Simmons, but I have to say it doesn't look good asking for a lawyer." Rogers flipped through a folder, tilting the top edge so Grace couldn't see the contents. She eyed him, and then Torres, who seemed to be growing more confused and uncomfortable by the moment.

"What other questions do you have then?" Grace debated if she should ask if she was free to go. Could she just stand up and leave? She wasn't sure, but she knew that wouldn't look good either.

"Can you continue? What happened after your father arrived?" Rogers continued.

"Yes, so——" Grace closed her eyes and tried to remember all the details. "He let my dad in, and he hid with me in the kitchen pantry. He wanted to jump out and surprise my dad." After the words came out, Grace cringed. She made it sound like it was a joyous occasion.

"So he forced you into the pantry?" Rogers asked, searching for confirmation.

"Yes. He had the gun, and once my father was in the kitchen, he jumped out. They struggled over the gun, and eventually, they were on the floor. It was terrifying. I grabbed a kitchen knife." Grace's voice shook as she continued. "I stabbed Noah in the back while he was wrestling with my dad. The gun went off, and I guess Noah must have shot my dad. Then, there was blood everywhere, and they were both dead."

Rogers and Torres were both nodding slightly.

"I need you to think carefully now." Rogers sat up straight in the chair. "Did you move the bodies at all before the authorities arrived?"

"Yes," she responded, thinking back to the cell phone. Torres shook his head and turned to face Rogers. Rogers looked back with the corners of his mouth slightly upturned. "I know you aren't supposed to, but I had to. We didn't have a phone. We needed to call the police, and Noah had taken both our phones."

"That's very interesting to hear, Miss Simmons."

"Interesting? I needed to call the cops. It was an emergency."

"Do you remember what happened after you called the police?"

Grace bit her bottom lip before answering Rogers.

"I dialed 9-1-1 and asked for help. But the rest is a blur. I think I must have passed out."

"What about when the police arrived?" Torres asked now, a small bit of desperation coating his voice.

"No. I don't remember at all."

"You were fully coherent when we arrived," Rogers began. "Miss Baker, however, was not." Grace shook her head. She didn't remember any of this.

"All I remember is being at the hospital. There might be like . . . flashes of memory. But nothing real." Grace blinked as she stared at her lap. *Why can't I remember?* she wondered. *Is it happening again?*

"Miss Simmons, I have to tell you that your story has some inconsistencies. Some major inconsistencies. Is there anything you want to admit before we move forward?" Rogers flipped the file folder shut and set it on the table. Grace could see now that her name was printed on the tab of the file.

"Move forward with what?"

Rogers sighed elaborately. "Is there anything in your statement you want to revise?"

"No. It's the whole truth." As the words slipped out of her mouth, Grace's brain nearly yelled out, *The gun,* she thought. *I touched one of the guns.*

"I'm sure you know we found your fingerprints on a weapon in the house other than the knife. In fact, your fingerprints were on the gun that killed your father."

"That's impossible! I never touched that gun!" Grace spat, confusion now filling her.

"*That* gun?" Rogers asked, a smirk spreading across his lips, infecting even his eyes.

"Well, there was more than one gun," Grace backpedaled. Both officers cocked their heads to the side, nearly in unison. Grace's hands flailed around as she struggled to explain. "There was a gun that I grabbed for protection, but Noah had removed the bullets. I tried to shoot him with it in self-defense, but it obviously didn't work." A small voice in Grace's head screamed out: *Shut up!*

Now, Rogers and Torres were looking at each other. Rogers raised his eyebrow, and Torres gave a tight nod.

"Miss Simmons, I think we are going to need to end the questioning here."

"What?" Grace was convinced she had misheard him. Torres rose from his chair and approached Grace.

"We are placing you under arrest. Please stand." Torres unhooked his handcuffs from his belt and stepped behind Grace's chair.

"Arrest, for what?" Grace couldn't decide if this was a dream or reality. Her thoughts zoomed around in her head, crashing and colliding.

Rogers stood even though Grace had not. "Arrest for murder. Jocelyn told us everything."

Grace felt tears prick the corners of her eyes. Nothing made sense. She pushed the chair back from the table, retreated like a scared animal.

"What? Where is she?"

Torres misinterpreted her panic for anger.

"Please stand. I will not ask again." One hand still held the handcuffs while the other was on his pistol.

Grace scrambled to her feet, flashbacks of Noah pointing the gun at her playing on a movie screen in her head. Torres clicked the handcuffs into place, first the right, then the left. Grace stared at Rogers in shock, but he was smiling.

"You really thought you could just pass it off as self-defense. That you could blame the dead for everything. People like you disgust me."

Grace felt like her stomach had dropped ten stories. She forced her mouth to stay shut, afraid she would make everything worse. Torres led her out of the room and turned her to the right. As Grace turned, out of the corner of her eye, she caught a glimpse of Jocelyn. She was smiling brighter than Grace had ever seen before. She knew then that it had never been over. Not really. She was never forgiven. And Jocelyn would never forget.

EPILOGUE

When the court date came around, Jocelyn didn't bother going. The district attorney had assured her that one way or another, Grace would be going away. Whether that be straight back to St. George as a permanent resident or to a "real" prison, she didn't care. Both were a form of hell. Both were enough revenge for her.

Jocelyn had been ready to let it all go. To call a truce. She told herself that she really was okay with what had happened. But then Grace had screwed it all up when she volunteered Jocelyn's life to Noah instead of sacrificing herself. Through her anger and despair, she formed a plan.

Originally, Jocelyn thought she would have to knock Grace out after she made the 9-1-1 call, but the stupid bitch had passed out almost instantly. She had dropped the phone, and Jocelyn kneeled down, straining to hear what the dispatcher said. *Please know where we are. Please track this call,* she begged. If she had to get on the line, the plan would become so much more difficult.

"We are sending units out to you now. Can you hear me, ma'am? Ma'am?" The dispatcher's voice remained calm. Jocelyn admired how well the woman could separate herself from reality. Jocelyn could do that too.

She needed to move quickly. Jocelyn scurried over to the maid's closet filled with cleaning supplies and pulled out a pair of latex gloves. Glancing over her shoulder, she saw Grace was still out cold.

"Perfect," she whispered. She moved over to the bodies and flipped Noah over, being careful to avoid blood splattering onto herself. The knife already had Grace's fingerprints, so that was taken care of. But she hadn't touched Noah's gun. Jocelyn carried it over to Grace and lightly pressed her hand onto the handle and trigger, even the barrel, before placing it to the side of Mr. Simmons's hand. It looked like someone had planted it there. Exactly like she intended.

Now, she found the gun that Grace had fired earlier, the one that was empty. She plucked it up carefully and carried it upstairs to her parents' bedroom. She was lucky that no blood splatter had landed on her during the scuffle. There was no way for them to know she was moving throughout the house.

She jumped up the stairs, taking two at a time. Inside the bedroom, she used a towel to wipe any prints off the gun before setting it back into her mother's nightstand. It looked like it had never been disturbed. Like Noah himself hadn't even touched it.

For a moment, Jocelyn thought she could hear the sirens in the distance, but it was only her imagination trying to rush her.

One more thing needed to be done. She rushed to the spare office upstairs. The one where they kept the security recording. It filmed from all the cameras, and clearly, Noah had been recording and watching this whole time. Nobody could see those tapes.

With the gloves still on, she deleted the footage from the past week, just to be safe. Then, she plucked out the discs and smashed them with a nearby three-hole punch. The discs shattered, a fleck of one flying up and cutting her forehead. She reached up and touched the blood that was now oozing from the wound. She decided it would only help her cause. Deciding the sketchier the scene looked the better, she left the disc shards in plain sight. She crumpled up the gloves and stuffed them behind the home server her father had. Nobody would be pulling that monstrosity out from the wall.

The sirens sounded again in the distance. Jocelyn couldn't tell if they were real or not, but she decided to act like they were. She slipped down the stairs, trying to scan the front of the house to see if they had pulled up yet. Finding the driveway empty, she moved back into the kitchen, relieved to see Grace still unconscious. At least she was none the wiser about what happened. Grace's confusion would only add strength to Jocelyn's testimony.

A frown settled upon Jocelyn's face. She had heard once that the average human couldn't inflict severe pain upon themselves. Instincts will stop them at the last moment. Lucky for her, she wasn't average. The sirens rang in her ears, louder and louder. By now, she didn't know what was real or fake. The little voice deep inside her head whispered, *do it.*

So, she did. She smashed the front of her face into

the marble countertop, hard enough to draw more blood, and toppled to the ground like a ragdoll. As blackness crept into the edges of her vision, all she could think about was seeing Grace's face when that moment came. The moment when Jocelyn had made it out safe, but Grace hadn't.

"I thought you were better than this, Einstein." Jocelyn soon lost consciousness, a small smile slowly disappearing from her lips.

ACKNOWLEDGMENTS

Being a writer was something I dreamed of ever since I was a small child. In actuality, it was a journey that took far longer than I anticipated. Despite this, there were so many people who helped me along the way.

To my parents, thank you for supporting me even before it was practical. You have always tried to foster my ambitions. Driving me once a week to a college campus, when I was only in ninth grade, to sit in a room full of adults easily twenty years my senior, is most notable. I will never forget all the nights you gave up for my dreams.

To my editor, Sarah Hawkins, you are unbelievable at what you do. I really flew by the seat of my pants on this novel, and you were there to fix all the loose seams along the way. Thank you for being my first reader and your kindness.

To my husband, thank you for humoring me while I chased after this dream. I know my anxiety about the project frequently caused you some as well.

Thank you to all my close friends and extended family who have been overwhelming supportive of this journey, even when I was keeping it a secret from most.

And to my readers, thank you for taking a chance on a new writer. It means everything to me.

ABOUT THE AUTHOR

Carley Wolfe spends her days listening to teenagers complain about American Literature and daydreaming about summer vacation. When she is not writing or eating good food, she is cuddling with her pets, and occasionally, her husband. *When We Lied* is her debut novel.

Printed in Great Britain
by Amazon

41931878R00192